# Stray Bullet

Written by S. G. Lee

First Edition 2017

# SB

An imprint of *Shillelagh Books*

London, Ontario, Canada

Acknowledgments:

Sincere thanks to Jodi and Sydney, without your constant support and encouragement, this book would not be possible. You are the best friends a writer could have. I dedicate this book to my daughters, my son-in law and my husband; who have supported my writing endeavours with encouragement and love. Special thanks to my beloved mother in heaven, who taught me dreams, can come true with hard work, perseverance and patience.

Preface:

In the small town of Driftwood, Colorado, under starry skies, residents went about their business. The town was now ready for the arrival of the new sheriff having gussied up the urban decay with a few coats of paint. The new sheriff would see the bad parts of town soon enough the mayor thought and turned over in his bed and went to sleep. The hospital looking after a few patients was unusually quiet under the full moon; other people in the settlement getting ready for bed and then turning on late night programs or setting alarms and climbing into bed.

Across town a man getting ready for bed after a long hard day at work completed his paperwork, stripped naked and stepped into the shower. As the water ran down in torrents the shower glass doors shattered, the man fell to the floor and rivets of blood ran into the drain. He was the first to die that night.

## *Stray Bullet*

A few doors over gunman entered killing the husband and wife in their beds and the children as they slept. Blood covered the floor and ceilings in those rooms. None of the neighbours heard a peep they simply slumbered on. Other homes across the town were entered and the residents, husband wife and children were also shot and killed. No one had time to shout out or call 911. It was all over in a few minutes with no time for whimpers only the muzzle of silencers doing their jobs and hitman scurrying into the night.

"It's done, boss. The teams are leaving the state. Yes, I'll do that now. He's coming in the morning. I'll check in after I meet him. His name? All I got is G. Bullet not sure of his first name, it's not on any paperwork. . See you, tomorrow… okay Friday," the man said into his prepaid cell phone and then took out sim card breaking it into pieces. Then he discarded it in a nearby bin at the now decrepit old pulp and paper mill. He had to go to work soon. A new sheriff was coming to town and he wanted to be there to greet him.

~0~

## Chapter 1 - Friendship Trumps Bullet

My name is G and I'm on my way to a new life to become a sheriff in a town called Driftwood. Sounds boring, doesn't it. If you'd asked me five year ago I would have told you of course it was; but now this is what I need and my daughter needs…a nice quiet life, in a quiet town, where I could raise my daughter without whispers and rumors. You want to more about that statement? I'll get back to that, but I'm told people will want to know about me a subject I'm not really comfortable talking about.

Asked to describe myself I would say I'm tall over six feet…okay six feet five inches. I am muscular, as I lift weights. I'm not overly muscular, just enough to take down the bad guys. Some people think I look like Tom Selleck in his youth, personally I don't see the resemblance.

G. is a short form for my first name but I don't like to talk about my real first name. Let's just say my parents grew up in the happy-go-lucky seventies and were heavily influenced by the weird names that people gave their children. What you still won't give up? You demand that I tell you my first name? You want to play the guessing game?

My first name is unmentionable I don't talk about it ever!! My last name is wait for it...Bullet...I know a clichéd name if you ever heard one. Honestly, it's my name. It has been mine my whole life.

My last name had raised a few eyebrows. Can you imagine how many chuckles I've gotten when I tell anyone my full name? Still can't guess? Some of you have deducted correctly. So now you know why I usually don't divulge my first name.

In order for you to understand the relevance
of my last name I'll have to explain more
about my family and their origins.

My grandfather when escaping persecution
in Russia came through at Ellis Island and
decided to Anglicize his name to Bullet; so
my dad used that and now I do.

What's that you like to know grandpa's
original name? Well so would I,
unfortunately he took that name to his grave
leaving no clues behind. But he was great
man, a hard working cop. I come from a
long line of cops. With a last name like
Bullet it tends to earn respect being a cop.

Grandpa was killed on the job by some
backward gangsters bent on destroying one
another. My dad swore he never be a cop
and went to San Francisco were he promptly
fell in love with my mother went to the

police academy there and then impregnated my mother.

After I turned one he decided he needed family and got a job as a cop in the city where his father had served and brothers now served as cops. When he worked there for six months he had planned to send for mom and me and marry her. Unfortunately the first day on the job he ran into a domestic situation and was killed in the line of duty. He hadn't told his family about my mother or me so we came as a surprise when mother showed up with me in tow for the funeral. They soon adapted however and accepted her and with her me.

When I was four years old, my mother learned she was dying of breast cancer. My dad's three brothers, James, Bennie, and Alfred also cops, stepped up to raise me. They were a demanding bunch always pushing me to be strong and tough. I had to be resilient and learn all the fighting techniques that they taught. Let's just say I am proficient in a number of fighting techniques.

Their younger sister, my Aunt Louisa was a teacher and just starting her career when they took me in; however Aunt Louise found plenty of time for me. She made my childhood more normal though my uncles would often say she shouldn't coddle me. My uncles drove her away with their constant beratement and by the time I was in my teens she moved to teach in Colorado to save her sanity. She still managed to chide the uncles into letting me visit her in Denver in the summer for two months; the best two months of the year for me.

Getting back to my uncles they hated my first name as much as I did (though I think they liked me even less; but did their duty). They also felt that I had come out of nowhere so they nicknamed me Stray and it stuck; that's what most of the cops on the force called me. Aunt Louise was the only one who ever called me; by my first name.

Why do I speak of my Aunt Louise? Aunt
Louise had recently retired to a small town
called Driftwood Colorado and I often
wished she had been closer especially when
I had run into the wall of blue at my job. Cut
to today as I told you earlier I'd taken a new
job as the sheriff in the same town,
Driftwood Colorado.

As I drove to the Sheriff station; I saw that
the downtown area was newly painted but
other parts were decrepit and rundown.
Stores had been closed and signs had been
posted that said for rent but the places
looked like they hadn't been rented in a long
time. The back alleys showed signs, of
hookers working their wares with discarded
condoms, beer bottles and other
paraphernalia.

The town was surrounded by trees; but the
main source of jobs in the past had been
lumber and the company had pulled up

stakes and moved away. Factories and brickyards were closed.

Some of the homes have seen better days and the downtown core was eerily quiet, with vacant storefronts lining the streets. Crime which in the past hadn't been a problem was suddenly up and maybe that's why the Sheriff had quit? But that was the reason I was here. I'd shape this town into a town we could all be proud of again if the re-elected mayor could do as he promised and bring in the jobs. I wanted to be happy here.

I'd just dropped off my three year old daughter with my Aunt Louise. Stella Marie, my daughter seemed okay with the new place and Aunt Louise; but was I? Aunt Louise was sixty years old and a retired school teacher. Why was I so worried? First day jitters obviously. Aunt Louise had my back. She knew what idiots her brothers really were and how they valued their friendships even more than family. Being a single father I needed her more than ever.

## Stray Bullet

Aunt Louise had urged me to apply for the vacant job of Sheriff after hearing about my troubles as a cop in a suburb of Halton, Illinois. I don't want to get into those troubles right now. Today was a new day and I decided it was going to be great even if it killed me. Just kidding! I was not going to get killed like my dad had on the first day of the job. Nerves were getting to me.

Sure it was hard settling into a new place for a child. A little voice worried that I had made a mistake; but this was a new start for both of us we should be happy. A month ago I had been offered my dream job, Sheriff of a small municipality in Driftwood, Colorado. Driftwood looked to me like a small town of three hundred people where I'd be happy raising Stella-Marie.

The streets were tree-lined; the cookie cutter houses had beautiful floral displays out front. The lawns were immaculate green and lush. Children rode their bikes up and down the streets with no fear of predators or gunplay. The people had seemed friendly and warm when I came for my interview for the job. What more could we want? I'd thought.

I'd done my research; but nothing had prepared me for the men all walking out on me. I stepped into the Sheriff's car.

This blue flu wouldn't do! I knew from the dispatcher that the other cops were not happy with my appointment because I was an outside hire; but damn it was my first day on the job and they had a duty to serve and protect the citizens of Driftwood.

# 12

## Stray Bullet

How could the four deputies just not show
up for the day? Calls to their residences had
gone to voice mail so they were even
avoiding talking to me. I had to put my foot
down hard or the men would never respect
my leadership. I'd already faced a wall of
blue in my old job; people pulling out the
old politics line and drawing in ranks on the
thin blue line. I'd wanted a new start to
change the harassment I'd faced in my not
so fair city over the last three years.

A bit of a long story which we'll get into
later but suffice to say the line in blue was
put up against me; simply because I stood up
to another cop who committed a crime.

Driving down the road to go to my new
deputy's home I grew angry. Hadn't I been
through enough of this crap from the guys in
Halton? I had been harassed day and night
by those assholes.

Parking the squad car and mounted the wooden steps on the house. I knocked lightly on Deputy Gregory Barnes door. No answer. I gave it my best thundering police knock and the door swung open of its own accord. I pulled my service revolver and entered the residence wily. A smell of dead berries and apples entered my nostrils. I felt in my pocket and then taking it out swished my menthol medicated lip balm under my nose. My adrenaline kicked in and suddenly I felt exhilarated and hyper aware.

I followed the putrid odor to a bedroom and found the late Greg Barnes with two bullet wounds to the heart surrounded by a dried rusty brown pool of blood. He'd been there at least two days. Nothing was disturbed in the home. No overturned furniture, nothing seemed out of place. He lived alone; so no help there. Was it a rogue girlfriend? Why was he dead?

What the hell? The first day on the job and my deputy is murdered? I needed those other cops that hadn't come to work today to help me solve this murder. Damn them and their blue flu.

I made the call to the coroner who was on call for autopsies. Then I secured the scene and called in the neighboring counties police force on loan until I could find my police force.

Less than an hour later, I had two officers, Alfred Jones and Paulo Scarlatti, I sent to the two of them to retrieve the first officer Joseph Paciocco on my list. Imagine my surprise when he called back to tell me that my other officer, Joseph Paciocco was dead too. Two shots to the heart and it looked like the same felon. Was I going to find all my missing officers dead?

A quick search of the other residences found all of the bachelor cops dead shot the same way. The family men with their families at home were dead too; but so were all their family members. They had all been shot with one shot to the head in their beds. They had not stood a chance. This was a professional job as each scene had been carefully scanned and nothing was left to find in the way of evidence other than the blood and bullets.

All in all the dead were Gregory Barnes, Joseph Paciocco, Jack Abrahams, Paul Jones, his brother and fellow officer, Harold Jones and Harold's wife Cheryl, and their two children, Gail, and Fred, Vincent Vecchio and his wife Paula Antrim (both cops on the force), their baby, Adrian a newborn was alive in his crib and was taken into custody of the Children's Aid until a relative could be reached. Also dead were Robert Di Salvio and his wife Rebecca and their fifteen year old son William and their daughter Helen eight years old, Kas Mahmoud his wife Dayita, and their three sons, Aaban, Aahil, and Aatif ages five seven and nine.

What in the hell was going on? Someone had killed whole families. Why? Did they know something someone didn't want them to know? Was it retaliation?

This meant looking into backgrounds and finding out things people didn't want you to know. Being the sheriff didn't make for a popularity contest in any case but this would have to be handled very delicately. The police officers on loan couldn't continue to investigate this after all I only had a temporary loan of their services for today. Even if I wanted to investigate I had to have help. I needed to call the FBI pronto and I knew just the guy my former partner, Gordon Chum.

I dialed Gordon's number by heart. He answered on the first ring asking me about the new job and then said he'd speak to his boss and get the okay to bring a team down as soon as possible.

Meanwhile I was trying to comfort the staff left at station and ducking calls from reporters from all over the country and residents of Driftwood who were demanding to know what had happened. I took deep soothing breaths…Gordon would be here soon we'd get to the bottom of this. Penny Ambercrombie the office dogsbody and police dispatcher took charge and hustled the troops off to their stations to work on the tasks I'd given them.

Penny was tall and lean possibly one hundred and ten pounds though it was hard to tell for her clothes hung on her in non-descript browns that did nothing to enhance her looks and she stood at least six feet tall. Her hair was a rich chestnut and was wound tightly at the nap of her neck into a bun. Her eyes were her most striking feature that not even her terrible clothes sense could hide as they were a glittering emerald green that showed immense interest and intelligence. She appeared to be in her late twenties though her skin was leathered with the weathering an outdoors enthusiast had.

I could see that Penny was be an asset to me and the sheriff's station in my job. But first I needed to call Aunt Louise and Stella- Marie and hope my daughter wouldn't get too upset that daddy would not see her until tomorrow at the earliest.

I picked up the phone and called the number by heart. There was no answer. Where could she be I wondered? My question was answered in the next few seconds by my office door swinging open. There my Aunt Louise stood with Stella Marie. Aunt Louise demanded, "Gunner is it true? Are they all dead?"

The next thing that happened was three year old Stella-Marie jumping in my arms and saying "Daddy, I missed you."

I closed my office door no sense in putting on a show to the remaining troops and I hoped no one had heard my aunt utter my first name. Stella-Marie took the chair nearest me.

"I want an answer Gunner."

"Not in front of the c.h.i.l.d."

"Ch. i.ld, child, that's me," my precocious daughter answered.

"Stella-Marie already knows all about this. She turned on the television while I was in the bathroom and she heard about all your deputies and their families being found dead. She insisted I bring her here."

"Then you both know what I know. I'm investigating and I've called in the FBI."

"Daddy, are you safe? In that movie with the Kung Fu guy they tried to kill him and then killed his family," Stella-Marie answered.

"What have you been watching?"

"I remember his name, now. I love Jean Claude van Damme movies," Stella-Marie stated.

"Me too, pumpkin and we're safe. I haven't been here long enough to be mixed up in whatever is going on here," I reassured.

"You'll find the bad guys?"

"Daddy will find them. That's what daddy used to do before he had you," I answered.

"Be careful," Stella-Marie said with adult wisdom beyond her years.

"Stella-Marie is correct. You need to stay safe."

"I promise both of you, I will stay safe."

"We'll trust you."

"Can we have dinner together, daddy?"

"Of course we can my apple dumpling."

"I'm not an apple dumpling."

"No you're my little pumpkin."

"You're silly, daddy."

"What would you like for dinner? Pizza? Chinese food?"

"Pizza! I want pizza!!"Stella-Marie chimed.

I ordered her favourite Hawaiian pizza and we forgot work for a few minutes as we ate. Stella-Marie told me about her day between bites. Stella-Marie sounded happy and was adjusting well to living in this new place. She didn't seem too worried about my job anymore. She kissed me goodbye and said, "Get'em, daddy. See you tomorrow, nighty, night."

I breathed a sigh of relief my daughter seemed happy despite all that was happening. I was the new sheriff so the danger to me from who ever committed these murders must be minimal if any, so my family was safe. Still I told Aunt Louise to keep Stella-Marie indoors and keep the doors locked reporting any suspicious activity to me.

Gordon arrived a few minutes later, "I'm Special Agent Gordon Chum FBI," he said showing his badge then continuing he said, "I'm here to take over this case."

"No. You're not you're here to assist me and the good people of Driftwood."

"I am here to serve the people yes, and if that means taking over the investigation in a town that has seen fit to kill all its police officers save one..."

"How dare you? This town is peaceable. There is a perpetrator or perpetrators who have committed a heinous crime but we will get to the bottom of this."

"You should have recused yourself Sheriff."

I heard Penny Ambercrombie gasp and then mutter under her breath, "What a maniacal idiot and a kook to boot."

"No, shouldn't! This was my first day on the
job. I was to begin tomorrow but I thought
I'd get in and do a little paperwork first. I
am imminently qualified to investigate this.
I hadn't even met these men or their
families; but I care very much about what
has happened to them. They are police
officers and my squad. Every one of them is
mine so this crime was committed against
me and my family. Do you understand?"

"I understand the feeling and I promise not
to step on your toes, Sheriff. My men and I
are at your disposal in this investigation.
You are in charge. Perhaps we could discuss
the particulars before my colleagues get
here?" Gordon stated.

"Please follow me this way to my office,
Special Agent Chum," I answered.

"Call me Gordon," my pal offered.

"People call me Stray, or G," I stated.

Gordon pretended to be shocked and lifted
an eyebrow at me. Penny looked at Gordon
with disgust but went back to the front desk
of the station.

Gordon entered my office and shut the door,
loudly. Spotting the pizza he said, "That
went well."

"Yes, it did. Did you see the dispatcher,
Penny Abercrombie craning her head and
her ears to listen to you?"

"I saw her when I came into the station. She
was frowning at you and giving you dirty
looks when you weren't looking like she
didn't believe you belonged here, Gee."

"I noticed those looks all day," I answered.

"That should be the end of that you can
thank me now. She is directing those looks
to me now and I'll wager she'll spread all
over town how you defended the honor of
the dead."

"Thanks Gordon for the assist; but how will
we can we keep up the lie?"

"We begin a new friendship," Gordon said calmly then continued, "I hope you saved me a few slices of that pizza, I'm starved and my team is checking into the No-Tell Motel down the street within the hour."

I smiled and nodded handing him a couple of slices. It was good to see my old partner again.

"You are staying with me and Aunt Louise aren't you?" I asked.

"Lucky for you or is it me they are limited space in this town to stay and of course this allows me to begin a new friendship with you. All my agents have taken up the last rooms in the motel so I'm grateful your aunt will put me up. You did ask her didn't you?"

"Didn't think I had to, you know Aunt Louise loves you."

Gordon raised another eyebrow.

"Fine I'll call her now."

I dialed and Aunt Louise answered her cell phone on the first ring. Aunt Louise said of course Gordon was staying here. I told her not to tell anyone we knew her and she agreed after I told her why. Then she said she had to go as she had pulled over to answer the cell phone.

"So it's settled?" Gordon asked.

I nodded.

"What a terrible first day on the job for you pal," Gordon commented, "Especially after what happened to you more than three and half years ago."

I thought back to what I had been through the last three and half years and I found myself reliving that chaotic time in my mind.

I'd been about eight years on the job in the city of Halton, Illinois, a cop, just like my dad and grandfather and uncles before me. The city had gone to the gangs. . It was two steps and one step forward. Every time we turned around; another shooting another victim of a drive-by. Just the other day the victim was a seven year old kid innocently riding their bike! Luckily the kid lived; but we actively hunted for the shooter or shooters. I should have took that as an omen seeing as my grandfather and my dad lost their lives in the police service, but I went merrily on my way doing my job not expecting my life to come crumbling all around me.

A routine call to a richer neighborhood for a disturbance started it all. The dispatcher didn't think to tell me it was a domestic disturbance and the man had a gun. I'm always careful in those situations; more careful then the average cop but if you don't know you can't take precautions.

I knocked on the door and announced myself and shots barreled through the front door grazing my forehead and tearing my knee apart. I burst through the door grabbed the shooter and he shot me again.

That should have got me accolades and medals right? After all I was shot doing my job, but no, all of those rightly went to my partner, Gordon Chum. The third shot resulted in a thigh wound that almost made me bleed out on the spot if it wasn't for the quick work of my partner Gordon Chum securing the prisoner and belting my thigh. Okay, so I got a medal or two, but Gordon was the real hero. See why he was the first man I called when my force had been gunned down.

Gordon is a second generation Asian American. A good looking fellow and kinder than most men, he speaks softly and carries a big stick. People underestimating him rather walk away unscathed. Gordon standing at five foot six weighed roughly two hundred and ten pounds of pure muscle.

He knew every fight technique I knew and more. He saved my life a time or two.

Gordon was arguably one of the best partners I've ever had. Gordon saved my life after I was shot on duty and secured the scene until back-up could get there. He also called for an ambulance for me. I was carted off to a hospital where I spent the next three weeks in intensive car being prayed over by my fellow cops, and the rest of the city.

Whatever chits they called in with the big guy upstairs it worked, I survived and I should have been happy about that; but all I could think was I missed my moment I was supposed to die like my dad and my grandfather before me on the job. It wasn't that I was that different when I came out of the coma.

Okay, so I had a few scars inside and out.
My forehead now sported a scar that I could
cover with bangs and temporarily bum leg.
The leg didn't seem to want heal in fact at
one point they threatened to take off my leg;
but good old Gordon helped me fight them
on that and the knee healed to the point I
could walk on it. But it wasn't good enough
for work, at least not then.

Suffering from self-loathing (and yes a little
post-traumatic stress disorder, if I truly
admit it); I began to be curt with everyone
closing myself off from everyone and
everything. My wife, Gina took the brunt of
all of this. I was cruel to her at every turn.
When she came to visit I'd ignore her.

I knew I needed help from the police shrink
but I couldn't accept or admit that I, the
wonder boy actually had a problem. Gordon
begged me to quit loathing myself so much
and making everyone else around me
miserable but I didn't listen. I was content to
wallow in my anger and self-loathing.

Weeks went by and Gina seemed unhappy
despite her forced saccharine with me. She
gave me an ultimatum get help; or she
would leave me. I decided I wanted Gina so
I found a shrink of my own choosing Doctor
Collins for his add in the Yellow Pages.

Doctor Collins turned out to be a woman.
Don't get me wrong she wasn't a fantasy
(that blonde fantasy with legs up to here and
hiding behind glasses); no she was more like
your grandmother. Non-descript, her silver
hair short and curled tight to her head. Her
voice was soft and she always offered me
milk and cookies before a session. I kind of
felt weird at first like she was family and I'd
never been all that chatty with family
anyway. I had so much trouble talking at
first that I'd just sit there and stare at the
walls; but after a few sessions she got me to
open up about my childhood and then finally
about the shooting. I began to feel better and
worked on getting my knee back in shape so
I could return to work.

I had a routine and I followed it. Therapy followed by afternoon sessions of psychotherapy. With the drugs Doctor Collins prescribed and all our talks I began to almost feel normal again. Okay, so I'm lying; I still had a few stray thoughts that I was a failure and that I should have died; but I labored hard to overcome them and worked on being nicer to my ball and chain. I even began to buy her flowers. As for my leg it was almost good enough to return to work.

Doctor Collins had scheduled my appointment for two p.m. on a Friday and I had looked forward to getting it over with and going home to surprise Gina. A cop buddy had offered me his family cottage and I planned a trip to the Poconos for the next week. I'd already called Gina's work and got her the next week off. It would be a fantastic surprise for her and a chance for us to just lay back and enjoy our weekend. I could even cook all the meals that I caught from the lake as it was loaded with fish.

I decided to change my appointment and let
Gina know that it would now be at noon
instead of two p.m... Surely I could charm
my shrink into seeing me earlier and if not
well then I see her next week after my trip. I
arrived at the doctor's office to find a note
on the door. It seemed my shrink. Doctor
Teresa Collins had died suddenly this
morning and they were rescheduling. A
number to call followed the announcement.

*Died!* And all they thought about was their
schedule? Devastating and only then
realizing how close I had gotten with my
shrink I fell to the floor crying and took
about a half- an -hour to recover enough just
to pull myself together. I told myself over
and over everything would be okay but I
didn't really believe it.

## Stray Bullet

Enough of this shit!! A little therapy and I
turned into a wimp; who cried at the drop of
a hat. I was a Bullet and we were strong
manly types; made of steel not mush!!
People died!! Get over yourself I
admonished myself. I had a life... a wife
who loved me despite myself. It was time to
man up and be the husband she deserved. I
just had to get away with Gina. I'd go home
and surprise her now.

Stopping at the gas station to fill-up and
walking into pay I spotted roses. I picked
some up and thought how pleased Gina
would be. She deserved this after all I'd put
her through the last two months. She'd
surprised me two weeks ago, telling me that
she was pregnant. I was overjoyed looking
forward to our baby coming in six months.

We had a new beginning and I would make
her as happy as Gina had made me.

I thought about the look on her face; her joy
at our baby and decided to book her
favourite restaurant before we left town. We
could then leave at nine p.m. I'd drive all
night and we reach there by morning. It
could be done despite my gimpy leg. Okay
so I lied, I wasn't fully recovered; but soon I
would be. My physical therapist was pleased
and said I might even be able to go back to
work in a month.

I went home opening the front door with my
key and... You know what happened? It was
that other old cliché...husband comes home
and finds his wife naked doing the tango
with another naked man.

I didn't recognize him from the back as he
jumped out the window, naked clothes in
hand. She could tell me who he was in her
own good time. And I had plenty of time as
I seethed and wanted to kill him but not her.
I didn't want to hurt her at all I just wanted
to take her in my arms and make this go
away.

I took huge breaths and then realized it takes two to tango. I had brought this on with neglect and coolness towards her when all she did was support and love me. I took deep breaths to calm myself and rationalized. I was sure this was just a one-time thing.

I'd heard women could get quite horny in pregnancy I obviously had let her down.

I had been a terrible husband moody brooding, distant and angry. Gina deserved better and I could forgive her this. Couldn't I? Sure I was angry, but I would never harm Gina despite my thinking for her lapse in judgement. I had stared at her five foot nine naked figure with its well-endowed breasts and tiny waist and wondered how she hid our baby in it.

Her curly black hair fell in ringlets to her waist. I realized I loved her. I loved our baby. It had been my neglect that had driven her to this; I was prepared to forgive her and take her on my planned trip. We'd been married fifteen glorious years, okay so not

glorious, fiery; but she was also pregnant
and I wanted my child to have a stable home
with two parents one of them me. I'd been
spared so my kid could grow up with a dad
it was as simple as that.

I told Gina all of this and she laughed. It
seems that she and her paramour had been
carrying on since day one of one of our
marriage. Once more she had an
amniocentesis last week and received the
results this morning the baby was his not
mine. I was devastated all those dreams of
playing catch with my daughter. Taking her
to daughter and daddy dances. Having her
look up to me, with hero worship came
crashing down. Yes, I know it could have
been a boy; but I had my heart set on a girl.

I admit it I went against all my principles
and begged her to stay and claim the baby
was mine. We were married so the baby was
legally mine. She laughed that twinkly laugh
that I knew so well and I had to restrain
myself from retaliating as she told me she
already left me I just hadn't noticed. Gina
said she was tired of living a lie. Now that I

knew it was all out in the open and she file
for divorce and move in with him. She
lunged at me slapping me and asked why
could I be like him?

I want to hit back at her but I couldn't if I it
back I wouldn't be any better than the men I
arrested who abused their wives.

Why couldn't I be like him? The man that
she slept with, she raged. I was stupefied
and getting angrier by the moment I knew I
needed to leave before I regretted losing my
temper; but I needed to know who had
replaced me.

She laughed again and said I find out soon. I
begged her to tell me and she did.

HIM?

I fell to my knees. How could it be him? No, it wasn't Gordon Chum; but someone else I considered a friend and brother. Gordon wouldn't do that to me. The dirty dog who had betrayed me had been a partner, a mentor and good grief the man was old...fifty five if he was a day and close to retirement.

Why had she cheated on me with my former partner Derek? He'd broken the cop code you didn't sleep with another cop's wife. He'd slept around I heard how many women he'd been with had she? I told her and she laughed telling me it was his cover story. She continued snickering and said at least every woman didn't try to pick him up in front of her. She packed her bags and then trounced out the front door to join him at his house.

I thought I could handle it all and maybe I could have if she hadn't come back a half an hour later saying she'd changed her mind. She stripped to her skivvies and begged me to change her mind. What's a hot blooded male to do? I wanted to prove I was the better man, the better lover, so I turned my back and began stripping too.

That's the last thing I remember before waking up in hospital. How I got there and what happened after that I couldn't recall until much later.

The doctor kept speaking to me but it sounded like gibberish. My brain didn't want to understand. I don't know why. I closed my eyes, but before I drift under I hear them talking.

"Will he be okay now, doctor?" Gina asked.

"We'll know better when he answers my questions," I perceive the doctor say far away.

I recalled hearing footsteps as someone left. A voice I recognized as Gina whispered in my ear, "You stupid son of a bitch. Why didn't you die? You'll wish you had now."

I struggled to wake before she could harm me; but I remember it was like moving under quicksand. I heard an alarm sound and footsteps run into the room.

"What did you do you now, you evil bitch?" I heard Gordon yell as I feel myself falling through layers of unconsciousness into nothingness.

# Chapter 2 -

# Taking My Life

# Back

S o I left a lot out, sue me. You want to

know what really happened? Gina grabbed
my gun and at close quarters shot me in the
chest as I stripped to my skivvies. Her
partner in crime, my former partner, and
superior Derek Chittwood then walked in
(while I hung onto to life by a thread)
quickly plugging me again placing the gun
in my own hand.

Lucky for me the neighbour heard and
called the cops and an ambulance. At first
my superiors and the other cops actually

believed I had tried to commit suicide like the bitch said.

I was taken to surgery and then intensive care where I lingered between heaven and hell but that's another story only waking to her comment in my ear.

The only one who didn't believe I had tried to kill me was Gordon Chum and he guarded me night and day so that bitch couldn't finish me.

Gordon managed to get her on video trying to kill me along with my former partner Derek Critchwood sneaking in and trying to help her finish the job; so they were finally arrested. As for me I lingered in a coma for six long weeks.

I know a lot of people say this but I was a changed man when I woke up a month later. The doctor said that sometimes this happens after a traumatic brain injury. My personality was different I was more

assertive and utterly calm except for my
burning hatred for Gina.

My attitude, the one that basically let people
roll over me was gone. I wouldn't be the
push-over or fall boy anymore. I could deal
with people better even if I had along
recovery ahead of me learning to walk all
over again. No, it was easy but I felt more
alive and strangely stronger than I had in all
my life.

That's when my long lost uncle, my
mother's brother came it my life. It seemed
he'd been searching for us. Finding my
mother dead; he was upset but he seemed
happy to find out my first name was Gunner.
I found out that was because my uncle's last
name was Gunnerson and his first name
Thomas like my middle name. Mother had
told me that I should avoid her side like the
plague should I encounter them because they
were laws only onto themselves but I was
curious.

Uncle Tommy as he told me had fallen out
of touch with my mother simply because she

didn't approve of her family's life style. Uncle Tommy was her half-brother (his father was my grandfather) and his step-father an enforcer for my grandfather the head of a mob family. Tommy had been welcomed into the family fold and became a fixture. You'd think that Uncle Tommy wouldn't have told me ant of this but oddly enough Uncle Tommy felt comfortable telling me this simply because he had researched how I felt about family. He was right as long as he didn't openly kill anyone or give me any ammunition I wouldn't arrest him.

Uncle Tommy had wanted to take that bitch out (as he put it) who had tried to off me and my former boss; but I refused. I didn't want my new found uncle to get into trouble that would send him to jail. He told me he approved of my friend, Gordon and said that he was a friend indeed; after all Gordon had saved my life.

I should have refused to have anything to do with him after all I was law abiding; but the fact that he looked like an older version of

myself with loads of charisma made him
more palatable.  I wanted that family
connection with my mother and I felt he
could tell me more of her story then my
presently known family who only seemed to
care about the Bullet side of the family.

Uncle Tommy was full of stories about my
mother and happily told me how she stood
up to their father and how shew as the
bravest woman he knew. She had run away
from their life of crime and had hidden from
their father finding a happy life if only for a
short while. He even said he envied her then
backtracked saying he'd made his life he
had to live with it.

Uncle Tommy gave me a phone number to
reach him at and said he'd be in touch. He
also said if I ever needed him urgently he
could be paged at a certain number. I
thought that odd and said no one pages
anymore. He said just because technology
changed doesn't mean the old is bad and
then was gone in a flash.

After that I'd see Uncle Tommy a couple of times a year when he suddenly appear, or at least talk to him occasionally by phone that is until a year ago when he suddenly seemed to cut ties; but we'll talk about that much later in my account. In the meantime Gordon helped me investigate why Gina had turned on me.

We found out that papers had arrived from a lawyer. An inheritance from an estranged great-aunt; my mother's great-aunt Matilda had died and had regretted her estrangement from me and my mother. She had not wanted my mother to marry a cop and had stopped speaking to her after their marriage. Now just before my great-aunt had died she had hired a lawyer to find me and had left her entire estate of twenty million dollars to me. The money would be settled on me with in the next few weeks; so Gina had decided that I was worth more dead than alive. She and Derek had decided that I would die through 'suicide' and then after a few weeks the bereaved widow would marry Derek and inherit my money

Gina could have gotten half of all my money. I would have given it to then; but since I had been comatose my mindset had changed; no more push over G. She would be going to prison and I would give her nothing!! Okay so I lied; I couldn't be that cruel even to someone who had tried to kill me; after all I'd once loved her. I'll get to that in a bit.

Gina lingered in jail awaiting trial as did Derek as I recovered slowly. It took months before I could walk again. Working as a cop was out for at least a year. Meanwhile Gina had given birth to a little girl in jail. The authorities had allowed her to keep the child but I felt bad for the child. Jail was no place for a child and she had no father either for Derek was in another jail.

The trial loomed and I looked forward to getting over with. I had also sought out a lawyer to get a divorce but stray thoughts lingered about the baby girl Gina had given birth to in jail. What proof did I have that she was Derek's child?

I demanded a DNA test through my lawyer and Gina tried to refuse but I was adamant. Gina offered a counter proposal she would submit to a DNA test if I put in a good word for her. I refused. My lawyer persisted even as the trial took place to get the baby tested.

Gina decided to plead guilty and throw herself on the mercy of the court. They took pity on her sentenced her to fifteen years. Derek went to trial and got thirty years. I thought it was all over but then first I found out the baby girl was mine. The DNA test proved it beyond a shadow of a doubt. I found out from the lawyer even though she was in prison for attempting to kill me, Gina had rights to our daughter. She could keep her there for at least three years. What a terrible place for our daughter. I begged my lawyer to help me secure custody of my baby girl. It should have been easy but it wasn't mostly because I was still not healthy so I worked on that but the custody issue dragged on and still I'd not seen my daughter.

Gina begged me to visit her. As she held our baby, Gina asked if I wanted to hold her and the guard let me. The little girl had dark brown curls tight to her head and she had eyes that were as blue as the sky on the most beautiful summer day. Her skin was pale with tiny rosy cheeks. Her lips were like little tiny rosebuds and my heart skipped a beat. Tears formed my eyes as I looked at the beauty of this little child. She looked like my mother when she was a baby and I was amazed at the genetics that had produced this combination.

The baby was now almost a year old and as she took my finger she said, "Dada."

I don't think I'd ever loved anything as fiercely as I loved that child. Gina told me her name was Stella-Marie and begged me to raise our daughter. She said that other inmates had threatened her and our daughter and that Stella-Marie wasn't safe.

Gina signed over complete custody to me and I took my daughter home that day. I promised to send Gina pictures and notes for Stella-Marie's sake but that any contact would be censored by me. After all Gina wouldn't be out of jail for at least fifteen years. Gina had sworn she'd never speak to Derek again. I took her at her word; but I'd never really trust her again but she was Stella-Marie's mother forever whether I liked it or not. If I didn't show her kindness that could hurt Stella-Marie; I spoke to the warden about the threats. Even if she deserved punishment she didn't deserve to live in fear of her own death.

I had money and a wonderful little girl but I wanted to be a cop again. So after a year and a half of recovery I went to work. The other cops blamed me for Derek's arrest like it was my fault. I thought it would settle down eventually; but the wall of blue just went higher and it became more difficult to police with no support except Gordon's.

My attorney advised me that I had grounds
to sue. If I ever wanted to work in policing
again then I had to stand up to them. The
way the department had supported a superior
who had broken the moral code, by one
sleeping with a junior cop's wife, then
plotting his murder had violate codes of
ethics and violate employment practices. I
won but it seemed like a hollow victory
when I didn't work as a cop in Halton
anymore. Gordon had had enough too he left
to work for the FBI.

With Aunt Louisa's help (at least at first) I
then became the father Stella-Marie
deserved. Gordon was her honorary uncle
and came to visit frequently before he was
transferred to his Colorado office. And now
we were all together again. I could show my
daughter I could be an upstanding citizen
and then this had to happen. My whole force
and some of their family members
murdered. Gordon and I had to find out who
did this.

I needed to take action. I needed to gather my troops and discuss possible suspects and motives. Usually with cop murders the suspects were perpetrators who had violated statues in some way shape or form. Drug dealers, wife beaters, gun runners, it was probably some low-life criminal and we could wrap this up fast and get down to the brass tacks of running my police station her in Driftwood, Colorado I thought. Little was to know how hard that would be and how much of uphill battle it would be.

~0~

# Chapter 3 – Driftwood

$\mathbf{M}$y phone buzzed it was Penny

Ambercrombie voice which I heard through the intercom, "Sheriff Bullet we've got a problem down at the high school."

"Problem? Can't someone else handle it? I'm searing through the crimes in the database to find a connection to our families' murderers. It's bad enough I have to shift through these police officers' lives and basically take them and their families' lives just because some asshole decided to kill them. "

"Gee whiz, Sheriff, I'm not the bad guy here. Save that shit for the perpetrator of these crimes. I knew each one of those cops. They were my colleagues and I'm grieving for them all. You're the top cop here and right now there's no one else to investigate crimes and this one is pretty serious," Penny stated sassily.

"You're right Penny. I'm sorry. Please put the principal on," I admitted. I picked up the line to hear from the principal of Driftwood High School.

"Sheriff Bullet here."

"Maggie Champlain here. I'm principal at Driftwood High. I understand with these awful murders you've got some staffing issues but we need some down here ASAP."

"Can you explain to me the problem?"

"I'll explain when you get here; but believe me I wouldn't call, if it weren't serious".

"I'll be there in five or ten that is after Penny gives me directions," I agreed.

"Thank-you Sheriff: I'll see you soon."

I shuffled the notes I'd made about investigating bank accounts and having Gordon check his sources for Cayman Island accounts or any other offshore accounts. I didn't want to think these cops were dirty, but I was practical. One of the biggest

reasons for killing them and their families'
had to be hiding evidence of a crime.

The other reason? That they were just a war
on the sheriff's department. After all the
reason I got the job was (I had found
out)because they were short one sheriff due
to a stray bullet. Maybe we should be
looking into that crime too?

I grabbed my keys only stopping at Penny's
desk for a moment for directions. The
sooner I became familiar with Driftwood
and its streets the better.

I noted from a distance that the high school
was like most in this country. It had been
built in the baby boom time in the fifties and
it showed its wear. A gray tattered brick
building that sprawled over a half a block; I
only hoped that the asbestos they used in a
lot of the other buildings wasn't present as
well. Maybe I'd check into that later; after
all at some point Stella-Marie would go to

school here as this building housed grades six to twelve.

As I pulled up to the high school I saw two ambulances arrive and I worried that this was more serious than I thought. Should I have brought some more cops? Did we have an active shooter?

No, it couldn't be that, or Ms. Champlain would have informed me and so would have Penny in no uncertain terms. So why were two ambulances here? No better time to find out then the present I parked my car and darted over to the ambulance before it left.

"Sheriff Bullet?" a woman asked standing beside the first ambulance.

The woman was knocked down gorgeous. Her hair fiery red and curly, hung in corkscrew natural ringlets about her face. Her eyes were blue like the prettiest summer sky. Her skin was pale and had the tiniest little freckles across the bridge of her nose. She had on a floral dress in a pattern of small poppies with a matching reddish orange jacket to cover her bare shoulders in

the sundress. Matching flat sandals
completed the look.

Frankly I didn't usually notice or care about
fashion, but this woman stirred something
inside me. Maybe I'd been without a woman
too long but she was hot! I shook myself. I
was on the job, no distractions besides in
this day and age sexual harassment was a
no-no. I should be better than this.

Stella-Marie and I were happy with Aunt
Louise another woman in the mix would
complicate things. Handle the task at hand
and bury yourself in work; then go home
and make a happy life for Stella-Marie.
Stella-Marie was my priority, no one else.

"Ms. Champlain I presume." I answered.

"This has been a horrendous morning. I'm
glad you're here."

"Why are the ambulances here?"

"There were two incidents. First we found a
baby in the staff room. It looks like someone
has given birth there and since it wasn't one

of the staff it only leaves one of our
students. If that student gave birth in a dirty
bathroom they need medical care... now!!
Without proper medical care the mother may
be in significant pain, may be bleeding
internally, and is at risk of a serious
infection...at least that's what the
paramedics said."

"Is the baby alive?"

"Yes, the paramedics seem to think it's a
full term baby and healthy; but they'll know
better when they get it to the hospital. If that
wasn't enough we found one of the students
had overdosed in one the boy's bathrooms.
The student that overdosed though is in
grave condition. Someone is dealing a new
drug in this school...a deadly drug the
paramedics tell me. It's possibly an opioid.
The boy might not even make it and I still
have to call his parents."

"I'm sorry to hear that. Is there a huge
amount of drugs filed through this school?"

"Are you blaming this school? I do my very
best but I can't be everywhere at once.
There's always drug dealing in every school
no matter how much you try to keep the

dealers out," Ms. Champlain answered defensively.

"I'm not blaming you there's only so much that you can do. I just want to get to the bottom of this."

"I think that it's best you speak with our head security guard Nathan Ricci about the drugs in this school; but first I want to tell you the rumors about this baby."

"Rumors...should I really put stock in high school rumors?"

"Normally I don't but if there's any factual basis for this rumor..."

"Tell me..."

"Right after the baby was found I overheard a bunch of girls talking about a pregnant teen,"

"Then you found the girl?"

"No, presently the young girls who gossiped are in my office being grilled by the vice principal, Hiram Grim. Poor Hiram! I've had to insist for his protection that he always have another staff member present when with students so my secretary is also there."

"Despite his name Hiram is what the young girls consider a hottie. Hiram acted when he was young and has a lot of screen credits as Richard Grim so the students treat him like he's a walking God," Maggie prattled on seeming nervous and flustered, "And of course there's also the aspect that they also said that the baby's father was your dead deputy.

"Wait a minute; you speak of my dead deputy, Greg Barnes?"

"Yes, the rumor is he had an affair with one of the girls here. Now if I can just track down which one. She needs medical help."

"That can't be true."

"Listen up, Sheriff Bullet.

"Call me Stray or Gee your choice," I retorted.

"Fine then Gee, call me Maggie; but if there's any chance your deputy did impregnate one of my teenage girls than that gives someone a motive for the killing. Doesn't it? So help me find that girl."

"Hey I'm not the enemy here. I'll help you anyway I can. Finding this girl is a number one priority. After all she needs medical attention; but as for ferreting out this information on the pregnancy I think you have better access to the sources. I also need to find out who is feeding drugs to the students and put a stop to it," I exclaimed rubbing my hand through my hair in frustration.

A woman of about thirty years old but appearing much younger, wearing a yellow sundress and strappy matching yellow sandals her long blonde hair perfectly curled and her make-up done expertly suddenly appeared at my elbow looking like she stepped off a magazine cover.. How had she gotten so close and I hadn't even heard or seen her until now I wondered?

"Is she in the ambulance?" the woman asked.

"Whom, ma'am?"

"My step-daughter Alicia. She called me but the damn cell phone cut out. She said someone at first that I thought ridiculous. I mean where does a one hundred pound girl hide a full term baby? It was full term wasn't it? Alicia insisted she's keeping her son. I told her to call 911 but she probably forgot to charge her cell phone again."

"Your step-daughter called you? Do you know where she was in the school?"

"You don't know where she is? But the ambulance... why isn't she in the ambulance? Is the baby alright?"

"Mrs. Jellnak we found the baby in the washroom but Alicia wasn't there," I answered.

"God damn that girl. I had to dress and do my make-up and hair before I came and of course I was groggy because we were at the mayor's party last night until four a.m."

"Where do you think Alicia could be?" I prodded.

"Alicia must have gone for help for herself. The call was pretty choppy. I bought her the top of the line cell phone and the best service and I still can't hear her half the time on that phone. I don't know why she couldn't have handled this herself. She better not expect me to take care of this baby. I'm not cut out to be a mother. I'm a busy woman I'm supposed to get a dress for the charity ball that's Friday night. I'm not sure she even heard me; but I think she said something about breaking.do you think she was talking about her breaking point?" the woman answered.

What a stupid woman, so shallow and brainless. The poor kid with a step-mom like that I thought.

"Break could she have said break room?" Maggie asked.

"Maybe; like I don't know. I'm only her step-mom. I've only been her step-mom for like six weeks and I can't reach Donald.

He's her father he should handle this not me."

Maggie instructed one of the ambulance attendants to come with her while the other attended the baby. We found Alicia on the teacher's break room floor. She lost blood and was found unconscious; but in her hand was a note that told where here baby was and how much she loved him and his name Anton.

The attendant radioed the other ambulance driver who brought the equipment and the baby. They then stabilized Alicia and with our assistance took both mom and baby to the waiting ambulance. The assured me that the hospital would radio me when she was stable enough to talk. I really needed to get to the bottom of this so I could confirm or deny that Greg Barnes was the father of a fourteen year old's baby. Good lord, what kind of department had this police force been running and what other secrets could they hold that had gotten them killed? I then went to speak to the security guard who had discovered the overdosed student.

Maggie led the way into the school, down a long hallway to where Mr. Ricci was breaking open lockers. Some students had voluntarily opened their lockers. Others milled around protesting as he used huge pliers to break into their lockers.

"All the students have to sign a code of honor and that means they can have their lockers searched at any time for drugs and any other contraband," Maggie explained.

Nathan Ricci stood about six feet tall His hair was dark brown short and cut in a military style. His smile did not meet his eyes and that alone made me leery of the guy. Not only that but his arms and legs were the size of tree trunks. I knew a few guys like this and either they were unsure of their manhood or they were genuinely health conscious. I wondered which category he would fit into?

"Mr. Ricci this is Sheriff Bullet."

"Nice to meet you," Mr. Ricci said as he outstretched his hand for shaking.

"Have you found anything yet Mr. Ricci?" Maggie asked.

"Now haven't I asked you to call me Nathan? Say can we get together for a drink tonight?"

"Mr. Ricci I've spoken to you about this. Given the nature of our relationship (after all I am your superior) this is inappropriate."

"Can't blame a guy for trying, can you?" Mr. Ricci retorted then turning to me he stated, "She's one hot tamale."

"Mr. Ricci I'd like our interaction to be productive; but your behaviour towards your boss borders on criminal," I charged.

"Geesh everything is about political correctness nowadays. I guy can't breathe without being admonished."

Maggie smiled at me after this and for a minute my heart beat a few extra beats. This woman was so beautiful inside and out.

"Oh I see what's going here. You like the law and order type. Security guards aren't good enough for you eh teach?"

"Mr. Ricci can we get back to the task at hand? Have you any idea which student or students could be responsible for dealing the drug that caused this overdose?" I asked.

"Well that Verma boy and his friend the Kassaba Muslim kid, then there's that no good, unruly violent, trailer trash, the Baker kid, all of these kids are suspicious," Mr. Ricci answered.

Maggie cleared her throat obviously in frustration with the man's clear racism and bias against the poor and different.

"Are there any with records of violations so you could help point Sheriff Bullet in the right direction?"

"There are the Donnelly boys. They are fifteen and seventeen years old going on fifty. Those lads have been in trouble since they were in diapers and nothing has changed. Their parents are degenerates and criminal types. Their dad serves a five sentence for assault. He's due out next year and the mom has new boyfriends every week; usually those biker types"

"Anyone else you can think of?"

"The Richardson's. Troy stole a car last year and got three months' probation. He's fourteen. Then there's his older brother, Calvin. Calvin is as slippery as an eel. You always suspect the guy but you can never get the goods on him"

"And that's all? The only kids that could have been dealing?"

"I guess there is those rich kids the Hollingwood's and the mayor's kids but you won't be able to touch them with a ten foot pole."

"Because they are rich they'll get off? Not in my police station Mr. Ricci."

"You haven't met Judge Purcell yet, have you?" Ricci smirked. "Judge Purcell is golf and poker buddies with the mayor. He also received large amounts of campaign money from the mayor. Last year when I submitted evidence that I found large amounts of ecstasy in his locker the judge ruled that the locker could have been tampered with and then let the mayor's son, Ethan float away free and that brat assaulted me too. He kicked my shins and tried to smash my face. You'd think that would have gotten him some time but the judge ruled that I provoked him. I hate that judge."

What a spectacular fuck-up this turned out to be. The mayor's kids being involved could screw up my retention next year; hopefully I'd find it was all in this racist hate spewing security guards mind.

I'd almost got to my car when this kid (if you could call a muscle bound three hundred pound solid mass a teenager) flew out of nowhere and tried to take me down. Okay, so he knocked me down. But I had him handcuffed and his arms behind his back before he was able to get up.

"SHIT!! Fuckin' unreal did you see that new Sheriff take down the Hulk?" I heard one milling student shot to another.

"Yah, that was so fast. That guy has trained in like martial arts or something," the other male student said.

He had the muscle mass and the skill but I had trained with the best. Did I forget to mention that my uncles were former marines? They had trained me since I was a baby to deal with whatever came my way.

"Name and age?" I demanded but all I got from my attacker were expletives. I marched the guy over to my cruiser and stuck him in the back of the car.

"The new Sheriff is so hot, he looks like a young Tom Selleck without the mustache," I heard a female student say as I reached over to buckle my prisoner in and shut the door.

"I think I'm in love. He's so much better looking than the vice principal. I hear he's single," a young teen said.

"Damn that cuts me out," said the disappointed teen.

"I think I've still got a chance," said the other.

"Dream on, Sabina," the disappoint teen stated; "The principal hasn't been interested in anyone since her husband died two years ago. If she likes him we haven't a chance."

That I didn't need! Teens fawning over me... Yuck!! But was Maggie making goo-goo eyes at me? She was so beautiful and single. A widow interesting, did I stand a chance? Did I want to?

I glanced over at her; as Maggie hurried to my side and said in a calm but clear manner, "Move along students; unless you'd prefer a detention?"

The students cleared out like there was a fire and soon only Maggie and I stood beside my car.

"Sorry about that. Not a great reception for you at my school. I saw what Reggie did to you but you handled that expertly. I can see why you're the new Sheriff."

I didn't say anything but the next thing she said was, "Oh, you're blushing. I'm sorry."

"Not at all I wasn't blushing I've just got a little too much sun today," I lied but I knew I didn't fool her.

"Er, his name is Reggie? I stated awkwardly.

Yes, that's Reggie Calladen."

"Calladen, any relation to the mayor, Ethan Calladen?"

"Yes, he's the mayor's oldest son. He's nineteen."

"Nineteen years old, isn't that a little old for high-school?"

"Reggie is a challenged student. He hates school but loves football. We've assisted him and he actually may graduate this year. I think he's hoping for a football scholarship; although he's dad can afford college for him. He's helped us win the pennant for our school and unfortunately he's also the overdose victim, Henry Balsom's best friend. I think he's afraid that if Henry lives you'll arrest Henry."

"Is Reggie Calladen a big user of steroids or any other drugs?"

"I wouldn't have thought so but you'd be surprised which students. Tread lightly careful Sheriff; the mayor will try to rake you over the coals if his son is charged. He tried to have me fired when Ethan Junior was expelled for three days."

"Thank-you for looking out for me. I'm inclined to let this go with a warning after a few hours in a jail cell and not because he's the mayor's son either."

"Did anyone ever tell you you're a nice man, Sheriff Bullet?"

"Please, I asked you to call me Gee, or Stray; you said you would."

"Sorry, Gee. I know this is rather forward; but would you like to meet for a coffee sometime?"

"I'd like that," I answered.

Maggie wrote her name and number on her planner she carried and then ripped it out and passed it to me.

"What no I-Pad?"

"Computers are allowed but no I-Pads. We had a rash of I-Pad thefts so the school council banned them."

"See you later, Maggie. I'll call you when some of this ruckus dies down."

"See you later. Gee."

I settled myself into my squad car and started the engine with Reggie kicking and screaming through the mesh and wire that separated him from the front seat.

"Calm down, Reggie," I ordered.

"F-off pig," he yelled.

I ignored him it would be a long ride to the station and an even longer day; once his father found out. I wondered if I'd made a mistake taking this job then I decided I was up to the task. I'd solve these murders and fix the drug problem at the high school.

~0~

## Chapter 4 – Reggie

W hen I arrived at the station I

escorted my prisoner into the station to gasps and whispered conversation. I ignored it all, even my prisoner's retort that I would be so sorry because his father would fire my ass. After I placed Reggie in the cell and he put his cuffs out through the opening I unlocked them and Reggie started up again by kicking the bars. Of course that's when his honor the mayor walked in. Ethan Calladen walked taller than his five foot six height. Some people would have believed him at least five foot nine or ten but not me. I'd seen his slick type before; the thing they cared most about was their image, followed by money, so this arrest was not going to curry me any favors.

Ethan frowned at me and then smiled it
didn't bode well for me.

Sheriff Bullet, I want to see you in private!"
Mayor Calladen demanded.

"Certainly Mayor; I believe I have a few
moments before my meeting in the
conference room with the FBI. My office?"

"Lead the way Sheriff Bullet."

"Dad it wasn't my fault."

"Shut-up Reggie, I'll deal with you in a few
moments."

"Gary? Can you handle the cells?" I asked
the new recruit, Gary Evans hired this
morning.

"You've got it Sheriff. Besides there's only
Reggie and the guy in the drunk tank," Gary
answered.

I'd no sooner closed the door then Penny Ambercrombie knocked at the door in her one hand she had a coffee in a mug and a Coke for me somewhat awkwardly held in one hand. Already Penny knew I preferred Coke or coffee this was kind of scary the woman was an enigma. The coffee she brought Mayor Calladen was perfect too. He seemed happy that she had taken the time to put it in a coffee cup and not a paper cup.

"Thank-you Penny, that will be all," I said and she closed the door frowning.

"Penny's good people. They've had the Ambercrombie ranch for more than a hundred years. My ranch touches theirs," Mayor Calladen commented.

"Mayor Calladen I'm sorry I had to arrest your son but..."

"Reggie was out of line. I heard Reggie lost his cool and blamed you for the overdose of his acquaintance. He's a bit of a hot-head and more like his wasteful, jet-setting, money grubbing mother than me, or his brother. Damn kid should lose some weight that's his real problem."

I couldn't believe the mayor; who chooses
one son over the other? If the kid had
troubles you could probably lay them right
at the mayor's feet. Reggie was product of
his father's lack of love.

"I was told the boy was his best friend and
therefore I need to take his statement."

"Poppycock, a mere recent acquaintance of
no consequence; believe me I don't want
Reggie hanging out with the gutter trash.
But how is the troubled boy will he live?"

"Do you really care?" I asked.

"Of course I care I care about my city or I
wouldn't have hired you. Now you will drop
all the charges and let my son out of that jail
cell?"

"He attacked me; but I'm prepared to let that
go provided he fills me in on his friend."

"I am your boss; but I can be reasonable.
Can I speak to him first?"

What was I to do? The mayor had me over a barrel. I nodded but I didn't like it. The mayor was actually being too nice I felt like he was holding something back. Would he retaliate against me later?

"You can speak to Reggie, after I take his statement," I agreed.

"So the troubled boy will he live?"

"The last update I had was that it was touch and go," I replied.

"That's good. Now the investigation into our dead cops and family, just how far are you on that?"

"It's in the beginning stages. Frankly, if I'm being honest with you there's a lot of investigating to do."

"That's certainly a first. Most people like pleasing me so much they give me colorful stories about how they're way ahead," Mayor Calladen responded.

"I am trying your honor."

"Don't get your hackles up Bullet! I realize investigating takes time and that the FBI can be a hindrance, but we also need this crime solved. Citizens are calling me day and night. Find the culprit or culprits and nail them to the wall. Now take me to my foolish boy."

"As I said I need to take his statement first."

I only hoped that the mayor wouldn't get Reggie to shut-up. I needed whatever information I could get out of him. I took the mayor to Reggie's cell.

The mayor was up to something he was being too nice. I had looked him up before I took the job and I knew he had a reputation of interfering with police business. I had been assured when I took the job that he wouldn't be a problem by the deputy mayor Geraldine Crocker, but I still was on my guard.

"I don't think that is a good idea."

"Really, Sheriff Bullet? I don't want to pull rank but I am your boss. Besides what will a few minutes with my boy cost you?"

"Fine," I answered.

"I'm not going to talk to him here; at least take him to a room so I can speak to my boy in private," the mayor requested.

"I'll take you both to Interview Room C. You can speak in private there. When you're finished come find me down the hall in the break room. It's two doors down," I explained.

I only hoped that the mayor wouldn't get Reggie to shut-up. I needed whatever information I could get out of him. I took the mayor to Reggie's cell. Now I could spy on them with the two way glass and at least know what the mayor said to Reggie even if it wasn't strictly on the up and up. I needed to protect my ass and the integrity of this station.

I pretended to go to the men's room as
Penny Ambercrombie watched; but as soon
as she turned her back I turned back and
entered the room where I could watch their
interaction through the glass.

"You stupid little punk!!"I heard Mayor
Calladen say and then he reached out and
smacked Reggie on the back of the head.

I almost went in then as a white rage burned
through me. I hated child abuse even when
the kid was of age. No one should hit their
child or anyone else. Reggie sat there not
saying a word.

"What the hell is wrong with you? Are you
trying to embarrass me or make me lose my
position?"

"No!" Reggie exclaimed.

"Do you have brain damage from playing football? What were you thinking attacking a sheriff? Have you lost your mind?"

"What are you talking about, he's a deputy?"

"The deputy is dead murdered! Did you do that too?"

"No, he isn't; he's out there and he arrested me."

"You idiot! That is the sheriff; the deputy was murdered three days ago. Where were you three days go?"

"What? He's not the deputy? But..."

"You thought he was the deputy? Now tell me Reggie, where were you three days ago."

"Don't you ever pay attention to anything I do? I was at that football tourney in Denver. You know the one I begged you to come to; but you wouldn't come? But what else is new?" Reggie whined.

"Thank God, you have an alibi."

"I'm glad that bastard's dead."

"You're glad he's dead? Don't you dare say that to anyone else! Wait a minute... it's that girl she has something to do with this. You haven't taken up with her again? You wouldn't do something so foolish after I warned you that she was jail bait? That's not my grandchild?" The mayor shouted while pacing up and down in the interview room.

"I love her but we never...How do I put it in your terms? She's a good girl, dad!"

"She's a fourteen year old slut with a baby. I told you she was looking for a fall guy to look after her! Her father is a businessman; but her mother was the town whore. She'd tried to get me to sleep with her but I was too smart to fall for those tricks," screamed the mayor angrily.

"What? She didn't try to get you to sleep with her take that back."

"She's a slut, boy!!"

"He raped her!!"

"What in the hell are you talking about who raped her? Is that her story? You idiot!! That's the oldest story in the book. She's stringing you along as her back-up guy."

"If I weren't handcuffed to this table ..."

"You'd do what? Hit me? Just try it boy! I brought you into this world I can take you out. I own your ass while you're living under my roof. And don't you forget that! And if you want me to help you out with that college you're considering you better stop talking to me with such disrespect."

"You don't understand, dad. I'm not trying to disrespect you. I just want you to know the truth. The deputy offered her a ride in his squad car and then he took her to Elk Woods and he raped her."

"Why would he have done that? You're mistaken!!Or she came on to him."

"She wasn't the only one dad; just the only one to get pregnant. Helena Harold, Taneesha Rollins, Carlotta Barnes are just a few."

I shook my head. With what I just heard this just gets worse and worse. I hoped I could get to the bottom of this but this would not go down well the hero of the community was now a pedophile and a rapist.

"If that's so then how do you know any of this?"

"The girls gossiped to each other and someone overheard and told me. The other girls say he wore a condom and told them he'd kill them and their families if they told anyone."

"This can't be true. I hired that guy. This will ruin me."

"It's not always about you dad. What about all those young girls he raped? And poor Alicia?"

"I'm the mayor. As for those girls they'll get help and deal. I'll start up a program to assist them and then I'll restore my good image. Watch and see."

I watched as Reggie rolled his eyes in response.

"You mark my words Reginald. Stay away from that girl, Alicia. You're an innocent when it comes to girls like that. She's nothing but a heap of trouble I know her type. I had to deal with someone like her in high-school. She tried to make me believe I'd fathered her baby and when that didn't work she tried to make me pity her. Alicia will try the same tactics. She's made from the same gutter trash cloth."

"You're cold, dad."

"If I'm so bad, why am I here trying to get you out of jail? You've given me nothing but trouble since the day you were born."

"Yah right, like you care. You only care about my brother, your clone, Ethan."

"Ethan is an upstanding individual. He doesn't get in trouble with the law or take drugs. If he hadn't been covering for you and hiding that ecstasy, he would never have gotten any blemished record."

"Is that what he told you? And you believed him? He's an even better model than you are at lying dad. He was dealing out of his locker. Where do you think he got all that money to go away on that ski trip to Aspen last winter?"

"Your brother worked day and night to earn enough money to go on that class trip and I rewarded him with a few extra bucks. He roomed with several others to save money. He earned that trip."

"You are so delusional. He took some computers from the computer lab to a nearby city and hawked them. He then told the school he wouldn't be on that trip that he was visiting an uncle. You being the mayor they didn't argue; they just accepted your forged signature saying he could stay with an uncle while on the trip. Of course there was no uncle Ethan took the computer money and the cash he got from supplying ecstasy and rented a chalet for himself and his buddies."

"You're lying! Why do you always make up these horrible stories about your brother? He always defends you too, even though you're a terrible example to him and are so cruel."

"You are so fucked!! I love my brother but the truth is he's a sociopath. He needs help that you can't give him!! I keep bailing him out; but he keeps tripping up and one of these days neither of us will be able to save him!"

"I can forgive you. You can't help being jealous of his good looks, model behaviour and charisma. Maybe I am to blame. I did favor him as he was so ill as a baby. That must have made you feel unloved for that I'm sorry but this has to stop. Do you understand me, Reginald?

"You keep living the life where I'm the screw-up and he's the perfect child; but one of these days it will bite you on the ass."

"I'll get you out of this Reggie; but you better shape-up, or I'm going to make you enrol in the military."

"You could never make me enrol in the military. I'm not a soldier."

"The military made your grandfather a great man. It could make you a better one. I could make it a condition of your release."

"Please dad, don't do that."

Reggie looked scared and contrite like he was ready to beg and I felt sorry for him. His father was an asshole. Reggie was right his father only cared about his other son and his job. When it came right down to it he probably loved his other son more because he saw himself in it.

"Do you promise to stay away from Alicia and sincerely apologise to the sheriff? You could tell him about Alicia and the other girls that would make him more amenable to dropping the charges."

Reggie looked like he wanted to refuse; but then he swallowed and said, "Fine, you win as usual."

"She's too young anyway, son, basically jailbait. I'm protecting you."

"Sure you are," Reggie said under his breath. The microphone picked it up but not the mayor luckily for Reggie.

I left the observation room at that point and walked to the break room. It wouldn't do to be caught eavesdropping by the mayor and I had received a lot of information that could help me in my investigation but there was still a long way to go. Entering the room I was thankful that no one was in it. I glanced at my watch my meeting with all the FBI guys would be soon I hoped the mayor would come here soon. I casually filled my mug and waited for the mayor to come to me.

~0~

# Chapter 5 - Getting to know council

The mayor wandered in a few minutes later looking his smug self. Looking at me expectantly I nodded at him and then I filled a coffee mug for him.

I asked "Cream, sugar?"

"Two creams, two sugars," he answered.

"Is Reggie ready to speak to me?" I asked.

"Reggie is. He's sorry about his behavior. He has mitigating circumstances. I'll let him explain, but it's not really criminal behaviour. I'm sure you can use any information he can offer in your investigation into Deputy Greg Barnes death. Something Deputy Greg Barnes did may have caused his premeditated death."

"Are you insinuating that a deputy committed a crime?" I exclaimed feigning that I hadn't listened in.

"Cut the crap, Sheriff Bullet. I know you listened in on the conversation because it's what I would have done if I were you."

"That's unethical and something I would never do!" I protested indignantly.

He looked taken aback and I think he believed me for he exclaimed, "I'm sorry Sheriff if I offended you. Reggie will be happy to give you a statement now."

"Does he want a lawyer present?" I asked.

"No, but of course I understand you have to ask him. That is if you are going to drop the charges?"

"Yes, I will drop the charges if Reggie apologises," I agreed.

I followed the mayor back to the interview
room. The mayor asked if he could sit in the
corner and he promised not to interrupt. I
allowed it as I thought he'd just watch
through the glass and interrupt anyway.
Besides I was still trying to stay on his good
side.

The interview was over after a few minutes
with Reggie apologising completely. He
reluctantly shared the names of the young
women who he had heard gossip of their
rapes by Greg Barnes. Reggie spilled
everything with prompting from his father
everything but what he'd said about his
brother. But I'd investigate his brother's
former crimes later.

I asked if Reggie if he knew the families of
the victims and he reluctantly gave me those
names. The mayor chimed in to asking me
to keep those details from the press until we

could get a handle and proof of this appalling news. I agreed as it might jeopardize my investigation not because the mayor wanted me to

.

The mayor then told me of his plans to set up an abused women shelter in town along with counselling for women who have been raped. He said a year ago the council had voted down funding for a new clinic/women's shelter but the mayor had voted for it. He had been working the last year to find sponsors of whom were willing to donate large sums of money and he'd finally been able to garner the funding. An unused building shuttered because of the economic downturn had been bought for a song and he hoped to begin renovating it in the next week.

I un-cuffed Reggie, cautioned him to respect the law from now on and he left the building. The mayor however did not; he lingered as if he had something else to say.

"You know I hate just calling you Sheriff
and having you refer to me as the mayor; I
think we should be on less formal terms
giving that were going to continually run
into each other while I'm dong city
business," the mayor started while following
me back to my office.

"Call me G," I offered smiling, but I didn't
really trust this congenial offering of his.  I
offered him a seat in my office and he
offered me his hand.

"I'm Ethan," he replied.

I shook his hand but vowed never to trust his
honor the mayor. He was slippery, slimy and
would stick a knife in my back if it made
him look good. All this fake camaraderie
was interrupted by a knock at the door.
Penny barged in and said, "You have an
interview with the new police candidates
starting at one p.m. and the meeting with the
FBI guys will start in fifteen minutes in the
conference room."

"Can't you handle the new hires, Penny?
I'm trying to conduct an investigation," I
complained.

"Sheriff, I work very hard at this station and
make sure all the paperwork is done and all
the calls are answered. But there's much
more than that I do. I don't have the time or
the inclination to conduct interviews, nor the
qualifications. I'm sorry you have so much
on your plate but if you hired some new
staff maybe we'd get some more work done
on this investigation."

"I'm sorry, Penny. You're correct you have
been working very hard and making it easier
for me and I appreciate all your hard work."

Penny positively beamed at me and I
thought maybe I should have complimented
her sooner.

"Mr. Mayor, you do know under the town
charter you have to be present for these
interviews too?"

"But I can't be here for one. I have too many things to do. I have to be at the new supermarket opening at one and cut the ribbon and a photo-op at 1:30 p.m. I could use you there if you're free Sheriff?"

"No, sorry I'm up to my ears in meetings and briefings myself," I answered.

"There are going to be times when you have to be available for photo-ops Sheriff. But I'm busy too. So I'll let you off this once." Then turning to Penny he said, "At two p. m. I have a council meeting to debate zoning laws. Let me make a conference call and get back to you Penny."

Penny excuse herself went back to her desk and Ethan then then took out his I-phone and setup a call.

"Harold, Winston, Douglas, Melanie, Gertie are you all on the line?" he asked.

I heard yesses come over the line.

"I want to change the charter so that Sheriff Bullet can hire the new police force with no interference or impute from me."

"If that's all I vote, yes," I heard a woman say.

A man complained that they should go changing the town charter, but was quickly voted down.

The mayor said goodbye put his I-phone away and then said, "It's done now you can hire who you want after you interview them. One caution though get us some law abiding cops we can't afford any more dirty cops and Penny did tell me her brother is applying he's a good man and he's been in Afghanistan."

"A former soldier?" I asked.

"I think so but you'll have to ask him these questions. I just think he might be a good man to have around," Ethan said.

"I'll put his resume on the top of the pile."

"I want you to do more than that. I want you to hire him," Ethan insisted.

"I thought you said I had total control over the hires?" I exclaimed.

"One favor for the other. You wash my back and I'll wash yours."

"Fine," I agreed, because what else could I do?

I then went to my morning meeting with the FBI to update them and get any feedback on the case it was going to be long day I just knew it.

I brought up to Gordon and his team about my idea to search for bank accounts in the Caymans and other offshore accounts but Gordon was way ahead of me and had already started the process with his team. We talked about the investigative process leads and what we could do to find the information we needed to find the killers of my cops.

am I ?” I asked.

“It was a half day for the high school students and some of the seniors left at ten-thirty a.m. after the assembly. They went to the swimming quarry where the kids like to hangout and partied,” Penny whispered then motioned me into the hall.

“So they’re what… drinking underage? Send Paul Grose. He’s great at handling calls like that,” I answered annoyed.

“No, Sheriff; you need to handle this. There’s been another incident.”

“An incident? What has happened?”

“Fourteen students are in critical condition after ingesting some drug. Another is zoned out on something else and there has been a fatality. You need to get to the hospital right away,” Penny stage whispered.

"Fourteen, oh my lord," came out of my mouth before I could stop myself and then I blurted, "What about the interviews for the jobs?"

"You can reschedule some of them for five and six tonight and do the rest tomorrow. I'll set it up," Penny offered.

"Thank you, Penny. I really need to see what I can do," I exclaimed.

I then stuck my head into the room and dismissed the meeting.

"Sheriff business? Anything to do with our case?" Gordon asked.

"I don't think so," I answered.

"Want some company all the same?" Gordon offered.

Gordon spoke happily about his new girlfriend, Perita He never mentioned her last name, but it was obvious he'd fallen hard. It was Perita said this, Perita said that; or Perita did the cutest thing. I'd never seen him so happy. Where had the cynic who said women were a dime a dozen go? Had those ideas become nebulous and unfounded? The more he talked the more worried I became he hadn't known this woman long and he was enthralled. I was the type to jump headlong into things not Gordon who was sensible.

"Got a picture?" I asked.

"Not yet Perita's a little camera shy. She had a bad ex who was stalking her; but he's finally moved on and lost interest."

"That's good but doesn't that mean she's has baggage?"

"We all have baggage, Gee. I'm thinking of asking her to move in with me," Gordon stated.

"You sure you're not rushing this pal? You've known her for what, a month?" I replied.

"It's like I've known her forever, Gee. I want her in my life forever. If I thought she'd say yes, I'd ask her to marry me instead."

"Marry her? Weren't you the same guy that told me that dames were a dime a dozen and with women like my ex who needed them?" I asked.

"With Perita I can see the appeal."

"So when get to meet this paragon of virtue?" I demanded.

"Soon Perita is really shy, but I've told her all about you," Gordon stated.

"Not everything, I hope. I'd hate for her to know about my ex-wife and her murder attempt on me."

Gordon looked guilty and for a moment I believed he had told her,but then he said, "Gee, I wouldn't reveal your confidence. Maybe someday we can fill her in, but that's up to you. I just told her you were divorced with custody of your daughter and that you'd recently moved to Colorado to become a sheriff here."

"Does she know about my present situation?"

"I think everyone in the country knows that your police department has had police officers murdered. I told her I would help you investigate and that I'd be away for awhile."

"What does Perita do for a living?" I asked.

"She's a businesswoman. She works for some conglomerate that sells high end clothing to stores. She's travelling in Mexico and some other places right now."

"Mexico? Isn't that dangerous?" I asked.

"They've got some fabrics and some clothing she wants to export and she's got bodyguards trained to guard celebrities in these countries. I think she'll be okay, but I do worry."

"When is she coming back?"

"Sunday, so I won't be available Sunday except in an emergency. I'm spending the day with her."

"You sound like a lovesick school boy buddy but I'm really happy for you. We're at the school. Just let me radio Paul Grose to see what statements he's gotten at the Quarry from the remaining kids."

Paul filled me in on the statements he'd taken, a whole lot of nothing. No one had seen anyone dealing drugs, no one had seen anyone taking drugs or even drinking. The kids had formed a wall of silence.

"I overheard Gee. Maybe we can get the kid who was zoned out on something else to tell us something," Gordon sympathized.

"That's the plan; if he's in a can talk and make any sense. Do you want to play good or bad cop?" I asked.

"You play good cop so well. Let me be the bad guy," Gordon begged.

As we went into the hospital, I hoped and prayed that the two weren't connected to my murdered cops; but every crime so far related to the high school students in town, would those murders too?

~0~

.

# Chapter 6 – Hospital

# Gossip

I noticed that the hospital though old

was up to date with the latest equipment.
The halls were long white and very clean as
well. The elevators were old and creaked as
we got on the elevator to go to Ethan's floor.

Gordon and I were stopped in the hallway
by a man in uniform. I asked the security
guard his name and how long he had been
working for the hospital as he checked our
badges. The man didn't answer until he
checked our badges thoroughly which put
him up in my esteem. I stared at him hard
and noticed his military bearing and his
brown hair in crew cut hair style.

"The name's Errol Ward. I've been working here for five years," he finally answered.

"What did you do before that?" I asked.

"What is this, a job interview?" he asked sarcastically.

"Actually if you're interested it is. He's got to find a whole new police force," Gordon answered.

"You're serious? I'm sorry for being so sarcastic. I've been waiting for an interview for a few years now. I was in the armed forces. I did two tours in Iraq policing. Then I came back and there was no room on the police force so I took this job and hoped to get hired soon; but as I said that hasn't panned out."

"Where were you when the murders took place?" I asked.

"A valid question. Lucky for me I was in Aspen. Here's the number of the people I was with," he said writing down details and his resume. "Now do I have a chance at that job?"

"You do if all your references checkout, Errol," I answered.

"You won't regret it," Errol answered, "Can I listen in on your interview with the kid?"

"Let the guy listen in," Gordon whispered.

"Sure, what's one more, but not one word out of you," I cautioned, "What's the kid's name?"

"They didn't tell you? It's Ethan Calladen, the mayor's son. Someone messed the kid up good."

"Great, another kid of the mayor's!!" I commented under my breath.

"You're really having a fabulous day," Gordon commented.

Ethan was a carbon copy of his father. He wasn't quite the mayor's six foot something height; but he was certainly inching up to it. He was sprawled out in the hospital bed barely fitting the bed.

"Hello Ethan, how are you?" I asked.

"He's fucking messed up! His no good friends roofied him," Reggie said from beside the bed.

"You got here fast," I commented.

"When my brother's friend called I booted it," Reggie exclaimed.

"Deputy, no Sheriff. ♫♪ *I shot the sheriff, but I didn't shoot the deputy!*♪♫ " he began singing then he broke into hysterically giggling.

"Ethan shut-up bro! That's not funny," Reggie interrupted.

"Reggie, Reginald the good boy always the good boy!" Ethan sniped, then suddenly zeroing in on me like he'd hadn't seen before he said, "Oh, you're really are here. Hi sheriff, no offence man. I was just singing, exercising my right to be joyful. I think someone slipped something in my drink. I don't feel so good, Reggie."

"It will be okay, Ethan. Don't pull at the intravenous line."

"Why do I have an intravenous line?"

"Someone roofied you, bro."

"Why would someone do that?" Ethan
asked.

"So Ethan what happened today?" I asked.

"Happened? Ooh, the colors, they are so
rad!!" Ethan said then grabbed at handfuls
of air.

"Not sure he's going to make any sense for
you Sheriff. He's coming down from
whatever someone slipped in his Coke,"
Reggie claimed.

I made a decision in that second.

"Can you repeat my questions and get your
brother to answer?"

"Yah, but if he says anything that's illegal
he's what's that word… immune," Reggie
said.

"He has immunity?" I asked.

"Yes, unless he murdered someone you have
to give it to him," Reggie stated.

I looked at Gordon and he nodded.

"You've got a deal kid. Now follow my lead and answer my questions." I answered.

About an hour later I had some answers with some prodding from Reggie. Ethan thought his pal, Hector Tomlinson had slipped something in his drink; but he wasn't sure. He'd seen some of the others doing lines of cocaine; but declined. A fellow student he refused to name invited him to partake. It seemed he'd promised his dad to be an upstanding student/citizen so he could go to Europe next year on a school trip. Reggie explained that if his dad had caught him doing anything criminal or anyone else did the trip was cancelled. All of this was for naught. I didn't have any real suspects except for Hector and Ethan was able to tell me for sure that Hector was really a suspect. Ethan seemed more coherent but he wasn't talking. Just when I thought I was getting nowhere the mayor barged having been listening in the hall.

"Ethan, if you know who supplied the cocaine you need to tell the sheriff now!!" The mayor demanded coming in the room, then continuing he said, "I've talked to the doctors and they think it was laced with fentanyl. These kids might die. Someone has to be held accountable. I can't be mayor of a city where kids are dying. My constituents will eat me alive."

"I don't know, dad," Ethan protested, "I feel sick. Don't you care that someone drugged me?"

"I've course I care but if you know anything or even have any suspicions tell the sheriff now!!"

"Zeus may have brought the cocaine."

"Zeus?"

"Brad Harris. They call him Zeus because he supplies the party supplies. Zeus offered me some but he didn't know about the fentanyl or he wouldn't have taken any. He overdosed himself," Ethan admitted, "I did good, dad. I called the sheriff's department and asked for an ambulance. I tried to save them despite feeling odd myself. Doesn't that count?"

"It does count. I'm proud of you son for that but you have to quit hanging out with this riffraff. They'll pull you down if you don't and destroy your life and mine."

"Thank-you Ethan, for your cooperation. We may have other questions for you when you're feeling better."

"You won't be charging my son with anything, will you?" the mayor asked.

"No, why would we? He's done nothing wrong," I stated in such a way that it implied Ethan had, just to rile the mayor.

"Now wait a minute. Anything my son said cannot be held against him a crime was committed against him and he admitted to anything in a drugged state," the mayor babbled on.

"Relax dad. He's yanking your chain. I already got a verbal agreement that he couldn't charge Ethan if he admitted to a crime," Reggie stated.

"I'm sorry if you misunderstood. Of course I'm not charging your son. He is a victim, not a perpetrator and a very helpful witness," I exclaimed.

"Good then. I gather then you'll be going to talk to the doctors about the other students and to this Brad?"

"Yes, Mr. Mayor. I aim to get to the bottom of this," I stated.

"I knew I hired the right sheriff. I'm off I have other mayoral business to attend to. Reggie stay with your brother for awhile! I'll be back."

"Don't I always dad?"

"Good boy, maybe you're worth something after all."

Poor Reggie cringed and I saw him die a little inside. But back to the matter at hand I had to go see if I could speak to Brad and get information from him. Maybe Gordon could be a help if we could question Brad. But he'd gone off to get us coffee and wouldn't be back for a few minutes to meet me in intensive care.

Seeing a vending machine I picked out an orange juice to bribe the doctor to be nice to me. As I walked through the intensive care doors the team was in action and I had to sit down out of the way in the hallway outside the actual unit; while they attended a patient. Soon with dejected faces they came back through and I knew it meant someone had died.

They went about preparing notes and other details in a scurry but I could tell the toil this had taken them. I waited patiently until the woman in a white coat went to leave then I approached her.

"Doctor?"

I have to admit the doctor was a man's fantasy. She was tall and leggy and wore cute little glasses for reading which she took off to look at me. Her eyes were a cat's eye green that sparkled with intelligence. Her hair was red gold and looked to be long but she had it in a bun at the back of her head. I imagined myself taking her hair down and then reminded myself, one that was sexual harassment and two I was on a job.

"I'm sorry I'm just going on break can this wait? I really need a drink."

"I'm the new sheriff, Sheriff G. Bullet and lucky for you I picked you up a drink. I hope you like orange juice."

"You're a lifesaver. Orange juice will hit the spot," she said taking the orange juice then she offered her hand, "I'm Doctor Tina Weldon. This has been a horrific day with all these students coming in. We have three other doctor's taking care of patients but we're really short staffed."

"Nice to meet you," I found myself saying benignly.

I felt like I'd known her forever. Her eyes, a cat's eye green that sparkled with intelligence seemed to focus solely on me and capture me as if no one else existed. I swear my heart began to beat out of my chest and words seemed to dry up in my mouth.

"You're cute, for a sheriff, Gee. So what's does Gee stand for?" she asked.

"If I tell you you'd have to…"

"I'd have to be sworn to silence or I'd be whacked?"

"The former it's Gunner, but don't tell anyone," I demanded.

"Gunner Bullet what a mouthful. I'll only call you Gunner in private; I'll call you Gee in public to make you happy."

"Call me Tina,"

"Can I call you Tina Bullet?"

"Is that a marriage proposal? So soon?"

I went to ask her out and instead blurted,
"Yes, will you marry me?"

Instead of being appalled and alarmed Tina
seemed to consider this for a moment and
then said, "I'll think about it; but you don't
even have a ring," she kidded.

I then pulled out my wallet and took out my
mother's ring that I carried in my change
part.

She laughed again a twinkly little laugh that
filled up my soul with happiness and I was
hooked love at first sight. What can I say?
She pulled out a condom out off the shelf as
we slipped into a broom closet and then
proceeded to unzip my pants and put it over
my rock hard cock. Tina's hands were
everywhere. Her long red nails raking over
my body. She was perfect from her pert little
breasts to her rock hard little ass. Satiated
with bliss I had trouble standing up. I felt
like I'd come home.

This woman was my soulmate and I wanted to stay here forever; but Tina abruptly straightening her clothes and switching gears. I felt a little foolish that I had given in to some afternoon delight when I was supposed to be working and then I realized that Tina felt the same way as I did when she smiled at me in such a way that brought me to my knees.

"That was amazing. I hope you don't think I do that all the time… I mean…"

"You are still one classy lady," I commented leered lifting my eyebrow and imitating Groucho Marx and pretending to hold a cigar and lift my mustache.

Tina laughed, as I expected her to.

"I definitely want to talk about this later; but for now we need to talk get out of the closet before someone notices I'm missing or walks in. And of course speak about the business at hand."

"How are your patients, Tina?" I asked fixing my clothes.

I then looked both ways and seeing no one I pulled Tina out of the supply closet.

"You have to understand that it's only because they got here so quickly that they are alive at all. Someone mixed fentanyl with cocaine and the kids took it. Fentanyl as an injection is used to relieve severe pain during and after surgery. It is also used with other medicines just before or during an operation to help the anesthetic work better."

"I have heard they use it for surgery but what moron decided it would be good in drugs they sold?" I asked.

"Fentanyl belongs to the group of medicines called narcotic analgesics (pain medicines). This acts on the central nervous system (CNS) or brain to relieve pain. That same pain reliever boosts the high the dealers believe but they're wrong the risk is too great. Cocaine, marijuana, oxycodone, ecstasy and heroin are some of the drugs often cut with fentanyl in pill, powder or liquid form. They are using it as a way to create a cheaper high and increase addiction not to kill but you can't see it, smell it or taste it, but if your drug of choice is cut with fentanyl, it can kill you… sometimes immediately."

"Wow, but I still don't quite understand this," I exclaimed.

"You know that fentanyl is a synthetic opiate also used to treat severe pain?"

I nodded.

"When used recreationally, the high can be similar to heroin but with deeper respiratory depression and stronger sedative effects, making it extremely dangerous. Those without a tolerance for opiates, unlike addicts, will experience stronger and more lethal effects. Street names used for fentanyl include Apache, Chuma girl, Chuma white, dance fever, friend, goodfella, jackpot, murder 8, TNT, as well as Tango and Cash. Users who knowingly or unknowingly take fentanyl may experience severe sleepiness, a slow heartbeat, trouble breather, slow or shallow breathing, cold and clammy skin and trouble walking and talking," Doctor Weldon explained.

"I heard that it's out there, but this could be an epidemic," I stated.

"An epidemic none of us are prepared for. I hope you can cut off the source for this in our town, sheriff because if you don't we're going to see a lot more deaths."

"More deaths?"

"Here's your example sheriff, we had sixteen students come in to emergency. One died on route here, another girl just passed away a few moments ago and one ingested something else. The others are in grave condition and could all die except for one, Brad Harris. They also ingested alcohol, Brad did not."

"Ingesting alcohol made a difference for Brad then?"

"Ingesting alcohol increases the risk of overdose. Brad (fortunately for him) ingested less of the drug than the rest and is now in serious, but somewhat stable condition. And the boy, Hamoud Al Khaled who died yesterday? He was also a fentanyl victim. Hamoud smoked pot laced with fentanyl, though we originally thought it was something else."

"Can I question Brad?"

"I don't know; the boy is still not out of the woods completely. Can you be gentle?"

"I can!"

"Fine then, I hope you realize I'm only doing this so you can stop this before more kids and other people in this community die. And of course because you're so damn cute I can't say no. However I have to be nearby to stop if my patient is at risk."

"I wouldn't have it any other way."

I entered the intensive care unit and pulled back the curtain around Brad's bed. Brad looked at me and mumbled "Cop?"

I nodded and he blurted, "I didn't know that it was Chuma White. We all just wanted to have a good time. I'm not a dealer. We just got some bad stuff."

"I'm going to stop you right there and read your rights," I interrupted.

I read Brad his rights and he clammed up for a moment and then stated weakly; that yes he understood his rights and wanted to make a statement to me.

"We were partying; it's the end of the year. There are my friends and they asked me for some smack. I said I didn't have any, but I had some crack and pot. It didn't taste any different. It wasn't tart, but the high was different and then I felt weird; you know?"

"And where did you get the product?"

"Just some people I know."

I didn't press him. I wanted more information then I'd get the name or names of his dealer.

"Why did you give only Ethan some marijuana?

"It was something underhanded," Brad slurred his mind not quite ready to lie then he backtracked and said, "Oops, I'm not supposed to tell."

Brad then covered his mouth with his hand like to keep from saying anything.

"Who asked you to give Ethan only the marijuana? Was it his brother, Reginald?" I pressed.

"No, Reggie's a straight arrow. Reggie won't do drugs. He preaches against them saying drugs ruin lives and abilities to participate in real life a lot he knows. He didn't even want to come to the quarry."

"You can say that after you almost died?"

"I'm alive, ain't I?"

"Are you aware that two students from the quarry have died?

"What? Not Melanie...not my Melanie," Brad asked the first I saw his bravado slipping.

I looked at Tina and she nodded.

"Aw hell no...not my girl... not my Mellie!!We was supposed to get married," Brad wailed, "God damn those assholes. I'll make them pay for killing Mellie and for trying to kill me. I'll give you all their names. They'll be sorry!!!"

"Start now."

"Charlie Watt works for them too and Tristian Hood, I've seen Omar Yeltzin around too, and the main boss is…"he began and then had to stop before he started coughing up blood then his eyes rolled back in his head.

"Code Blue," Tina yelled going into full doctor mode and numerous staff arrived pushing me out of the way.

I walked into the corridor to wait hoping I hadn't cause this reaction in the young man. Gordon arrived with the coffee and I took a huge jolt of it filling it curse through my system and wondered if coffee too could be considered and addiction.

An hour later Tina came back out; she told Gordon and I, that Brad had died but they had managed to revive him once. She said an autopsy had to be done because Brad coughing up blood was unusual. I asked her if Brad had said anything and Tina replied, "Brad said, "She." But I'm not sure what he was talking about. People have seen loved ones when they crossover."

"You believe in that hooey, Doctor? Gordon commented, "So does my pal Gee here."

"I don't believe I caught your name," Doctor Weldon said in crisp tones finally noticing Gordon.

I liked Tina's reaction to Gordon. She looked leery and appraised him with an eye not his looks; but who he was in relationship to me. Something about him satisfied her and she smiled at me and then him.

"Special Agent Gordon Chum of the FBI," Gordon stated holding out his hand to shake.

"I thought the sheriff was in charge here?" Doctor Weldon exclaimed.

"He is the FBI helps out the Driftwood Police Services because his entire police force was murdered," Gordon answered.

Doctor Weldon turned to me and stared then blurted, "Yes, I heard about that what an awful start to your new job, Gee and what and awful day this has been around here, too."

"I'm sorry, Tina, it must be hard to lose patients," I commiserated.

"Yes, it is. Thank- you, Gee."

Gordon noticed my growing attraction to the good doctor and hers with me and sat down on a bench nearby giving me some elbow room.

"You know Gee, I have to tell you, you remind me of someone," Doctor Weldon stated.

"Really?" I responded flirting.

"I'm not sure who... wait a minute I know you are similar in looks and face shape (though more masculine and rugged) to Louise Bullet. Of course why didn't I put it together before? You have the same last name since Louise took her last name back. Of course you're related!"

"You know Aunt Louise? We're living with her right now."

"We're living with her?"

"I'm divorced and have full custody of my almost four year old daughter. Aunt Louise helps me out with child care," I answered, "What did you mean when you said Aunt Louise took her last name back?

"About fifteen years ago the mayor, John Calladen was murdered."

"What does that have to do with my Aunt Louise?"

"Your Aunt Louise was married to him and someone murdered him. It was a real scandal because the present mayor, Ethan Calladen's wife was knocked out by the murderer and found naked near the mayor's bed. The Mayor was Ethan's brother and Ethan was the deputy mayor at the time. Everyone was suspect but they found some drifter had broken into John Calladen's house thinking no one was home and murdered John Calladen while Rita (that's Ethan's ex-wife's name) was in the bathroom. Ethan Calladen, the present mayor, became very vindictive and sued and won custody of his two boys. But poor Louise Bullet she was really hurt the worst in all this."

"Good grief, Aunt Louise must have gone through hell," I blurted.

"I probably shouldn't tell you this since you didn't already know, but everyone else in town knows. Louise Bullet lost the baby she carried; when she heard he had cheated on her with Rita. I heard the baby was a girl and she was devastated when they told her she never have a living child. She quit her job at the school and retired and became a bit of recluse until about four years ago."

I was astounded poor Aunt Louise. Her family hadn't known about the marriage or the baby. To lose a baby was bad enough but to be told that was your last chance at one? How had she kept such a secret from me or her other family members? We would have been there to help her but maybe that was the point she didn't want her brothers to know and be their mean selves but I would have helped her somehow. Wouldn't I?

I felt ashamed that she hadn't turned to me.
Poor Aunt Louise! And now it seemed Aunt
Louise was related to the mayor by
marriage. What a horrible crime but the
drifter being the culprit seemed a little
convenient. It wasn't my case told myself.

I even felt kind of sorry for the mayor. His
brother had cuckolded him and then been
brutally murdered. That had to hurt, no
wonder his sons lived with him and he was a
bit of a dickhead. But this old story didn't
get me any further with my case. They'd
caught that murderer. I needed to catch mine
and Brad's information wasn't enough
though Gordon and I could move on the
names Brad had given me.

"I'm sorry. I've hurt you with this
information. Maybe I could make it up to
you with dinner, my treat? You were going
to ask me out weren't you before the
marriage proposal?" Tina asked laughing.

"Okay, what time?" I found myself
answering.

"See you at the Double Dee diner at 5 p.m.," Doctor Weldon stated smiling.

"Unless I'm called away to more business. I'll need your cell number so I can text you if that happens," I replied.

"That works both ways. I'd like lots more information about you," Doctor Weldon said then took my cell and tapped in her number then handed it back.

She then walked back into the intensive care unit.

"You're asking for trouble buddy. You should stick to one woman at a time," Gordon commented.

"I won't hide anything from her. I was attracted to her and Maggie both and it's only dinner. But she's the one now," I answered.

"It's never only dinner with you. Women just usually fall all over you and you never notice. Now you're starting to wake up to that. Be careful buddy. I wouldn't want this to backfire on you," Gordon commented.

"It won't. I'm breaking up with Maggie. Tina is my soulmate," I answered.

"You said that about Gina and look how that turned out," Gordon commented, "Take it slow Gee."

"I will I said."

I checked to make sure that none of the patients were the men Brad mentioned and then decide to head back with Gordon to the police station.

~0~

# Chapter 7 - Killing Ground

I realized later in the car that I had

forgotten about my dinner with my daughter and Aunt Louise. It was scheduled for five p.m. as well. I texted Tina and asked to meet at 7 p.m. Two dinners wouldn't kill me this once after all I'd skipped lunch.

Gordon and I went to the police station and tried to dig up some information on Charlie Watt, Tristian Hood, and Omar Yeltzin and hoped I could find them. Gordon told me he found bank accounts in the Cayman's for a number of the cops that were killed starting with Greg Barnes. Crap, dirty cops, just

what I didn't need another shit-storm to fall
into where it would pit cop against cop.

In my world crime was black and white cop
or civilian if you committed a crime you did
the time; but there were cops who thought
that being a cop allowed you to be protected
by the brethren of other police officers; like
what had happened to me in Illinois.

"It's not going to be like last time Gcc."
Gordon said reading my thoughts, "You're
the sheriff and were going to bring justice to
Driftwood and clean this town up."

"Thank-you, Gordon," I replied.

"What's a pal for?" he asked then hearing
his cellphone buzz he read the message and
said, "Got to go. I've been called backed to
head office. You're on your own my men
are at your disposal."

Gordon then left.

With Penny's help I found the address of
one Omar Yeltzin in some old police files.
Omar was a surprising fifty years old. I
thought he might be a mid-level employee
possibly thirty years old; but Omar had been
just that twenty years ago. Omar had been
released from prison two years ago and to all
extents and purposes had appeared to be
reformed. He had a job at the local gas
station as mechanic. Could Brad's last
words been a lie. Was I really chasing
nothing but stories? What about Mellie did
she really not mean anything to him?

I had to go ask some questions and get the
facts. Then I'd speak with Omar and get to
the bottom of this.

I pulled my squad car up to the home of
Omar Yeltzin on Pine Grove Road. The
house if you could call it that was a
ramshackle rundown place. The boards on
the house looked weathered for about a
hundred years; which made sense given that
it was an old farm house encroached on by
the city.

The roof looked like it needed replacement and the building itself looked like it had shifted sideways. The building should be condemned, but instead I saw an old swing set, with children happily playing. A light rain fell as I exited my car.

A woman about thirty years old with long dark hair and brown eyes yelled at them to come out of the rain with a Mexican accent. Then she spotted me and my car and her mouth dropped and she yelled, "It's the fuzz; run."

I heard the back door open and the sound of boots on the wet ground as Omar exited the back door.

I ran pursing him as he tried to flee through the nearby woods. Branches hit me in the face and I started to slip as the now torrential rain pooled and made rivets of rain water and piles of mud. The man was fast but I was younger and in better shape I caught him taking him down into the mud and placing my handcuffs on him.

I marched him back to my squad car through the forest. I had almost reached the squad car shots rang out, the first one hitting me in the leg; the next one hitting Omar between the eyes. My leg bled out and realizing that Omar was dead; I struggled to remain up right. I took my belt off and placed it around my upper right thigh. I found myself blinded by light coming through the clouds now that the rain and worried about where Omar's wife and kids were with these shots ringing out. I saw one of the kids at the window of the house and Omar's wife pulled them away and downward. Aiming my gun I managed to fire back and I swore I heard a grunt before the next shot grazed my temple at the world faded away.

~0~

# Chapter 8 - Hospital Suck

I dreamt that my leg was on fire and it felt like my leg seared off in small pieces continuously over an open flame. I could hear the beep- beep- squeal of the fire alarm. I tried to flee; but I could feel the flames touching me. I was hot, so hot it felt like a scorching sun was burning me out from the inside out.

I opened my eyes but nothing seemed real everything was far away and shimmery. I closed them again and felt soft hands on mine.

Aunt Louise said, "Hang in there Gunner. Fight back. Stella-Marie needs you."

I tried to open my eyes again but I was just so tired and I found myself drifting off again.

When I awoke again sunlight streamed in the room and I could hear a machine beeping. A male doctor in a white coat had my wrist in his hand. The guy was about 6 feet 2 inches and looked a little like Jimmy Stewart.

"Well lookee here. Look who is awake, Tim," Doctor Weldon stated from the doorway.

"I'm your doctor, Tim Burton." The man in the white coat said looking me straight in the eye.

"I must be hearing things I thought he said his name was Tim Burton, Tina," I commented still feeling quite not there.

"It is my name. What's worse, my daddy's name was Richard and my grandpa's name is Pierre."

"The Richard I get, but who is Pierre?"

"He was actually Pierre Berton. My grandfather was Canadian and he's named after a Canadian author of Canadian history and a well-known journalist and television personality."

"I've never heard of him," I commented, "But at least talking to you I know I'm alive."

"For now but if you don't follow through for a replacement date…,"Tina replied.

"Don't make me laugh Tina that hurts."

"Sorry, I'm sure you'd like a few minutes with your fiancée, sheriff, I'll be back in ten minutes," Doctor Burton said leaving.

"Fiancée?" I asked weakly after he left.

"Don't tell me you've forgotten already?" Tina asked showing me my mother's ring on her finger.

I hope you don't mind. I took it out of your wallet when you came in. it was a cinch to slip it on my finger before anyone saw. Your bulldog friend Gordon didn't want anyone by Tim to see you."

"Gordon's a good friend."

"Is he gay?"

I laughed and it hurt, "No, Tina were just really good friends that have been through a lot. I had an ex-wife who was a handful."

"You attract them like flies should I be worried?

"No," I answered, "I'm taken."

"Good because I'm gaga for you. I guess I should have thought about putting on you ring more; your Aunt Louise and your daughter have seen the ring too."

"What did they say?"

"Your Aunt Louise said we should have along engagement and your daughter said, "You're prettier than his last friend."

"Oops about that…" I said.

"Oh don't worry, I met Maggie."

"And you're not mad? I mean I slept with her before I met you."

"That's right, before you met me! I'm not mad about that; but she was. She called you a few choice names."

"At least I don't have to break up with her," I quipped.

"Don't make me laugh. You're still not out of my bad books buddy boy."

I raised an eyebrow.

"Am I interrupting something?" Tim asked.

"Sorry, Tim the man promised me a date and then he gets himself shot to get out of it."

"You can have your date with your fiancée in about a week's time, that is if these antibiotics start working better," Tim answered.

"Hey, what about me you two; I'm the one in pain here," I complained.

"You should hurt. You took two to your legs and one to the side of your head," Tina commented.

"Two, but I only heard three bullets."

"Tim took two bullets out of your legs and one bullet that grazed that thick head of yours. Idiot!!" Tina griped.

"Thick head? Why are you so mad at me?"

"You could have died. You almost did from the wound itself if Omar's wife Maria hadn't put towels on your wounds enabling you to live…"

"Omar's wife saved me?"

"Yes, she had one of her kids' call 911. She then stemmed the bleeding until the emergency technicians got there. Tim did the best he could to seal up your wounds; but then you got an infection from your bullet wounds."

"Infection?" I asked feeling kind of dazed.

"It's okay, Gee. You're on the mend. Some powerful antibiotics and three units of blood and you're starting to mend."

Up until that moment I swear Tina had
mesmerized me. I hadn't thought of my job
accept in the recess of my mind; but I started
thinking of where the investigation had to go
and how I had to get back to it. Omar and
his connections needed to be investigated
and I needed to urgently speak with Gordon.
Where was he when I needed him?

"I have to get back to the station," I said
trying to swing my legs over the bed but a
bar was in the way. I pushed it out of the
way and promptly fell on my ass. I felt weak
and frail like an old man and I got really
angry at myself. I had to get to the station
and help Gordon investigate.

"Idiot, not a chance, buddy boy," Tina said
helping Doctor Burton pick me up.

"You're staying put; until I say so. You
better not have ruined my stitches," Doctor
Burton exclaimed.

I continued to try and get up myself, not
succeeding.

"Your fiancée is a stubborn one, Tina," he continued, "Are you sure about him?"

"Very sure," Tina answered.

"Then that's good enough for me."

"I need to get back on the case. Gordon needs me," I protested weakly as I was tucked back in bed.

"Gee, it's been a week and he's got a few more men on the case. At least that's what he told me," Tina stated.

"A week? God damn it that's too long. How could I have been here a week?"

"He can manage for another week until you get back, Gunner," Tina stated.

I just shook my head.

Meanwhile Doctor Burton responded by
sneaking pulling out a needle I didn't see
and putting something into the intravenous
in my hand and I felt my eyes grow heavy
and the world fade away.

~0~

## Chapter 9 - I can't be a patient I'm a cop

Awakening again to the sound of

something dripping and feeling wet through my blanket, I then heard Aunt Louise whispering loudly, "Stella-Marie you're spilling your drink."

"Sorry, Aunt Louise, I squeezed the juice."

"It's okay," Aunt Louise said, but she sounded sad and I felt guilty.

"Daddy? Look his eyes are open," Stella-Marie shouted and then jumped on my leg resulting in a muttered oomph from me.

"Stella-Marie, don't you be jumping all over your daddy."

"Did I hurt you daddy?"

"No, pumpkin," I exclaimed trying not to wince.

"Maybe she should have," griped Aunt Louise.

"I'm sorry Aunt Louise," I said automatically.

"Sorry for what? Being stupid? Going in without back-up, getting shot up, almost dying, or getting engaged without telling your aunt and daughter?"

"All of the above," I admitted.

"We're still a little mad," Stella-Marie said looking at Aunt Louise for confirmation then continuing she said, "You promised you'd stay safe."

Stella-Marie then crossed her arms in a move I recognized as my own.

"I'm sorry," I said again.

"I forgive you; but you better be more careful," Stella-Marie sternly said sounding older.

"Do you like Tina, Doctor Weldon?" I asked Stella-Marie.

"Are you really sure daddy? She seems really nice but you liked Maggie before her, I could tell. You should get to know her really good before you marry her. Bobby Keller's mommy and daddy didn't and they divorced when Bobby was a baby," Stella-Marie said sounding extremely grown up.

"I'll try to take it a little slower baby; but she's the one."

"You love her more than you did my mommy?" asked Stella-Marie.

"I thought I loved your mommy very much, I explained this to you baby. Your mommy made a big mistake and she hurt me."

"That's why she had to admit her mistake and go to jail?"

"That's right."

"But you forgive her?"

"Yes, I forgive her but I'm never going to forget what she did or trust her again. Sometimes trust is never found again when you do something really bad."

"When will you tell me what she did?"

"When you're older Stella-Marie and can understand it better."

"It's not fair you should tell me now!!"

"Sweetie I'll tell you when you're older."

"I miss having a mom. Other kids' moms do things with them. Will Tina be like a mommy?"

"I'd like to be likc a mom, but you know I can never take your mom's place, right?" Tina said coming in the room.

"Yes, but we can do mother daughter stuff, right? Like you braiding my hair my friend Helen's mom braids hers. Dad tries but he doesn't braid in French braids," Stella-Marie asked.

"I'd like that and I think I can handle French braids," Tina answered patting her hair and showing off her own.

"Just remember, pumpkin, Tina's a busy emergency doctor. She saves people so she is sometimes called into the hospital."

"I'd like to be a doctor and a cop someday," Stella-Marie said.

"You can be anything you want to sweetie," I answered.

"Your daddy looks tired and we need to go visit your friend Bobby for your playdate. We'll come back and see your daddy at dinnertime," Aunt Louise stated.

"Bobby's my boyfriend," Stella-Marie whispered to Tina.

I raised my eyebrow and Aunt Louise said; "It's puppy love don't worry. Now you behave yourself and maybe they'll let out in the next few days. Gordon should be by soon. That boy has been working night and day on your case so don't you go thinking your needed sooner. Aw speak of the devil here's that boy now," Aunt Louise said then touching Gordon's arm, "Don't tire out my nephew now."

"I like my living quarters; but you know I'm moving out this week Louise."

Aunt Louise turned red and looked like she would blow her top.

"I'm not arguing Louise I'll be quick just an update and then I'm out of here. Promise."

"Very well then Gordon. Let's head out, Stella-Marie."

"Bye Daddy. And you both do what Aunt Louise said," Stella-Marie ordered her finger pointing at us reminiscent of Aunt Louise.

"Bye, pumpkin see you later," I commented.

The hospital room door closed and Gordon began speaking.

"We investigated that forest area you chased Omar into."

"You found something?"

"Yes, a trailer where they were making meth and synthetic marijuana."

"In the same trailer?"

"It was sectioned off and a very sophisticated trailer; it even had an air filter system better than a hospital quarantine unit."

"This sounds like a whole new drug trade. It's not what we're dealing with the fentanyl at all. Is this whole county a drug dealers' paradise?"

"You got that right; it maybe that the two different types of drug trade are entirely unrelated. I tried to find Charlie Watt and Tristian Hood, but they're in the wind after Omar was killed."

"Now where are we?" I asked.

"I've got some leads," Gordon said.

I started getting dressed and Gordon said, "What the hell do you think you're doing?"

"Getting back to work."

"You're an idiot."

"I'm going back to the job. I can't be a patient, I'm a cop."

"Your Aunt Louise will kill me."

"Just sneak me out," I answered.

We waited a few minutes then Gordon snuck me out and into his car. As I maneuvered myself into the car Gordon reached into the trunk and took out a cane which he handed to me.

"You'll need this. I've had it since I was shot last year," he said.

"Thank you Gordon," I answered.

"Don't thank me your Aunt Louise is going to have my head for aiding and abetting you in your escape from the hospital," Gordon exclaimed.

"I'll try to smooth it over so she only blames me."

"You do that. I don't want your Aunt Louise as an enemy."

"To the station, James."

~0~

# Chapter 10 - Nothing like Family

Gordon dropped me off at the station

and I limped through the doors. Gordon went off to chase down some leads while I thought about the paperwork waiting me in my office.

Penny Ambercrombie grabbed my arm and said, "Sheriff you should be in the hospital. We can manage here until you get better."

"I'm okay, Penny," I answered, grumpily.

"Likely story, you're very irritable. But I can see I can't change your mind. Errol Ward is a good cop and a great hire on your part. He's been really working hard on the drug case and the murders. The guy, Nathan Ricci, who the mayor hired from the high school? I don't think he's going to work out. He's so lazy and incompetent. But you can see for yourself."

"The mayor hired Nathan Ricci?"

"Yes and no one hired my brother, Andrew Ambercrombie, though the mayor promised he would."

"I'm sorry Penny, give me his number and I'll give him a call."

"Thanks Sheriff."

"Call me Gee, Penny when we're in private."

"You need to rest that leg while you work. Let me get you that soft chair in the other office," Penny said.

"Thank-you Penny."

Penny came back as good as her word with a soft chair and I propped up my leg. It hurt like blazes but I had worked to do. I just hoped it wouldn't get any more infected.

"There's a guy in the lobby waiting for you. He just showed up out of the blue; but looking at him I think he's a family member."

"Send him in, please Penny," I replied wondering which uncle it was.

"Okay, after you're done with the guy in the lobby I'll send in Errol Ward. He's been hot to tell you some information he found," Penny said excusing herself.

"Don't worry Penny this won't take too long," I said not really sure why one of my uncles would come this far to see me. Did they really care I'd been shot? And which one of them was it?

The door opened slowly and a man swaggered in. Frankly I didn't recognize him, but something seemed very familiar about him. I warily pulled my gun hiding it under my desk.

"Hey sonny. You're looking better than when I saw you the other day."

"You saw me the other day?"

"Sure at the hospital."

"Who are you?" I asked starting to get irritated.

"And here I thought you were a hot-shot detective;" the man laughed and then continued, "See the nose here and the space between my eyes. The top of my head is a little bit salt and pepper when I don't recondition it, but it was once the color of yours."

"Are you saying we look alike?" I asked incredulously.

"Look in the mirror pal. Those apples don't fall far from the tree."

He was right of course that's what had been so familiar about him. Possible in his sixties he looked more like Tom Selleck than I did. From his bushy black hair to his dyed eyebrows and black mustache and his high cheekbones; he was very like an older version of me. He took out a picture of a woman and laid it out on my desk.

I glanced over at it. It was a picture of my mother I'd never seen before. She was young maybe eighteen or nineteen and her hair was pleated in braids. She wore a sundress and looked happily at the camera.

"Where did you get that?" I asked.

"I took that picture of Marie."

"Who are you?"

"I'm your Uncle Thomas, Thomas Gunnerson. I explained this to you at the hospital but I guess with the dope they had you on it didn't take. Marie was my sister. She named you Gunner Thomas for me. Please call me Uncle Tommy."

"How come I haven't met you before?" I asked suspiciously.

"You lived with a household of cops. But I did see you a time or two when you were younger and I made sure you were well cared for. Plus I came when that bitch your ex-wife shot you; but I can see why that time was hazy. I'd want to forget that too!!"

"I don't get it; why would me living in a household of cops bother you?" I asked then it dawned on me. "Are you in trouble with the law? Because I'd hate to arrest you!"

"I'm not right now. How much do you know about your mother's family?"

"Next to nothing. In fact I thought all of you were dead."

"That sounds like a story your Uncle James would tell."

"What does Uncle James have to do with this?"

"James introduced them... Marie and his brother...course he didn't know about Marie's family connections then,"

"So?"

"Our family has been in the criminal business a long time and James had no idea that Marie was a Gunnerson who was part of the family. When he did discover Marie's background he tried to discourage your father from Marie but it was too late. So your father got Marie to distance herself from us."

"Are you trying to say you're mobbed up?"

"I was. Not anymore. Our whole family was with the exception of Marie. I'm the last one standing. All the rest have gotten themselves knocked off. So don't worry I won't compromise you. I'm in the witness protection program, anyway. I slipped my minder to come here. I testify in Chicago next month against my old boss Carmine Luciano and his boss, Lucas Kelly."

"I heard that trial was coming up. Those two would kill you in a heartbeat. Are you sure you're safe?"

"When are we really safe? Those two have no idea about you Gunner so don't you worry. That's why I stayed away from you all these years. But I had to come when I heard about your shooting."

I found myself charmed by this man. I
should have been appalled and horrified to
be related to a man who was clearly mobbed
up but I wasn't I liked him and saw some of
the same good qualities of myself in him.

"Where were you when my wife shot me?"

"You probably don't remember but I snuck
in and saw you then too. I almost put a hit
out on that wife of yours; but she was
pregnant with that kid of yours so I let it go.
When she had the kid; I saw how the kid
would be hurt if I knocked her mom off so I
let her live."

"You're confessing this to a cop?"

"I'm confessing this to my nephew. Anyway
it's good to see you son. You take better
care of that leg."

"Will I see you again?" I asked.

"You will when I can get away. Oh, but before I go the other reason I'm here. I heard that someone tried to muscle their way into the drug trade in Colorado. Though this is a new player in the state this person has been building up the drug trade in other states for years now. They want the state and they are prepared to do what it takes to get it. I'll try to get you a name, Gunner, but this person is very secretive and only the upper echelon of the organization seemed to know the name and the leader. They ordered the hit on your cops and their families."

"Why are you doing this?"

"No one is going to try and kill my nephew and get away with it."

"You wouldn't do anything stupid?" I asked.

"I won't kill anyone. Those days are over I don't want to jeopardize my deal. But I can and will protect you, Gunner."

"I don't need protection," I protested.

"We all need a little help oh golly, oh, Gee. Best you remember that. Your little girl needs her daddy. I have to get back before my minder notices I'm gone."

"Will I see you again? Can I have your phone number at least?" I surprised myself by asking.

"Gunner we're family. I'll stay in touch. Meanwhile take it easy and rest that leg," Uncle Tommy said and then with a flash he was out of the door and gone like he'd never been there.

I was at once horrified and amused at the same time. On one side I came from a long line of cops the other side it seemed were a long line of criminals. But Uncle Tommy was charismatic and illusive all at the same time. When I had more time I'd look up his criminal record and look into more details about him and the other side of my family, but for now I had to speak to Errol Ward and get down to brass tacks. I'd stop the drug trade and if it was connected to my officers' murders then I'd nail their murder or murderers to the wall. Or my name wasn't Gunner Thomas Bullet.

I wondered why half the reports weren't on my desk and whether I should demand them from Penny and then thought maybe someone else kindly did them while I was gone? Dream on Bullet. I'd look for them later for now I needed some information on the two investigations, or was it one? I thought. Could the two be connected? It would be a good way to run drugs through a county if all the cops were chasing their tales looking for cop killers. Could anyone be that diabolical? Of course they could! Hadn't I seen the under belly of the criminal world in Illinois? But to prove that it was one investigation and not two as I suspected I had a long way to go.

"Penny, send Errol in please," I demanded through my antiquated speakerphone.

Errol came in a few moments later looking excited.

.

"Have you heard of a Troy and Calvin Richardson?" were the first words out of his lips.

"The names sound familiar. Troy is a car snatcher on probation; so what about his brother Calvin?" I asked looking at Troy's file that Errol handed me.

"Calvin is like quicksilver and nothing has ever stuck to that boy since he was fifteen years old. He's twenty-one years old. But he is into prostitution and is a low-level drug dealer. The word on the street is he's come into a lot of money lately from a new enterprise. We also got a tip through our tip line that he might know something about our cops and their families' deaths. "

"Is there anyone else we could talk to about this, Errol?"

"I've got some feelers out and called a snitch; but I had to leave a message. People are scared out there boss. There's a big player in town that's making them quake to their very toes."

Errol's cell phone rang and he said, "Speak of the devil. It's my snitch. Excuse me", he then spoke into the cell phone as if I wasn't there, "Ty? Do you have that information for me? What do you mean you can't talk now you called me! Yes, I understand it's dangerous. I can offer you a hundred bucks. You want what? Immunity?"

I nodded saying, "As long as the information will get us an arrest ad he's not one of the triggerman for the killings of our officers."

"That's my boss; he'll offer you immunity provided the intel is sound. I know you didn't do the killings! You heard the chatter afterwards? Okay, then we probably have a deal but I need to hear more. Come to the station. What? Sure, I can understand being scared. Meet you where? Okay, your strip club, two hours."

I put my leg down and grabbed my cane.

"Boss. I can handle this."

"Don't go off half-cocked you need backup! I shouldn't have gone in with backup."

"Boss, no one knows Ty wants to talk with us. Very few people know I work for the Driftwood police force now. I can slip into the strip club and then bring him back here, and bring him in through the back door of the station."

"Take Nathan Ricci he can wait outside if need be. Just be cautious; don't put yourself or anyone else at risk and keep your radio on so I can hear you're safe."

"Will do boss. First I'm going to get some lunch so I'll be ready for the meet in a couple of hours. Do you want anything?"

"No thanks, Errol," I replied, "Just ask Penny nicely if someone could bring me a coffee."

Frankly I wasn't hungry only in pain my leg felt on fire and it was time for my pills. Errol left and went to get lunch. I finally felt like we were getting somewhere in the investigation. Maybe his snitch could point us where we needed to go.

Reading over the reports, I heard my office door creak open. I looked up to meet Tina's glare. Oh, no I thought I'm in trouble now.

"Sorry?"

"Sorry is not good enough. You left against medical advice and you didn't even call me," Tina complained.

She then sat down in a chair with wheels which she swiveled toward me.

"I should have called you. I'm sorry. I just knew you'd be mad."

"And why would I be mad?"

"Because you like me?" I exclaimed grabbing her and pulling her off the chair so she was now sitting on my lap.

"Damn right and it's more than like; I love you, you big dope. If we are to be honest I have to know. Do you love me too? Or is it just a mere attraction on your part?" she relented.

"It is attraction and love and many, many, more things. I've never felt like this in my entire life either, Tina."

She gazed into my eyes and smiled. My heart did a flip flop and I felt so incredibly happy. I smiled back at her and everything seemed right with the world despite the chaos of these two cases.

"Why didn't you talk to me before you left the hospital? I could think of a thing or two we could have done," Tina said her tongue sliding between her teeth.

"You could, could you have?" I dared.

Tina stood up and then slid her hand up my leg and started to unzip my pants, teasing, "I could have taken some time off and made you very welcome in my bed."

"Lock the door," I said choking out the words.

Tina obediently walked to the door; but before she could lock it Penny knocked and without waiting walked in. With one hand I zipped and buttoned my pants and with the other I pretended to be looking at documents on my desk hoping Penny hadn't noticed.

"Here are the reports from the last two weeks. I took care of them but you need to sign off on them," Penny said not looking up and setting them on my desk, and then she realized Tina was there.

"Oh hi, Doctor Weldon. So it's true then, you and the Sheriff; you're engaged?"

"Yes, Penny. See he even gave me a ring." Tina said.

"It looks old. I thought you would have given her a big rock with lots of carats," Penny sniffed.

"I think it's the most beautiful ring I have ever seen. It was Gee's mother's."

"That's different then. I heard your mom was dead, Sheriff." Penny said looking pointedly at me "You're sure about this marriage Sheriff? I mean this was awful fast. No offence, Doctor Weldon."

"I'm not offended and call me Tina. I'm glad someone's looking after Gee. Sometimes if you're really lucky you meet someone and it's like a bolt of lightning has hit you. You fall instantly in love with someone. I know that's how I felt," Tina replied.

"Me too! I saw her and I was totally head over heels," I commented.

"I think you both better think about this. Lightning can burnout fast."

"We have thought about this Penny and we're getting married," I stated gently.

"Congratulations then!" Penny conceded, but turning back to Tina, she cautioned, "The Sheriff has had bad luck with the ladies, I understand; so don't hurt him. Or you'll answer to us here at the station. Now I have to get back to my desk. Drop those reports back on my desk Sheriff, no later than three this afternoon. The city comptroller wants to look over our budget and we have to justify the overtime we've been putting in."

Penny then left closing the door. I felt flattered that Penny had cautioned Tina. Obviously the troops were beginning to like me. That would make my job easier.

"She likes you. You're just a chick magnet aren't you? I'm going to have to beat them off with a stick or maybe I'll just keep you so satisfied you won't be able to think of anyone else," Tina declared licking her lips again and flitting out her tongue and then locking the door.

The image she had created in my head, made me want to leave right now and go home with her but I had a case to solve. Cops and their families had been murdered this had to take top priority. I couldn't be distracted. Tina unlocked the door realizing this was going nowhere.

"Will you come home with me tonight? I'd like to spend a night in your arms not just a few minutes in a locked closet at the hospital," Tina asked.

"But that was a pretty interesting half-hour; wouldn't you say?"

"Let's say I'd like to go back to the closet; but I bet you'd have a little trouble balancing; that's why a bed would come in handy," Tina quipped.

"I should go home to my daughter; but if I tell her I'm under doctor's care…"

"Then it will be alright. Now what was Penny talking about and how does she know you had bad luck with women?"

"I can only think that Penny researched me. Damn, I was hoping no one knew here in Driftwood besides Aunt Louise."

"Knew what?"

"I told you I'd been married before but I never felt this way about Gina."

"So that's her name. But you're still avoiding telling me whatever Penny already knows. Gina must have been a real piece of work. The way you say her name tells me you have a lot of unhappiness and rage over something she did. What did the bitch do? Did she cut out when you were injured on the job? I saw the gunshot wounds."

"She caused the gunshot wounds."

"She did what?"

"Gina screwed me over literally and figuratively. She had an affair with my superior officer and then she and her stupid boyfriend plotted to kill me when I found out."

"She what? That fucking bitch!!! Is she alive? I'll kill her!!" Tina exclaimed.

"Gordon saved me from her. Gina and Derek had planned on me dying or looking like I had committed suicide."

"How did you get mixed up with the likes of her?"

"Just unlucky I guess and maybe a little too trusting."

"Do you trust me? You didn't call me when you left the hospital."

"I guess I've gotten into the habit where I've not considered anyone; but me and that has to change because I care about you and want you in my life. I've never felt like this about anyone in my entire life. I looked at you that day outside of the intensive care and I forgot about my all my troubles and even my job. But you have to know I have to put my job first."

"I know you do and that's what we have in common. I put my patients first too; so I'll forgive you this once. That is as long as you call me when you're going to do something stupid like this next time. Here's your medicine. You should take some of this antibiotic now and maybe some of this painkiller. You're looking a little green around the gills  But don't go shooting anyone under the influence of these painkillers. Then we'd both have explaining to do," Tina laughed.

I hesitated taking the pain pills and only the antibiotic. I needed to be alert at work, Tina was correct in that respect.

"So where is this Gina and do I have to worry about her?"

"She's rotting in Statesville. She's still got about eleven more years to serve."

"Poor little Stella-Marie. I'd ask if she wasn't your daughter; but you can see that she's the spitting image of a female you. So I'm guessing you have full custody."

"Of course, I do and she'll never see my little girl as long as I have a breath."

"How will you finagle that? Stella-Marie may go looking for her mother when she gets older."

"Yes, I know that I'll have to deal with it, when I come to it."

"If we're going to be together you're going to have to not make me look so bad in front of your daughter and aunt."

"I don't understand," I commented.

"Your Aunt Louise is just getting to know me and so is your daughter; then you go off and run off from the hospital…they are less than enchanted with me."

"Again, I'm sorry. I should have considered that."

"Lucky for you your daughter has all the brains in the family. She told me never mind, nobody can stop daddy when he wants to do something and then your Aunt Louise agreed."

"Now I know why I'm so attracted to you."

"It's not my body?" Tina asked sounding insulted.

"Babe you've got brains, and body to die for. Who'd forget that?"

"A sweet talker and charisma to spare; no wonder I'm mad for you," Tina said kissing me full on the lips then she stopped abruptly saying, "You distracted me so much I forgot the other reason I came here."

"There was another reason?" I said joking that I was insulted.

"Yes, Gunner besides the fact that I'm hot for your body; I do have other pressing concerns."

"My office door locks. I told you this before," I offered.

"Maybe another time; right now I have to inform you a large quantity of fentanyl has gone missing at the hospital and it has to be someone who worked at the hospital and has access to it but we haven't been able to determine whom."

"When did this occur?"

"Before you started working here at the police station. The powers that be think maybe as long as a month ago, the drugs went missing."

"Powers that be?"

"The administrators annoy me; it's my pet name for them."

"Why isn't it the missing fentanyl in any report that came across my desk?"

"The hospital thought that they could take care of this internally and discipline the offending party when they found them; but they found more missing this morning."

"This morning? Again why wasn't I called?"

"I don't know. I'm telling you now! You wouldn't believe the number of people who come through our emergency room with overdoses with fentanyl. The problem is (and you should pay close attention to this) we as physicians are getting second-hand exposure."

"How does the exposure happen?"

"We get it from their clothing and other belongings. Tim had to take naloxone nasal spray a year ago. He became addicted and had to undergo some addiction therapy; before he could come back to work. Yet none of that was his fault. He was just doing his job."

"Poor Tim, is he better now?"

"Yes. Of course he is. He had nothing to do with the missing drug; if that's what you're asking."

"What about you are you safe?"

"I wear a mask and full hazmat gear at all times when dealing with drug overdoses at the emergency department. You should be really careful too Gunner. You don't want to get exposed. You should also caution your officers not to go into any of these drug dens without the proper gear. Get some naloxone nasal spray and get your officers to carry it; maybe even double doses."

"I will. I don't know why the hospital couldn't have informed my department of this development. If a huge large of drugs go missing that's a serious crime."

"Fentanyl is to easily accessible. If I were to do a simple online search of "buy fentanyl online" I find a number of sellers who would be only too happy to sell me fentanyl. It's a growing epidemic and don't get me started on all the derivatives of fentanyl that you can. There are Alfentanil (brand name: Alfenta), Carfentanil (brand name: Wildnil), Sufentanil (brand name: Sufenta), Remifentanil (brand name: Ultiva), and then there's Brifentanil ,Lofentanil, Mirfentanil, Ocfentanil, Ohmefentanyl,Paraflurofentanyl, Acetylfentanyl, Butryfentanyl, Alphamethylthiofentanyl, Betahydroxyfentanyl, Betahydroxythiofentanyl, Furanylfentanyl, Methylacetylfentanyl, N-Methylcarfentanil, Methylfentanyl, Methylbutyrfentanyl, Flurobutyrfentanyl, Allylfentanyl, Phenylfentanyl, Methylthiofentanyl, Beta-Methylfentanyl. These derivatives are far more dangerous. Carfentanil alone is a synthetic opioid so deadly, as little as twenty micrograms would be fatal to the average person, with one microgram being smaller than a grain of salt."

"Less than a grain? Are you kidding me?"

"No!"

"How do you know all this?" I asked.

"I'm a doctor; but also call me curious, when so many patients come through my department with drug addictions to one source I wanted to know how and why they could get access to the drug and don't forget fentanyl is not detected by standard urine screens; so someone might not even know they took it if it's mixed with another drug and it also makes it harder for the hospital to find the culprit."

"I've seen those same websites and more. One foreign pharmacy that promises "one hundred per cent anonymity and privacy," and "undetectable" parcels packed carefully so they can skip through customs' X-ray machines"... It's a terrible epidemic with huge societal implications and I have to stop it here. I won't have Driftwood over run by drug addiction and start to be called Actiq town or some other crazy drug name like Murder 8 town because they've mixed it with heroin. This is my town and I'll solve these murders and take it back from the drug trade too; which means I have to go back to the hospital and speak to the administrators and find the culprits."

"I thought that's what you say so I'll drive you back. I have to get back to work anyway I'm just on a half-hour break. I'm working until six and then we have a command performance for dinner."

"Command performance?"

"Your Aunt Louise and Stella-Marie have requested our presence at a dinner they're making."

"Damn, I'm supposed to be on call for Errol. In about fifteen minutes he's meeting a source. He took Nathan with him; but I'm at edge with all these blatant shootings at cops."

"Tell you what give me a few minutes to fresh up in the washroom and then I'll call in a favour and get another hour off so I can drive you back to the hospital," Tina exclaimed smiling at me.

"I hope you can receive your favor otherwise I'll have to get George Henning to drive me and I hear he might need a refresher course for driving. Penny signed him up for a defensive driving course but he hasn't completed it yet."

"I'll get the time, Yasmin owes me she'll cover for me," Tina claimed, "Excuse me now I'll let you get your work done and be back in a few minutes."

glanced over some reports at my desk and waited for Errol to meet with his snitch at the strip club and wished that I had been able to go with him but my leg being the way it was right now would be a liability.

"Sorry, Yasmin says it's a no go. She can't cover for me. I guess George Henning will be your driver. Tell him to drive carefully and bring you back in one piece. I'll see you later. Bye," Tina fired rapidly as she came back into the office. Tina then quickly kissed me goodbye and went back to the hospital.

~0~

# Chapter 11 - Errol's Source

I procrastinated a little after Tina left but

finished my paperwork in time for the meeting to take place. Normally you wouldn't worry so much when an officer was meeting a source but these weren't normal times. These criminals knew who the police officers were but we didn't know who they were that had to change. Hopefully this meeting would change that and give us the upper hand.

I turned on the speakers on my end at the appointed time and listened intently as Errol told me through his microphone that he had arrived at the strip club.

I heard Errol's voice come through clearly on his wire, "Testing one, two, three, text me if you're getting this boss."

I signalled that I was through his ear piece and Errol continued, *"Entering the strip club."*

*"Were closed, sir, until five p.m.,"* a woman said.

*"Tyrell around?"* Errol inquired.

*"Is Mr. Spector expecting you?"*

*"I'm Errol Ward, Tyrell expects me."*

*"Oh so you're his buddy from Iraq. From eight years ago."*

*"You seem well informed Miss?"*

*"It's Mrs. Sally Spector."*

*"Ty didn't tell me he got married."*

*"Ty and were married in Vegas last weekend."*

*"So I'm interrupting your honeymoon?"*

*"No we'll go next week. I'm sorry we didn't tell you but we didn't tell anyone. We'll have a party in about three weeks I hope you'll come."*

*"I'd be glad to."*

*"Ty says he offered you a job working security here, but you turned him down."*

*"I did because I had another job offer."*

*"Sally, quit grilling the man. Come into my office, Errol. Errol, buddy. I hear you've joined the police force here. That's a dangerous occupation with most of the former police force dead."*

*"You know once a cop always a cop. You are keeping your nose clean buddy, aren't you?"*

*"I'm still grateful for all you've done for me. I'll never forget how you went to bat for me in Iraq when that Sergeant was out to get me. I could have spent years in the stockade."*

*"It was mostly symbolic."*

*"Like hell it was! You finding me a lawyer saved me from the Sergeant. You even put your career in the line and testified. I appreciate all of this more than words can say."*

*"We're friends; that's what friends do,
"Errol insisted, and then changing the
subject he said, "You've picked up a
beautiful wife since I last saw you."*

*"Sally is a peach. She was desperate and
came in here to audition as a stripper, but
couldn't do it. I hired here as a waitress and
then as my manager. We were married after
six weeks."*

*"Love at first sight."*

*"You betcha, Errol. Maybe you need to find
a good woman to settle down with too."*

*"I think I'll wait on that a bit. I'm not ready
for the domestic life yet."*

*"Quit listening at the door Sally and come
in," I heard Tyrell say. There was a brief
silence and then I heard, "Who are you and
why do you have a gun pointed at Sally?"*

I heard a loud crack followed by a sort of whine in the background and some shouting. I recognized that sound and I signalled Nathan Ricci to move in. I went out into the outer office and gestured to George Henning to drive me to the strip club still intently listening to the action at the strip club on my radio. My heart dropped into my mouth as I heard more shots ring out and I hoped that Errol and my other officers were all right.

~0~

# Chapter 12 – Shit-Storm

I arrived at the strip club with a lot of

squad cars and an ambulance. I was glad I had forgone my painkillers and could keep my head. It felt like I could have been back in Illinois as I looked around. This was in an older decayed part of town I never noticed before. The storefronts were empty here and signs said for sale on buildings that looked old and decrepit. The store next to the strip club said variety store; but it too was closed and shuttered. The paint on it was faded like it hadn't been open in years. There were young men in the alleyways openly doing drugs despite the huge police presence. The first person I saw at the strip club was Errol in the back of an ambulance being patched up.

"I was winged boss. A through and through, the fleshy part of my arm was struck. Thanks to my vest you made me wear. I have a few bruised ribs, but I'm fine," Errol explained.

The emergency technician nodded but said, "He still needs to be checked out at the hospital."

"He'll go," I said and then looked pointedly at Errol who nodded.

I then turned to Nathan and asked, "Can you tell me what happened?"

Nathan answered and then became silent as he let Errol explain the rest of what had happened, "Three guys all dressed in black with ski masks burst in the adjoining room in the back of the club, one of them gathered up Sally and came into the office. The others opened fire while I was dealing with the gunman who had Sally. Sally seemed so alive, so bouncy. You know the type of personality I'm speaking of? You think they're vapid, but underneath they are really smart."

"I'm sorry I can tell you cared about them,"
I commented.

"I can't believe they killed her."

"Any more causalities. Errol?"

"Unfortunately yes, we've also got a few
dead women, strippers and waitresses; the
security who were at the front door and
some other people. I tried to save Tyrell
Spector boss. I really did. I pulled him out of
the range of fire; but he'd already been hit,"
Errol continued.

"How is Spector? Can he give us any
information?" I asked.

"He's dead. I think I may have gotten him
and like I said his wife, Sally was killed too.
She fought back got away but the other
damn gunmen shot her, too. This was an
assassination squad and they hit their targets
before I could do a damn thing," Errol
stated.

"We will get them Errol." I commiserated.

"I think they followed me boss. How else
could they have known I was at the club? I
didn't tell anyone but you and Nathan."

"Maybe they hacked the airwaves and picked up on the conversation you had with Tyrell; if so it's my fault." I answered.

"I get what you're saying boss; but I still feel guilty."

"Guilt gets us nowhere…,"I began before Errol interrupted, "You're saying let's just get the buggers."

"Before he was killed (when your microphone wasn't on) did Tyrell share any other information with you? Anything at all?" I asked grabbing at straws.

"I wish," Errol said.

"So we don't have a clue what Tyrell was going to tell you?"

"I'm sorry boss, I blew it," Errol said sadly.

"I'm just glad you aren't dead. I can't afford to lose another officer let alone an officer of your caliber."

"Then I'm not fired?"

"No, but you have to be seen to at the hospital and take a couple of days to recuperate. I've taken your report of the situation," I said then turning to the paramedic I said, "Take good care of him."

The ambulance driver then got in and the ambulance took off with sirens going. I had just started to process the scene when my cell phone rang.

"What the hell is going on, Bullet?" asked the not so dulcet voice of the mayor.

"Excuse me?"

"There's been another shooting in my town."

"It's my town too. This started before I came here. Two innocent civilian are dead, others wounded and my police officer has been wounded. I'm investigating a crime here. I'll call you back later," I said as I went to hang up.

"Wait, don't hang up."

"What do you want?" I demanded.

"Be here at six for a special council meeting."

"What part of I'm in the midst of an investigation, do you not understand?"

"We hired you, be here, or you're fired," the mayor shouted then abruptly hung up the phone.

Just what I didn't need explaining myself in front of a closed council session. Then I remembered I was supposed to have dinner with Tina, Aunt Louise and Stella-Marie and what about Tina? Tina would be worried sick if I didn't call her. I asked the Bluetooth connection in my patrol car to call Tina and she answered after three rings.

"Hello Gee. Miss me all ready?"

"We've had another shooting."

"So I've heard the victims were brought here but were dead on arrival. I thought you were in your office so I wasn't too worried. Although someone told me you had arrived after the shooting."

"I'm sorry. I'm not going to make dinner. I can't make it until eight."

"I'm not going to be there until eight either. Will your Aunt Louise be mad?"

"I'm sure she'll understand, but my daughter will be disappointed," I answered.

"I'm sorry I was looking forward to getting better acquainted with your daughter."

"They'll be lots of time for that."

"Will you tell Aunt Louise, that I could come later if Aunt Louise doesn't mind feeding me that late? I haven't time to make a call. I should even be talking to you, but I saw your number and had to answer. I have to go now a patient needs me. See you at eight."

"I'm sure she'll be happy to feed us then."

"Bye now," Tina said as she disconnected.


I then instructed the *Bluetooth* to call Aunt Louise.

Aunt Louise answered with, "Thank god, you called. I heard a cop had been shot by the strip club. I was worried it was you."

""I'm fine really, Aunt Louise."

"No, you're not; you should still be in the hospital."

"I'm sorry but this investigation needs me."

"What good will this town be if you are dead?"

"Dead, daddy's dead?" I heard near the phone then Stella-Marie crying.

"No, Stella-Marie your father is not dead. Would you like to speak to your father? He's on the phone."

"Daddy?"

"Hi pumpkin."

"I'm mad at you for leaving the hospital. Aunt Louise says you should have stayed. Is your officer okay?"

"Yes, pumpkin he's going to be okay."

"I don't like this daddy! Are you wearing your jacket?"

"Jacket?"

"You know like in the movies, the cops wear jackets that protect them from bullets; kind of like superman.""

"I'll put it on right now. I promise."

"Okay, then maybe I'll forgive you. See you at supper." "I'm not going to make for your suppertime, baby."

"Why not? I want to see you daddy?" Stella-Marie whined.

"I'm sorry Stella-Marie I'll be here by eight to tuck you in, I promise," I offered.

"We can find out about Tina better while you're not here anyway. We expect you at eight and no excuses," Stella-Marie stated sternly.

I laughed I couldn't help it she sounded just like Aunt Louise.

"Don't laugh at me be here at eight p.m. no later. I'll be waiting!"

"Tina has to work later and can't get there until eight either so she can tuck you in too, That is if you want."

"No! That's our time," Stella-Marie said.

"Don't be too hard on Tina. I really care about her Stella-Marie."

"Fine, I'll try but I can't promise for Aunt Louise. Just remember, I want you to tuck me in not her. I'll say hello but that's all tonight. Here, Uncle Gordon wants to speak to you. He just drove over."

"As I was having a late lunch with Perita, I heard on the radio that a shooting had occurred; so. I dropped her off at my motel room and I came over. I thought Aunt Louise would appreciate it if I were here. You know in case there was bad news about you."

"Thanks buddy. No rushing to the hospital, huh?" I joked.

"You're welcome."

"So you're not ready for Aunt Louise to meet Perita?"

"Perita's a little shy. I'll let you all meet her soon when Perita's up to it. Now do you need me at the scene?"

"No, I can handle it. Thanks Gordon. You keep working on those leads you had to the killings of our officers."

"That's what is so strange the leads have dried up and even forensics can't pull us in the right direction if we don't have clues. But I'll keep plugging at it."

"I'll keep working with snitches someone has to know something about these hits," I answered, "Got to go give my love to my girl and Aunt Louise and tell her Tina can't come until eight either."

"Ducking the annoyed auntie talk, huh? I'm sure she'll save it all up for you until she can corner you later. I'll tell Aunt Louise. My cell phone is ringing I'll talk to you later, Gunner."

I sent Jack Hoskins to the hospital to investigate the missing fentanyl and then I went back to supervising the scene. The forensics technicians were almost finished. Noticing it was nearing six o'clock (and having dismissed George Henning) I got in my squad car I drove myself to the inquisition. Maneuvering my leg around I was able to drive with minimal pain.

Penny had sent the papers with one of my officers to the strip club scene so I was prepared. I needed to justify overtime requisitions. Now with all this paperwork I had and my silver tongue; hopefully I'd still have my job when I was done at city hall.

~0~

# Chapter 13 – Questions Unanswered

Entering the building the security guard

told me the mayor demanded to see me in his office first; telling me exactly where it was.

I knocked on the door and the mayor said, "Come in."

The mayor's office was as pretentious as he was. The walls were oak and his desk was an antique oak too. On his desk was a silver frame with a picture of a woman with dark hair. He saw me looking over at it and actually blushed.

"My kids put that on my desk I've been meaning to give it back to them. It's a picture of my ex-wife and I hate looking at her. Now the council session starts in about five minutes; but I wanted to speak to you first," he claimed conspiratorially.

"How are Ethan and Reggie?"

"Ethan is getting better. I sent him to rehab. He's one of the lucky ones. As you know the other fourteen students are dead. I hear that drug that killed the others was a derivative of fentanyl. This community is being decimated by drug dealers funneling their product through my town. Your job is to stop them; but so far all I've seen is cops getting shot and more wreckage."

"Are you insinuating I'm not doing my job?"

"Crime had gotten worse since you arrived."

"You had this problem before I landed; otherwise you wouldn't have dead cops or kids dying."

"Point taken. So you think the drugs and the killings are connected?"

"It sure looks that way."

"Then that's a different kettle of fish and I'll back you in front of council for now. But we have to see results soon, our constituents are scared. We've been getting phone calls about how they are feeling unsafe in their homes and there's an election coming up this November. That affects you too. You must run for office to keep your appointment; but you knew this didn't you?" the mayor stated.

"I knew I had to run when the election came up; but I thought that was two years away."

"Nope we have to both run and win to keep our jobs and I for one would like to show the people they are safe and that I made the right choice in hiring you," the mayor exclaimed, "Now let's go convince the council so you can stay until the election."

The council meeting was over in a few minutes and I held unto my job by the skin of my teeth. I lied telling them I thought I was close to finding the drug dealers suppliers and the killers of my police officers. I would have to hustle to make these lies a reality. With Gordon's help I'd find the killers and the drug dealers but it was going to be a lot of unpaid overtime.

My thoughts were interrupted by a call on my Bluetooth. My newest officer (a lucky find as he was a highly decorated cop and a Portland transplant) was on the horn. It seemed he had been stonewalled at the hospital passed around from person to person until he, Jack Hoskins, spoke with a head nurse who insisted she couldn't give him information on the staff working at the hospital whom may have had access to the locked cabinet which contained the missing fentanyl. I asked him if he had spoken to Tina, but he said she wasn't available apparently she was working on some more overdoses and of course the shootings at the strip club that had come into the Emergency room.

I assured Jack that I would handle it and put
him to work on the shooting at the strip club
hoping that the city council wouldn't balk
on more overtime.

I then called the hospital and demanded to
speak to their president and chief executor,
Murray Trenton. They of course told me he
wasn't available until after 8 a.m. tomorrow
morning so I went home to my daughter to
tuck her in bed.

Arriving hone I didn't see Tina's car. Was
she running late? I stepped into the house
only to be grabbed around the legs by Stella-
Marie.

"Of all the hare-brained, idiotic things you
should be in a bed, not running around
running stakeouts and having your officers
shot. You aren't able to take care of yourself
right now. You could have been the one
shot," Aunt Louise greeted me.

"Thank you for listening to me daddy. Steven Segal's character was safe when he wore his jacket now take it off because you're safe at home."

I obediently took off my flak jacket as Stella-Marie smiled.

"So your policeman's arm okay?" Stella-Marie asked.

"How did you know it was his arm?" I asked.

"I heard it on the police radio," Stella-Marie replied.

"Stella-Marie…"

"I know no listening on your police radio in your office."

"My office is out of bounds."

"I'm sorry Stella-Marie snuck in there when I was in the bathroom."

"Stella-Marie should have known better," I insisted.

"I promise I won't do it again," Stella-Marie claimed but I noticed she had her right hands fingers crossed behind her back.

"See that you do, "I cautioned, "Now I believe it was someone's bed time."

"Can't I stay up until Tina comes?"

I was about to give in to her plea, when my cell phone rang. I put up a hand as if to say just a minute then I walked into the other room so Stella-Marie and Aunt Louise couldn't hear the conversation. It was the hospital administrator Murray Trenton. He had received my messages and wanted to assure me he knew who was responsible. All he wanted me to do was to arrest her. The hospital administrator was sure the head nurse responsible for the locked cabinet was responsible for the missing fentanyl.

He believed Helga Bruin was guilty as she had previously been suspected of stealing oxycodone and morphine. I told him wanted to investigate more and he agreed that I could. I decided to pull Jack back off the strip club shooting and have him investigate.

My cell phone rang as I hung up.

"Gunner? I 'm not going to make dinner. It's been a long day and I think I'm coming down with something, Tina's voice croaked.

"Do you want me to come over and make you some soup," I offered seductively.

"No, I'd never get any sleep if you came over and they expect me to work tomorrow. I may be wearing a mask all day to keep people safe from my germs."

"You could wear that same mask and I could come over and take care of you," I offered.

"What jumping around on one foot? I'm supposed to be looking after you," protested Tina.

"So I can come over?"

"No, your little girl misses you spend time with her and Aunt Louise and I'll make it up to you tomorrow if I'm better."

"Okay I'll explain to Aunt Louise and Stella-Marie. Get some sleep and feel better."

"Thanks Gunner, I love you."

"I love you too, Tina," I replied and then hung up the phone.

Stella-Marie seemed disappointed that Tina wasn't coming. Aunt Louise just frowned; even after I told her that Tina was sick. I could tell she thought badly of Tina. I decide to talk to her later about and not in front of Stella-Marie. As for Stella-Marie she somehow talked me into sharing desert with her; before I tucked her in bed and read Robert Munsch's '*The Paper Bag Princess.*'

Stella-Marie somehow talked me into another two books. The kid's books today were fun and educational as well. The Mare the Hare book by S .G. Lee that I read to her had me smiling and I admit to a tear or two while reading Robert Munsch's, 'I'll Love You Forever'.

Stella –Marie went to sleep and I went to talk to Aunt Louise. It didn't go well. Aunt Louise was mad at me and said I was rushing things with Tina. She agreed we'd disagree; but I was angry. I left the house supposedly to go to the station but I went to Tina's and took care of her. I slipped home in time to have breakfast with Stella-Marie and then I went to work.

Jack reported in the next day that the case had come to a conclusion at the hospital. The fentanyl which had been sold to Troy and Calvin Richardson had come from a marked supply traced to the hospital. It seemed too easy that Helga had coughed up the Richardson's' name; but Jack told me he'd promised to speak at her trial if she gave up the name of the person or persons she'd sold the drug to.

Troy and Calvin Richardson were too dumb to have conceived a huge drug organization like this. I wanted the real name of the people behind the drugs in my town. I decided while talking to Gordon that it would be prudent to investigate the Richardson's some more before arresting them. I would protect Driftwood and make this town safe or my name wasn't Gunner Bullet.

~0~

## Chapter 14 - Penny's Secrets

It was two weeks before I saw Tina again.

She was so busy working as a physician I didn't see here even when I arrived for therapy. I was keeping busy too. I'd been going a half-hour daily and then doing the exercises at my desk while filling and reading reports so my leg was getting better but I still had a pronounced limp and had to work really hard at balancing but of course I was a tough guy so I didn't complain.

"Coffee and some aspirin, boss," Penny said as she came into my office. And also handed me some more paperwork; there always seemed to be paperwork.

"Was I that cranky?"

"Just a little. See you later boss," Penny said as she shut the door.

I stared into space, thinking about how easily the missing fentanyl case at the hospital had wrapped up. I had wrapped up the case of course; I'd followed up some leads on Troy and Calvin Richardson but so far they'd come up clean despite the fact that these pair looked more and more like the guilty parties. The testimony of the head nurse would go a long way in helping to convict them.

They had motive and means; but it felt like someone else was pulling their strings. Who was their boss? My instinct that I always relied upon tingled like there was something I wasn't seeing. I could arrest the Richardson's and try to sweat it out of them; but I feared I would get nowhere so I put them under investigation by my men waited and watched.

As for Gordon he'd been called back to head office but I kept him updated. The investigation was a slow go. I decided I needed a coffee and went to the break room. I was only there about five seconds when Nathan Ricci walked in. Nathan looked at me for about five seconds as if he was hesitant then abruptly said, "I've seen your election signs around town. They're okay; but I think your opponent's signs are better and bigger. They are also in more strategic positions."

"I have signs?"

"Of course you have signs," Penny laughed as she entered the coffee room. "You know you only have roughly six weeks until the election, Sheriff. Nathan's correct your opponent's signs are bigger. You have to do some campaigning. I've put up some signs for you but you have to start taking this seriously or you'll be out of a job come November 8th."

"I hate campaigning. I just want to do the job," I complained.

"Sorry Sheriff, but I've got to say your opponent's looking pretty good. He says he can solve all these crimes and that you're doing a piss poor job not only in solving the cries but in allocating money and resources," Nathan replied.

"He can allocate some money right now by firing you if you want," Penny threatened.

"Hey don't kill the messenger. No offence meant." Nathan responded.

Who did this little shit think he was? I'd given him a job and he was stabbing me in the back with this kind of talk to my face what did he say behind my back?

"Aren't you supposed to be relieving Errol whose watching the Richardson's?" I asked my eyes narrowing.

"Yes… in about fifteen minutes. Guess I'd better hit the road," Nathan said looking at his watch.

"Yes, and you better get going and don't forget to report back to your sheriff those Richardson's doings. I'd better not hear you've been spreading these same lies that Perry's telling. Don't forget Nathan, I know your mother and she was grateful to the sheriff for giving you a job," Penny whispered to him as he went out the door but I still overheard.

As soon as Nathan was out of earshot Penny started in, "Do you have any idea who is running against you?"

"Some guy named Percival Derrickson."

"Not just some guy; his father was killed on
the job. Twenty years ago his father, Hiram
Derrickson held the position as sheriff. He
was killed apprehending bank suspects and
he left a wife and an eight year old son
Percival or Perry as those who know him.
Perry will use that to win. You have to solve
the murders of your police officers and their
families and stop the flow of the fentanyl in
this county then people will see you are the
sheriff they need and want. Because Perry
knows how to pretend his good and has
charisma that sways crowds but he's an evil
vindictive soul who would make a terrible
sheriff."

"Tell me what you really think…"

"Don't joke this is serious. You do want to
be sheriff still? Don't you?"

"Yes, I do and I appreciate that you're
helping me. You've been a good friend to
me since I came to Driftwood."

"I know how hard it is to be a single parent.
I had a little girl once."

"Once?"

"I met a guy and I thought I was in love; but he didn't. He left me; but not without a present…the greatest present of my life, my little girl Lorna. Lorna was healthy for a couple of years but then she got really sick with leukemia. I tried to find her a bone marrow but her father was the only one to match even the slightest. He was tested but he refused to give her his bone marrow. I begged, I pleaded; but he wouldn't give his bone marrow and Lorna died."

"Who was this guy?"

Penny hesitated then said very quietly, "Percival Derrickson."

"He is truly evil. What kind of father wouldn't give his child anything, even his own life? I'm so sorry Penny. I will do everything in my power to make sure he doesn't get this job."

I then left and went to my office but Penny
followed a few seconds later carrying papers
in her hands.

"I'm glad you said that you would do
everything in your power to get this job. I
like having you for a sheriff and I think you
are the man to beat Perry. I'm not
exaggerating there is something innately evil
in that man, Now if you really mean to win
then you have to give a speech this
afternoon at the community center at 3
p.m..."

"I hate those things but I understand that I
need to be seen so they can judge I'm the
better candidate. I don't have a speech
prepared. I guess I'll have to write one
before then," I answered.

"I've already written you one," Penny
replied handing me piece of paper.

I glanced over it. It was a great speech and touched all the right points; but Penny was right I need to show the citizens of this county I could do the job or I'd be out on my ear come November 8th.

"I'll leave you to get some of this paperwork done, now," Penny said.

Penny then left the room shutting my door and I was left with my mountains of administration and for me to tinker with the speech and make it mine.

~0~

## Chapter 15 – Perita

T wo hours later my door creaked as

Gordon came in unexpectedly.

"Hey buddy, how's it going?" I asked.

"Fine," Gordon answered.

"Were still slugging it out if you read the reports I've been sending you."

"I have read them, but I keep hoping one of us will find the answers we need. I need to wrap this one up," Gordon stated.

"I'm working on it. Two of my best are surveilling the Richardson's and their associates day and night." "So are my FBI men. It's under control. Now come have lunch with me. I've invited Tina. She's meeting us at the restaurant. I want you both to meet Perita."

"We finally get to meet the illusive Perita," I blurted.

"Be nice she's really shy and I care about her."

"She must be really special if you love her, so I'll be extra nice," I joked winking.

"Not that nice. I don't think Tina or I would appreciate that."

"Gottcha Gordon."

"You...."

I just grabbed my coat and limped out the door. When we got to the curb I climbed into Gordon's car.

"So how is it going? Are you going to ask Perita to marry you?"

"Maybe but not yet; unlike you I want to wait a little bit before proposing marriage."

"I love Tina and I'm going to marry her so you'd better get used to Tina hanging around."

"I can see that Gunner; but if she makes you unhappy she's going to have to answer to me," Gordon said.

"The same goes for Perita. If she hurts you she'll answer to me," I exclaimed.

"Touché. We'll agree to try and like each other's significant other," Gordon agreed.

"Wait a minute; where are you heading? I can't go out of town I have a campaign speech at 3 p.m."

"Campaign speech? So you've finally decided you want to keep your job?"

"I'm not going to let Percival Derrickson win."

"I'll help you anyway I can, Gee. It's only eleven a.m. I'll get you back way before 3 p.m."

"Thanks Gordon."

"Earn it by welcoming Perita."

"I will Gordon. I only want my pal happy."

The drive took a half- an hour and we soon arrived at an upscale restaurant in nearby De Ulibarri, Colorado. De Ulibarri was named after Spanish conquistador, Juan de Ulibarri who claimed Colorado. Some people were fighting to change the name and saw it affront to the native peoples who were driven from the land by the conquistador in the early seventeen hundreds.

As I entered the restaurant with Gordon by my side; I saw his face light as he gazed at the woman whose back was turned to us. Tall and beautiful, her hair was like liquid chocolate as it flowed to her waist. As she stood up her dress moved like it was glued to her, it was cut expertly to accent her larger bosom, tiny waist and rounded bum. Her dark chocolate brown eyes flashed with intelligence. Glancing at her twice, I knew something about her reminded me of someone I seen recently; but I couldn't think of whom or what.

"Perita, this is Gee Bullet, my best friend
and the Sheriff of Driftwood. Gee, this is
Perita Castillo."

"It's very nice to finally meet you," Perita
replied in a sweet soft sultry voice with a
slight Spanish accent.

I looked at Gordon; yes he liked this voice
of hers. Frankly I was suspicious of it. He
had described Perita as shy and retiring.
Women who had figures and voices like that
knew what they had and they used it to
ensnare males. They weren't shy and
retiring. What was her angle why was she
playing Gordon?

"Gee, Perita and I've been talking and it
seems we know a lot of the same people,"
Tina interrupted my thoughts.

Oddly Perita frowned like she didn't like
Tina sharing their conversation. Tina noticed
and gulped as if she had offended Perita and

then changed the subject, "So how has your day been, Gee?"

"Pretty busy. I'm still trying to find some clues for the case I'm working on. I'm also trying to do a bit of campaigning. In fact I have to back to Driftwood Community Center by 3 p.m. to give a speech."

"Sounds like a very busy day, Sheriff, I'm so glad you found the time to have lunch with me," Perita stated.

Perita followed this up by smiling the kind of smile that can bring a male to his knees and I was no exception, I found myself smiling back and saying, "Please call me Gee. My boy, Gordon here is mad for you so that makes us friends, I hope?"

"I'd like us all to be friends," Perita exclaimed and smiled again at Gordon.

The smile for Gordon was different solely focused on him and with warmth that was

palatable and for a moment I saw what
Gordon saw in her.

I ordered steak and potatoes as did Gordon
and surprisingly Perita. Tina ordered shrimp
and rice on a sea of vegetables and frowned
at my steak. Tina had been cautioning me
lately about the food I ate and my over
dependence on red meats. I silently
promised her that I would eat better later.

But as we talked some more over lunch, I
noticed (as Gordon had said) that Perita
didn't seem shy at all but a bit on the
manipulative side, or maybe my suspicious
mind thought she's hiding something. But
that was ridiculous, was I actually jealous of
Perita? I felt her eyes drawing me in until I
forcefully pulled my eyes away.

Gordon had supported me and protected me
from my vicious ex – wife. That was it. Of
course, my scars from Gina had made me
suspicious of a perfectly nice woman who
was just being sociable and I had taken it all
wrong. I needed to support Gordon's
relationship with Perita not be a suspicious,

judgmental friend. I attempted to be a better friend and told some fun stories keeping the ladies in stitches.

We finished our meal and I excuse myself to go the bathroom. I had just finished using the urinal and zipping my pants and going to wash my hands when Gordon came in.

"Do you like her?"

"Yes, Perita seems very nice," I answered.

"And it does hurt that she's hot, huh?"

"Yes she is beautiful," I responded knowing the answer he wanted.

"I'm glad you like her Gee. It means a lot to me."

"I better get back," I stated not wanting to get into anymore conversation and say the wrong thing.

"Okay, I paid the check. Go join the ladies. I'll be back soon."

Leaving the bathroom I reached into my
pocket to check the time on my cell and
realized I left my cell phone on the table. I
hurried and got to the table to find only
Perita sitting there finishing off a piece of
chocolate cheesecake.

"Wow for someone so skinny you can really
put the food away," I blurted out and then
realizing how that sounded I backtracked,
"I'm sorry that was rude. You are a beautiful
woman you can eat what you want."

Perita laughed a tinkling laugh that made all
the men in the room turn and smile at her
then she said, "I had you pegged all wrong. I
thought you hated me. I just make you
nervous."

I nodded.

We began talking and I finally started liking
her. The conversation was running smoothly
and I let my guard down. Perita seemed to

look over my shoulder and then said, "Look at the ring Gordon gave me isn't it lovely."

"Yes," I replied.

"Look at the cut the clarity," she responded putting the finger that held the ring directly in my hands.

I clasped her hand looking at it closely and her face turned fearful and then she yanked her hand from mine as Gordon appeared over my shoulder.

"I want to go home," Perita said sinking into Gordon's arms as he gravitated to beside her.

I was puzzled. Did she worry Gordon would think she was flirting with me? Perita whispered in his ear and the next thing I knew Gordon started glaring at me and then he abruptly took her hand and walked away.

What had just happened? My best friend of
more than fifteen years had just walked
away from me. I tried to dial him on my cell
phone but he didn't answer me.


Tina then arrived at the table.


"Where are Gordon and Perita?" She asked.

"I don't know one minute we are talking
then Gordon came back and she says she
wants to go home," I explained.

"What exactly happened? Tell me exactly
what you and she did?"

"Did? I didn't do anything!" I protested.

"No you didn't, but she's done something.
So tell me what did she do?"

"She was sweet and charming and
apologizing that we didn't hit it off. She said
she'd misjudged me, and then she had me
look at her ring."

"Look at her ring?"

"I don't know but Gordon is mad at me. He
left without speaking to me."

"Oh dear that doesn't sound good."

"No kidding and not only that he was my ride. I have to get back or I'll be late for my campaign speech."

"Hopefully this will blow over." Tina said comforting me, "I'll drive you to the community center and you can give your speech. You have to win the election. So clear your head and give a rousing speech. Okay?"

"Thank-you, honey. What would I do without you?" I asked.

"You'll never have to find out." Tina cried kissing me on the lips then she took out her keys, "Let's go it won't look good if the candidate is late."

We stepped into the car and Tina as good as her word got me to the community center in time and I gave the stirring speech that Penny had written for me.

~0~

# Chapter 16 - Storming the Richardson's

A week went on and I didn't hear from Gordon, no matter how many times I called. I thought he would answer work calls, but he didn't. The continued surveillance of the Richardson's continued with nothing but reports of low level drug dealing.

I was fast asleep when I got a call from Errol who was at the stakeout of the Richardson's.

"Boss you better get down here to 450 River Road. The FBI are here and they're about to storm the house and arrest the Richardson's," Errol stated.

"Thank-you Errol. I'll be there in less than five," said disconnecting my phone and throwing on my uniform in about two seconds.

I buttoned up my pants with one hand, while grabbing my keys with the other. Running out to my squad car, I put on my flak jacket; I then drove flipping on the lights, but not the siren as I went to the scene. When I got close to the scene I turned off my lights. Gordon and his FBI team were starting to move in and I jumped out of the car and joined them. Gordon glared at me, but nodded at one of his man who asked by a look whether to let me stay.

I wondered what the fuck was his problem. All I knew was that he better get over it quick and not let it interfere with police work.

Entering the mansion we arrested a number of men and women immediately but we knew there were rooms that had yet to be explored that could hold the evidence we needed to hold them and probably other perpetrators too.

The schematics that the FBI had showed sectioned off rooms; but even those diagrams were no match for what they actually done to the home. Rooms were sectioned off unlike the blueprints. Additional circuitry added inside the home brought electrical power to other parts of the home probably to power the equipment to make the drugs and grow the pot. There were extra chimneys lined with metal in the house to ventilate the place. We managed to scoop up a number of people in the front room working bagging pot and counting money with a currency counter.

Much of it was sectioned off; but one section held steel doors and no way of getting through without keys. Gordon sent for the local locksmith and a blowtorch just in case. I wanted to yell at Gordon for not telling me about this bust; but now was the not the time this could wait until later. Right now I needed to caution Gordon and the other FBI that we needed gear in case fentanyl was being manufactured in site.

I told Gordon about the full equipment Tina had advised we wear and Gordon said his FBI truck held all the gear we needed and offered it to me and one of my men. We left some men inside while most of us suited up and then those men came back and suited up.

While we waited for the locksmith that my one of my men was retrieving; we explored the house that we could and found the basement easily accessible and it held a grow-up complete with ideal greenhouse conditions including illegal hydro hook-ups and lighting, along with a marijuana grinder and bundles of marijuana.

One room peered into had long counters and chairs plastic lining the walls and the people still in there wore protective clothing that Tina had advised for fentanyl. We went in and took them all down in a matter of minutes. Seventeen men and fifteen women were arrested from within that large sealed room and ten others from the other rooms.

The criminal network extended from
Colorado to Montana and had ties to
Manitoba, Canada and Mexico.

We found Fentanyl powder that had the
potential to create more than 35,321
Fentanyl pills (worth an estimated $706,000)
and other drugs, like $22,000 worth of
Methamphetamine and $40,000 worth of
Cocaine and $9,000 in Heroin. Also found
were varying amounts of marijuana,
MDMA, Oxycodone and morphine,60
grams of meth and a large amount of Hash,
Cocaine, Psilocybin "Magic" Mushrooms,
Ritalin, Oxycodone, Hydromorphone,
Synthetic THC, marijuana. We also found
70 tablets of a drug that had yet to be
determined. Also found was GHB, also
known as Gamma Hydroxybutyrate or the
"date rape drug, turned to be after testing a
few vials of GHB and a vial of liquid
Fentanyl. We also find a new derivative of
the drug that Tina had mentioned to me...
furanylfentanyl being distributed in
counterfeit oxycodone tablets, which were
marked with a 30 on one side and an 'M' on
the other side.

Furanylfentanyl, the Opioid Analgesic that was an analog of Fentanyl and was being sold as a designer/ party drug was present which shook me. This was worse than I believed. These could possibly have come from China. They'd gotten it past customs how could I stop this all from coming to Driftwood? I mentioned it to Gordon said the FBI would follow up with customs walking away from me.

My officers found a cache of weapons in the home, including three shotguns, two rifles, a handgun and a crossbow. Various amounts of ammunition for the guns and body armour were also seized. A search of a vehicle found discovered $37,115 in cash.

The drugs seized were worth an estimated $825,000. Fifteen (pay as you) go burner cell phones. Also found was $500000 in cash.20 stolen driver's licenses and 20 stolen credit cards and a number of stolen items of property.

The Fentanyl and Cocaine, Methamphetamines (Meth) and Oxycodone were founded bundled in baggies ready for sale. Also found were a pill press used to make fake Oxy pills that contained Fentanyl and Carfentanil used to mix with other drugs.

The amount of Carfentanil seized could have produced more than 50 million doses. The greatest danger of all to these men and women making the drug concoctions was the consumer blender; with all their other precautions wearing full body suits and keeping environmentally safe rooms. None of this would help if they failed to realize that reusing this blender for foods could be deadly.

Of all our finds, the best of all was the proof that the Richardson's had carried out the shooting deaths of my officers and their families. We found the guns and the plans they used. They were obviously not the smartest tools in the bunch, so should I trust this evidence? Gordon said the FBI trusted it so should I.

We jointly released a press release saying *"The apparent prime suspect, 30-year-old Calvin Richardson is accused of recruiting members for a criminal organization, trafficking Cocaine and Fentanyl and other drugs and firearms offences. Calvin Richardson has a criminal history dating back to his childhood when he pled guilty to manslaughter at 13. He was released after serving eight years of a ten year sentence. A youth who cannot be named was also charged with trafficking and other charges along with some other people. A list of those charged will be passed out in a media release. But we want to stress that it is important that the community know just how dangerous these drugs are and how important it is for the community to report any information about anyone who may be illegally trafficking these drugs but that we felt we had apprehended the murderers of these cops and their families so the community could feel safer."*

Gordon and my department were hoping to find some more important details to sew up our cases. I found myself jockeying with Gordon to interview suspects a clear waste of labor and time. All the information from the FBI side was now lopsided and attention seeking for Gordon and his team. My team was getting very little credit which I wouldn't stand for. My team needed to know they had done a good job in the public's eyes as much as the FBI did.

We found the guns used and some of the people we nabbed offered testimony to the guilt of the Richardson's in my police officers and their family's deaths for more lenient sentences. Still I kept at Gordon about my feeling that wasn't satisfied that we had the right men. He froze me out. Damn that Perita, she had Gordon refusing to even listening to me in police matters. How had it come to this? What had Perita said to him that made him end our friendship? Gordon planned on wrapping up the FBI' send of this case and then he was leaving Driftwood until the trial. I thought we were kindred spirits Gordon and I but that woman had changed all that.

I tried to speak to him this morning but was
rebuffed. It seemed that our friendship was
at an end and I didn't know how to fix it.
Sure the Richardson's were high level drug
dealers that we took off the streets; but
something about how easy it was to find
them made me uneasy.

A week went by and Gordon went back to
his FBI headquarters and was promoted to
Denver Of course I only knew this through
the grapevine. He still wouldn't speak to me.
If only I knew why!

I spoke with Aunt Louise and she told me to
apologise for whatever I had done. I tried
again, issuing my congratulations on his
promotion but Gordon's heart was hardened
and he said except for work we were done
he never wanted to speak with me again.
Heartbroken I knew that I could do nothing
and I went on with my life.

# Chapter 17 - Election Day

Life went on and I got into a routine. I went to the office handled the mundane cases, a few drunk and dis-orderlies, some kids tagging, no big crimes. The election was tomorrow and it looked like in the polls I would win by a landslide. It probably didn't hurt that city council had given me a medal for my devotion to duty. Take that Percival Derrickson!!

Everyone seemed happy with the wrap of the murder investigation and drug busts. Driftwood had become the town I thought it was; but still I was uneasy. It just seemed too perfect.

Maybe I was just an adrenaline junky, I
thought but still the lingering feelings
remained of unease. Election Day loomed
and I dressed carefully proudly wearing my
uniform. What would I do if the polls were
wrong?

Tina, Aunt Louise and Stella-Marie
accompanied me to the polling station and
proudly posed for the Daily Driftwood's
front page if I won or lost. Aunt Louise cast
her ballet then told me she voted for me. I
cast my ballet for myself and crossed my
fingers that I would win.

After much discussion with Aunt Louise
Penny, we decided the Driftwood café
would be reserved for my victory. The
Driftwood café was small intimate not too
flashy and just big enough for a few of my
supporters.

As I came into the restaurant on election
night I noted that the remodel that had
closed the restaurant for the last month had
not replaced the aging and cracked nineteen
fifties furniture, but had repainted and
resurfaced it making it look like you stepped
right back to the fifties again. The vintage
red wrought iron ice cream parlor chairs at
the counter looked new again. The rest of
the restaurant had been remodelled with new
red leather seating material in a diamond
tuff pattern in the booths. The outside of the
restaurant new red and white awning looked
great with the brick red paint that now
covered its façade.

Although people came to greet me and wish
me well I saw that just as we hoped
everyone was having a good time eating and
talking in the booths and at the counter. All
my officers who weren't on duty were
waiting there for me awaiting the results the
results; except of course Nathan Ricci. I was
sure he was at my opponent, Percival
Derrickson's headquarters.

Tina came to my side giving me a passionate kiss and whispering in my ear that win or lose, she was going to rock my world later. Stella-Marie gave me a hug and kiss and pulled me to a booth where she whispered, "They made two cakes for you daddy and I get to wipe off 'Sorry you lost' when you win. I can hardly wait to do that since you will win!"

"But what if I lose pumpkin?" I asked gently.

"You won't you're a hero. Aunt Louise says they all love you."

"I hope so sweetie."

Two hours after the polls were finished I was elected by a landslide just like the polls predicted. Percival Derrickson called the café and conceded. My police officers with the exception of Nathan Ricci congratulated me.

The next call I received was from a unknown cell number. I laughed when I realized it was from my Uncle Tommy. I excused myself went into the hallway to speak to Uncle Tommy.

"Congratulations, nephew. I hear you won. I'm looking forward to you staying on the next four years as sheriff."

"Don't be thinking that will win you any favors."

"Now would I expect that?"

"Thank-you, then I'll accept your felicitations. No congratulations on closing the cases?"

"Are they closed?" Uncle Tommy said mysteriously.

"You don't think so either?"

"I don't know it seemed a little too easy. Don't you think?"

"Maybe," I admitted.

"I'll keep my ears open. Maybe I'll hear something for you," Uncle Tommy said.

"The trial is over?"

"Yes and I'm still in witness protection; it's so freakin' boring."

"Uncle Tommy, please don't contact your old contacts. You could get yourself killed," I exclaimed.

"I'll be careful, Gunner. I've got a new life I'm not going to ruin it. Now go back and join your friends at the café."

"How did you know…?" I asked.

"I have my sources. Bye now. I'll keep in touch. Whoops, heads up boyo, incoming," I heard and then the cellphone call cut off.

What did he mean by incoming? I thought as I took my seat back in the booth with Tina, Aunt Louise and Stella-Marie. I didn't have long to wait. Nathan Ricci came in like whirlwind, his big size ten boots stamping across the floor of the café until he reached me sitting in a booth. It was obvious by his stance that he had a few to many drinks.

"You didn't deserve to win. Perry
Derrickson is worth ten of you! You are a
neophyte, misogynist piece of shit with
allusions of grandeur!!" Nathan slurred.

How he got the words out clearly I didn't
know; Nathan was barely standing.
Everyone in the café stopped talking and
stared at Nathan. Errol nodded at me as if to
ask, "Do you want me to handle this?"

I shook my head.

"Hello Nathan," I said quietly, "Would you
like to sit down and have a coffee and
something to eat? Maybe a piece of cake?"

"No, you stupid son of a bitch! Shove that cake up your ass!!" Nathan said and then he threw his badge at me and exclaimed, "I'm not working for you anymore. Take this badge and shove it up your ass."

Nathan looked like he was going to swing at me but he seemed to think better of it and then stamped out like a petulant school boy prompting Stella-Marie to say, "He shouldn't swear. That's bad!! He should have had a nap this afternoon, like I did. He needs a timeout."

Which prompted the crowd to laugh and agree and the party was back on. Nathan then glared at me one last time and left I hoped he was taking a cab.

I told Stella-Marie it was time to go home and she protested stamping her feet, but then Aunt Louise said, "Do you want a timeout?"

Stella-Marie then agreed and Aunt Louise took her home. I re-watched the election results to find the five members of city, Harold Thorne, Winston Steadwell, Douglas Banks, Melanie Halton and Gertrude Fines were all re-elected along with Mayor Ethan Calladen, as well. Surprisingly Harold, Winston, Douglas, Melanie, Gertie all dropped by to wish me well. It was a great night filled with friends and family but by two am. I was exhausted and I had to be to work at seven a.m. so I left saying my goodnights.

~0~

## Chapter 18 – Surprise Birthday Present

Two weeks went by and it all seemed

that Driftwood had turned into the town I had thought I was moving to. I should have been happy but I was restless and thought there was something more to the case. I know I should have been satisfied the case had been closed up in a bright red bow but maybe that was the point it was a little too pat. The nagging little voice I had had before was magnified by Uncle Tommy's comments.

I talked it over with Tina in the evenings when I saw her and she tried to convince me to relax and enjoy the quiet and relative calm and I tried; but I just felt uneasy, like I had missed something important.

Even Penny Ambercrombie had voiced concerns. Penny said she heard rumors about the hospital being mismanaged and wanted me to investigate, obviously I couldn't do so outright, but I'd kept my ears and my sources ears open. I stopped talking to Tina about the case and let her think I had put it aside. I quietly continued to investigate.

We had never truly proved the head nurse, Helga Bruin had taken the fentanyl at the hospital and that disturbed me greatly. We only had the hospital administrator and some of her colleagues to insist that she was the culprit and those people didn't like her. Could they have lied? Suspiciously the nurse died last week from a fentanyl overdose. That was a little too pat, a little too easy, or was I just grasping at straws?

A few days before Thanksgiving, I celebrated six months on the job. I wouldn't have noted it at all but Penny found out it was my thirty fourth birthday.

Penny figured out that I had an aversion to
birthdays and changed the cake from a
birthday cake to a six month on the job cake.
But I didn't get off that easy. Penny waited
and gave me a birthday gift when the other
cops weren't around. She gave me a silver
frame with Tina, Stella-Marie and Aunt
Louise in it. I found out that she had taken
that picture the night of the election with her
cell phone. She said we looked so happy she
had to take it. It was such a lovely
thoughtful gift that I was overcome with
emotion but it stirred an unconscious
memory in my head…a fleeting recollection
so quick that it passed before I could truly
capture it. I told myself I would recall it; but
I beat myself up knowing that whatever this
was it was important.

I began some more paperwork when my cell
phone rang. Tina called and begged me to
meet her for lunch she seemed stressed and I
wondered of something was wrong? Had she
decided I was too much trouble?

Coming into the diner I saw Tina sitting at the table. Her face looked worried as she stared into space not noticing me at first. I also noticed for the first time that her face had put on a little weight. Was I stressing her out? Was my job a problem?

"Gee, over here," she yelled.

I sat down at the table

"I ordered you your favorite cheeseburger with bacon and fries," Tina stated.

"You're not complaining about me eating red meat? Scandalous!! Is that because of my birthday, or do you have bad news?" I joked.

"I didn't know it was your birthday…,"Tina said biting her lip.

"It will be okay Tina; whatever it is just spit it out. I can take it."

"I have a present for you, that is if you consider it a present. That is ...I'm five and half months pregnant," Tina said and then because I didn't react fast enough she added, "I'm sorry."

My brain scrambled for a moment. I thought what that hell is going on? Is this my baby? Of course it's my kid. But do I really want to marry this woman? I hardly know her; but then my heart kicked in and I knew I cared about her and most of all I loved this new baby.

"Why are you sorry? This is wonderful news. This could be my best birthday present ever," I stated feeling slightly overwhelmed, but wanting to say the right thing that would put a smile back on Tina's now tear streaked face.

It worked she wiped her tears and started smiling tentatively, "Do you really mean that?" she asked.

"Of course I do. I love you Tina and a baby that will be just icing on my cake."

"I love you, Gunner," Tina cried kissing me soundly on the lips.

"Why don't you two get a room?" Marcy our favorite waitress asked coming over.

"Why don't we," I asked.

"Get a room?" Tina enquired.

"No, get married tomorrow."

"What? But it takes weeks to prepare and you only want to marry me because I'm pregnant."

"If you recall I asked you to marry me the minute I met you. I love you, Tina. As for it taking weeks to prepare for a wedding it could, but not if we get married in Vegas," I declared.

"You remembered I wanted a small intimate wedding?"

"Of course and you can pick whatever package you want. You probably think I'm a little secretive now because I didn't tell you; but I have a few dollars… okay if I'm honest more than a few. I got a huge settlement from my last job," I offered.

"I guess we should have talked finances. I'm independently wealthy. My parents left me and my brother a vast fortune when they died," Tina stated.

"Brother?"

"That's the other thing. I have a brother …"

She had a brother and she hadn't told me? Maybe I should reconsider my proposal? No, it was just the jitters. She was having my baby and we could be a happy family.

"When do I meet him?" I asked, sounding positive.

"I should have told you before …it's Tim…Doctor Tim Burton."

Her brother was Tim Burton?

"But you have different last names."

"Tim's my half-brother. We have different fathers."

"Bring him to the wedding. I liked him and he's your family."

"I think he's working, but thank-you for not getting mad because I didn't tell you," Tina replied then looking pensive she said worriedly, "Do we know enough about each other to get married?"

"We know enough. I know I love you more than any other person I've ever been with," I answered.

"Okay then let's get married. I'm off for the next five days anyway," Tina explained.

"And I'm off until the day after Thanksgiving. Can you wait until after the baby is born for our honeymoon? I'm sure Aunt Louise could be trusted to look after our baby for a couple of weeks."

"What are we waiting for let's go tell Aunt Louise and Stella-Marie," Tina exclaimed.

For better or worse I was getting married. Hopefully everything would work out just fine. Besides that Stella-Marie would be a big sister. Life would be good I convinced myself

.~0~

## Chapter 19 - Wedding Day

We told Aunt Louise and Stella-Marie of our wedding plans. Aunt Louise seemed okay at first. Tina went to the bathroom and Stella-Marie went to her playroom to find her princess dress then Aunt Louise told me what she really thought...so much for all champagne and roses. To say that Aunt Louise was unhappy was an understatement. She told me that she liked Tina it wasn't that; but how well did I know Tina?

I can still hear the conversation in my head

"I've always supported you in everything you do but I'm not happy about this quick wedding Gunner. You've been like this since you were a little boy rushing into things without thinking things through. I know it's my fault. I didn't fight my brothers enough and nurture you the way you needed…the way you would have been if your mother had lived and you look for that mothering in every relationship you seek. That's not healthy. Can't you postpone the wedding for awhile?"

I wasn't ready to tell her that Tina was pregnant that could wait.

"No, it's what I want…what Tina and I both want."

"Please, Gunner. I'm not trying to harm you. I love you but you're making another mistake. You rushed into marriage with Gina looking for that mother figure. I should have said something then, but I didn't, so I'm doing that now. Be sure this is what you really want to do," pleaded Aunt Louise.

"You can support me or I can walk away from you right now, Aunt Louise it's your choice," I exclaimed.

"I love you; so I'll support you whatever you choose. I just want you to be sure, Gunner."

"I'm sure," I insisted, knowing I was lying but sure that I wanted my children to have two parents unlike me.

"Then let's go plan a wedding," Aunt Louise said.


Lucky for me that is when Tina came back hearing only the positive. Tina was overjoyed thinking Aunt Louise had accepted her. Was I really ready to be a husband again? I was terrified that I would fail. I failed once before and my wife had cheated on me and tried to kill me.


I looked over at Tina. She wasn't Gina. Tina truly loved me and she was having my baby. It would all work out I just had to believe.

For now I had to find that happiness again and give Tina the wedding she deserved. I came abruptly out of my thoughts as I heard Tina say to Aunt Louise, "Were going to Las Vegas tomorrow to be married in a simple ceremony. Can you be ready?"

Aunt Louise agreed and the next day after a quick flight to Las Vegas I let Tina pick out a wedding chapel. Tina picked out a package that she claimed would be magical. The ceremony was tactful and Stella-Marie served as our flower girl. Aunt Louise dabbed back happy tears as Elvis pronounced as husband and wife. I was overjoyed when Stella-Marie asked if she could call Tina, Mama. Tina said Mommy was reserved for Gina. I told her I understood because even though Gina didn't deserve the title she was still Stella-Marie's mother and Stella-Marie felt conflicted.

Tina was overjoyed to have Stella-Marie call her Mama. Stella-Marie wanted to tell her about the baby, but I wanted it to be a Thanksgiving surprise and Tina agreed to make me happy. We were married and it was the happiest day of our lives. I followed up the wedding with a conversation about dinner.

"I want fish," Stella-Marie declared.

"That's good because I have reservations at Gordon Ramsay Fish & Chips at The Linq Promenade," Tina declared, "I think you'll like this place Stella-Marie. It has old telephone booths to exit and enter the restaurant."

"What's a phone booth?" Stella-Marie asked.

"You'll see," I replied.

"The younger generation needs more education," Aunt Louise commented.

"I just want fish with French fries," Stella-Marie said.

"I'm going to have shrimp," Tina stated.

"Can I have that and fish?"

"Sure," Tina said.

"What about cake? There's supposed to be wedding cake," Stella-Marie complained.

"I ordered a cake," Aunt Louise stated.

"How did you know I picked Gordon Ramsay's restaurant?" Tina asked.

"I'm afraid I overheard you making the reservation so I called back and they promised to produce a wedding cake."

The meal was wonderful and we all had a wonderful celebration. I couldn't believe me good fortune. Here I was married to the kindest most beautiful doctor in the world. Life was good, everyone was happy so why did I have this bad feeling at the bottom of my stomach. Nerves, I thought just left over feelings from the past and my bad marriage. Tina truly loved me and we were going to have a new child to love. I was truly blessed.

I smiled at my bride and then my child. It would all be bliss as Aunt Louise always cautioned me I had to quit borrowing trouble, I was a married man with two kids I was lucky! But Tina had been giving me looks all evening like she wanted to say something but didn't.

We flew home that evening and Aunt Louise took Stella-Marie for the night while we went to honeymoon at Tina's house...

~0~

## Chapter 20 – Revelations

T ina's house was small, but held three

small bedrooms. It was a back split with only two levels. A cookie cutter home, except for the bright yellow color she had painted it; it had a white picket fence around it. I had come home, I thought as I saw it through new eyes. It was like a breath of fresh air. We'd all be happy here even if Aunt Louise would miss us. We'd visit lots and she'd already promised to continue babysit Stella-Marie for me. I smiled this was a good thing. We'd all be happy, the new baby, Stella-Marie Tina and I.

Carrying Tina over the threshold she giggled like a school girl.

"I have a present for you," Tina said.

"Really Mrs. Bullet?"

"I like how you say that. Here's your present."

I opened the gaily wrapped paper to a new I-Phone. Complete with a case.

"The case is metal and they assure me it will stand up to most disasters, like dropping your phone. Like I've seen you repeatedly do. Keep it in your front pocket like a talisman; because keeping it in your back pocket case, or no case it will not be good."

"Thank you, I love it."

"I put in all your personal numbers so you don't have to store any."

"Thank you sweetie." I said admiring the cell phone and then proclaiming, "It just so happens I have a present for you. This was my mother's."

I pulled out a lovely piece of jewelery in a
box. The heart was encrusted with rubies
and diamonds surrounding it and through the
middle an arrow. It hung on a gold chain
that hung just between her breasts. It was the
one gift my father had ever given my mother
and I treasured it.

"Oh Gunner, I'm so honored. It's lovely but
I have something I need to tell you."

All of sudden I didn't want to hear any
troubles. They could wait; right now I
wanted to make wild passionate love to my
beautiful new wife.

"It can wait honey. It's our honeymoon
tonight. Tomorrow we can face any troubles
together," I stated and she smiled widely.

I felt like I was twenty again and proved it by taking my wife in my arms and making mad passionate love to her all night long. About five a.m. we fell into a deep sleep. Through deep layers of sleep I heard a persistent ringing that penetrated my brain. I realized with growing awareness that it was the special ring I had for Aunt Louise and Stella-Marie and I reached out answering my phone. Glancing at the time I realized we'd slept until eleven a.m. We? Tina was no longer in the bed. Still saying, "Hello" into the phone I got up looking around for Tina. She didn't seem to be in the house. Where was she?

I spoke to Stella-Marie and Aunt Louise for a moment and assured both of them we'd be there in an hour for Thanksgiving and the dinner she was making. I just hoped I could find Tina by then. Maybe she snuck off to the hospital? Or to get coffee?

I decided to take a shower and then look for her. Stepping into the shower I showered quickly and was just stepping out when I heard the front door open and close and then Tina yell out, "I have coffee."

I toweled off and threw on my boxer shorts. Maybe I could convince her to have a quickie I thought. I opened the bedroom door to go to Tina when I heard the doorbell ring and Tina open the front door.

The next thing I heard were a cadence of sounds, a muffled bang, bang, a high-pitched scream and a sound I recognized as two double taps from a revolver. I grabbed my gun, loading it as I stayed close to the floor, while crawling quickly to the front door. I found Tina in a pool of blood near the door. As I tried to stem the bleeding and move her away from the open door, another shot rang out. I slammed the door shut, but not before I heard running feet and then a car starting. I had seen a red car out of the corner of my eye but where? To my right my brain screamed.

More shots were fired into the door. It was obvious from the sounds that the shooter was moving fast, because of the change in direction of the sound I heard from each shot. In that general direction there was only one road close that would allow travel at the shooters apparent speed. I knew I should go after them; but I couldn't leave Tina. I looked out open the front door, but the red car was gone as I called in a description of it and ordered an ambulance for Tina.

"I'm sorry," Tina stated.

"For what? Getting shot in the stomach? You and the baby will be okay. An ambulance is coming you'll be fine," I lied.

"I can tell by your face you're lying; besides I'm a doctor I know I'm dying...we're dying. I'm so sorry..."

"No, you'll be fine," I argued.

"I should have told you last night about her."

"Her? Does that mean you know who shot you?"

"She decided to take me out personally"

"Who Tina? Who are you talking about?" I demanded.

"Don't hate me please don't hate me. I couldn't bear it," Tina said her voice sounding ragged and getting worse with each sentence.

"Tell me Tina. Whatever it involves it won't change my feelings about you; as long as you weren't pretending to love me."

"I wasn't. Rita demanded my obedience. At first it just seemed she was mischievous, and misguided; like she was testing me. She seemed a little broken and sad; but she was really a Machiavellian nightmare. She was playing on my sensitivities. "

"I don't understand," I insisted.

"Rita wanted me to get close to you it is true; but I'd finally found love, home and family with you, Stella-Marie and Aunt Louise. I couldn't love you more. I decided to tell you the truth today, because I love you and trust you and you'll protect us," Tina explained and then her face started turning a grayish blue color, her face turned ashen and then her chest rattled.

"Where's that damn ambulance," I cried.

"I have to tell you Rita is…."Tina managed
to gasp out.

Tina's breath became labored and then I
heard a rattle and her breath faded away. I
began the chest compressions like I had
been taught in first aid; but it was too late,
my baby and my new wife lay cold and
lifeless in my arms even as I begged Tina
not to go.

The ambulance arrived a few seconds later
(all the ambulances had been out on calls for
a ten car pileup on the highway and that's
why this one was delayed).

I didn't want to leave Tina and hoped and I begged God all the way to the hospital that they could somehow magically revive her and bring her and the baby back to me.

The hospital staff hurried to Tina and seemed cold and impersonal, until I realized they had put aside all their emotions to try and save Tina and my baby.

I called Aunt Louise and told her that Tina had been shot and that I didn't think she would survive. Aunt Louise wanted to come to me; but I told her that Stella-Marie needed her worse. I didn't tell her about the baby. Tina had wanted to tell Stella-Marie and Aunt Louise today but now it was probably better that they hadn't known. If the baby survived I'd tell them…If…

It seemed like hours; but it was less than a half an hour later that a doctor came out of the room and said, "Sheriff Bullet?"

"Yes," I answered.

"We did everything possible but your wife was dead on arrival and we were unable to resuscitate her."

"And the baby?"

"I'm sorry we were unable to save your daughter. She was just too early and her lungs and heart had not matured enough. I'm sorry. Would you like to see them and say your goodbyes?"

I choked back tears and nodded. I followed the doctor into a cubicle and saw them. Tina's arms held a baby that if I hadn't looked closely I would have thought she was alive. The baby was tiny, but fully formed. Her hair had tight blonde ringlets knotted close to her head. Her rosebud lips looked like her older sister, Stella-Marie's when she was born. Her eyes unfocused and staring into space were the shape and color of mine.

I choked back unshed tears as the nurse standing beside the bed asked gently, "Would you like to hold the baby? It's a girl."

I nodded again, not trusting my words.

As I held her in my arms, I apologised to her for not protecting her from whoever this Rita was. The nurse left and I stared down at my tiny baby and wondered what Tina would have called her and in that moment I picked a name as if Tina whispered in my ear. I kissed the baby's soft cheek, now cool to the touch and then for a moment I lost it. I felt my body slide down the wall and to the floor in a heap still holding my daughter in my arms and crying over the lifeless body of my baby girl. I felt arms reach out and try to take the body from my arms and I resisted. But the other person just put the hands under my arms and helped me up.

"She's beautiful Gunner," the voice said softly, "May I take a picture and then hold her?"

"She is… isn't she?" I said wiping my tears away. Regaining my composure I allowed Penny to take a picture of the baby and then I handed the tiny soul to her.

"What are you going to call her?" Penny asked.

"Tina-Marie," I answered.

"Her mother, your girlfriend would have liked that," Penny replied.

"My wife. We were married yesterday," I stated.

"Oh Gee! I'm so sorry somehow that makes this all worse. I'm here for you. I know we haven't known each other long but I'd like to think were friends and friends are there through thick and thin. I want you to remember that and call me if you need anything. Now is there anything I can do for you right now?"

"We need to find out who did this," I insisted.

"And we will, but right now you need to take some time for yourself and your family to deal with this."

"I should call Tina's brother," I said my brain coming out of the fog and starting to function.

"I didn't know she had a brother who is he?" Penny demanded.

I didn't answer but continued my actions I dialed the switchboard (since the hospital still did things the old fashion way) and asked for Doctor Tim Burton. This was met first with silence and then with a few ums.

Penny's gasp should have alerted me but it didn't and I continued my conversation with the switchboard, "This is his brother-in-law. It's urgent I speak with him," I insisted.

"Just a moment let me transfer you," the person on the switchboard answered.

The phone rang and someone answered, "Hello?"

"Tim?"

"Sir, I don't know how to tell you this." the person on the other end hesitated, "here talk to this gentleman he'll explain."

"This is Sheriff Bullet just tell me!" I demanded.

"This is Errol, boss," The new voice said, "I arrived about fifteen minutes ago on the scene, it seems that Doctor Burton was found dead in the doctor's lounge a half an hour ago.

"How long do they think he was there, Errol?"

There was a whispered conversation near the phone then Errol stated, "A few hours. I think it was a suicide boss; but of course there will be an autopsy. There's a note addressed to you. I was just about to open it up but I'll wait for you and Tina before reading it."

"Tina's dead."

"What in the hell is going on? I'm so sorry, sir, I forgot myself. I'm so sorry for your loss. Was that the shooting call that came in boss?"

"Yes, I'm coming up, what floor?"

"Third floor, sir," Errol said then hung up.

"Will you stay her with them and arrange for the funeral home…to pick them up? I'll speak with the director Hiram Packer later about the arrangements," I asked Penny.

"I'll make arrangements for all of them Gee. Don't worry now, go see about Doctor Burton. But first give me your cell phone."

Obediently I gave it to her and Penny did something with it and then handed it back to me a few minutes later.

"What did you do?" I asked.

"I installed an app on your I-phone it will record all incoming and outgoing calls, It will also record and conversations if you wish you just press this button and say aloud I wish I could record this and it instantly records," Penny explained.

"But why did you do that?"

"You're going to need an edge just to carry on in the next few days. Conversations may escape you, your mind will wander of its own accord and your brain will fog in and out this will help. But for heaven sake if you figure out who did this and go after them take back up. Promise me boss," Penny pleaded.

"I promise," I answered obediently knowing full well that I wouldn't wait for backup if I found this perpetrator.

I laid my daughter down and kissed her sweet cheek goodbye and said, "I'll be back, Tina-Marie. I have to find out who did this. I promise you baby they'll pay."

I wiped away the tears that threatened to overtake me again and pulled myself together I had a job to do and I would do it. I stiffed my back and rage shook within me. Whoever had killed Tina and my baby girl would pay.

In the elevator I wracked my brain, who was this Rita and why did the name sound so familiar? I tried to root out the memory in my brain and then I recalled Ethan Calladen's ex-wife's name. Her name was Rita.

She was that awful woman who had been found naked beside a dead John Calladen, (Aunt Louise's husband). It couldn't be her. Could it? Why would she come after Tina?

I stepped off the elevator and went to the doctor's lounge. Errol was examining the scene and I was grateful for his thoroughness.

"Gee, are you sure you should be working? I can handle this boss."

"I know you can and I expect you to; but I'd like to see the note."

"Sure. Normally I would have read it; but since it was addressed to you…"

"That's okay Errol. Always read the evidence. I'll give it back to you so you can log it in after I'm done."

"That's the other thing boss, even though I suspect a suicide the drug he used was fentanyl."

"You're sure?"

"Yes, he had some packets in his hands."

"Were they from the hospital pharmacy?"

"Yes, they were."

Before I picked up the letter an idea formed
in my mind of something else. I had seen
that picture on Mayor, Ethan Calladen's
desk of his wife; Rita and she had reminded
me of someone else I'd met recently. With a
lot of surgical work, some dramatic weight
loss and some make-up... could it be?

I put the thought aside until I finished the
letter. I read...,

*To my new brother-in-law, Gee*

*First of all thank you for marrying my sister
and making her happy. I know you'll keep
her and my new niece or nephew safe. I have
done something that has entrapped an
endangered them both. A year ago I became
horribly addicted to fentanyl when I was
exposed in the emergency room. I went to
rehab, thought I had beaten the addiction
and then once I went back to work I became
embroiled in the addiction again. I tried to
hide it by going to dealers on the street (I
didn't want to get caught at work after all).*

*I thought I could handle all of this but that's when she came along. She was my dealer's boss and she saw a way to use my addiction to her advantage.*

*She saw how deep my addiction went and when she realized Tina would do anything to protect me she pressured her to be her ally or she'd harm me either with jail or cut off my supply or taint my drugs. Tina didn't want to work with Rita she hated her but she had no choice if she wanted to save me. If you'd ever meet Rita when she was I her nice mode you'd understand the pull she has but when she is in her 'I'm going to get you mode' she's the devil incarnate. Rita slowly helped me to become addicted again... although I could have said no. Of course I didn't and I must take the blame for being so weak. I should have said no and have gone back to rehab instead I let my addiction own me and my sister.*

*You see Rita runs a big drug organization and I know she is the one you're looking for who killed the cops and ran drugs through Driftwood.*

*She set up the Richardson's they were
becoming too much competition. Please see
that that bitch pays for her evil deeds and
her crimes against Driftwood and my sister.*


*Now Tina and her baby can be free. Rita has
no hold over her and she can be free to live
out her life with the love of her life… you
Gee. Rita made Tina cozy up to you; but
Tina fell in love with you at first sight and
Tina refused to harm you. This made Rita
angry; but then she became amused and
thought she could control Tina more. She
decided to get to you and your organization
another way which I'm sure made you really
mad. Just remember when you feel angry at
my sister that Rita threatened to tell you that
Tina worked for the very drug organization
you were searching for and to get Tina's
medical licence revoked. That would have
killed my sister. She loves helping others
and is a top notch doctor. Tina Told me she
would tell you all of this so I'm not telling
you anything new or you wouldn't have
married my sister.*

*Tina thinks you can protect both of us but I know I'm just a liability that Rita will exploit. So to save us all I'm ending it now. Tell Tina I love her and take good care of my sister.*

*Make that bitch pay for ruining my life and for all her other crimes; but protect my sister at all costs. She is an angel and you are lucky to have her. Remember that she was between a rock and hard place and that Rita threatened to kill me if she didn't comply. Please comfort Tina and tell her not to be too sad and it was my turn to be the hero and save her.*

*Your brother-in law*

*Tim*

I took a picture on my I-phone of the letter and then I said, "Thank- you, Errol. You can take the letter for analysis, I'm heading home for a little bit, and then I'll swing back to the station later this afternoon."

"We can handle this boss. You need some time…"

"It's Thanksgiving we're short staffed I'm going home to pretend to eat a little turkey and be with my family. Then I'm coming back to the station. Aunt Louise said that dinner would be ready at three and it's almost that now."

"If you need anything…"

"I'll be okay Errol and I'll eat some turkey for Aunt Louise's sake."

Errol looked like he wanted to say something else but he swallowed and then tried to sound normal, "Bring me back a plateful?"

"I'll do that Errol."

I was grateful that Errol hadn't pushed me to stay home. As I got into my car a few minutes later my brain began racing. Rita was the kingpin? But who the hell was this Rita? She couldn't be the housewife married to the mayor at one time, could she?

Crap what was wrong with me? I thought as it suddenly dawned on me who Rita really was. I knew her and she thought she'd bested me. I wouldn't let her harm anyone else. I pinned on my badge and stuck my cell phone in my front pocket.

I called the station and let them know who I was going after to gasps from Penny. Penny promised to send me back –up that would meet me at my house before we went after Rita.

I picked up the phone to call Gordon so he could meet me at Aunt Louise's but there was no answer and when I called back again my cell phone indicated another call was coming in when I was a block from Aunt Louise's house. I pulled over so I could safely answer but turned on the app that Penny had installed so I could remember the conversation.

"Sheriff Bullet," I answered.

"Hello darling Gee. Having a great day?" a woman's voice asked.

"You bitch Rita." I sniped.

"So you did figure it out? I had hoped one of the bullets from my gun would have pinged you when I saw you run to Tina's side; but no such luck. Now my sources say you are looking for me."

"How? Who? "I said without thinking.

"Are you discombobulated? Good! But I'm still waiting for you."

"What do you mean you're waiting for me?"

"Louise welcomed me into the house. Your daughter on the other hand bit me. You and Louise ought to have taught her better manners when someone is holding a gun on you."

"If you've harmed one hair on either of them," I threatened.

"You know how this works Gee. Such a funny name Gee, Gordon said it stood for something; but he wouldn't tell me what. The damn man is so loyal to you even when he's angry with you. How did you make him into your lap dog? Oh well no matter that obstacle will be finished today. I'm tired of competing with the oh so perfect friend, Gee Bullet. If he hadn't proven himself with me I think he was gay. Then one of my men would have killed him. They are not so politically enlightened like me."

"You enlightened? Let my family go!!"

"Not to worry I won't harm a hair on their pretty little heads. I'm only holding them prisoner until you come home. Then I'll let them go after you give yourself up to me."

"How do I know you even have them?"

"Would I kid?"

I didn't answer. I should have answered
though because in the next second I heard
Stella-Marie scream and Aunt Louise cry.

"What did you do to them?"

"I pulled Stella-Marie's hair and I slapped
that holier than thou bitch Louise."

"You said you wouldn't harm a hair on their
heads so how do I know you haven't killed
them? Why should I risk myself and come to
you?

"Because if you don't I'm not going pull
hair, or slap; I'm just going to shoot them
between the eyes and let you hear them
plead and scream for their lives."

"I'm coming don't do that," I pleaded.

"Now that's more like it. I'll be waiting lover and maybe I'll even give you a kiss before I shoot you. You'd like that wouldn't you? Isn't that what your ex-wife Gina did before she shot you?"

"I'll be there soon Rita or should I call you Perita?"

"I hate that name Perita. Rita is such a stronger name. You hear Perita and you think soft, feminine and weak. Personally I've never been the shrinking violet type. So you'd better remember that. You'd also better be here in the next half an hour or you'll be burying your girlfriend, your daughter and your auntie." Rita said in menacing voice.

I attempted to turn off the app and close my phone. Terrified out of my mind I found myself closing off the terror in my head and plotting my next move against Rita.

~0~

# Chapter 21 - Family Comes First

I had almost arrived in front of my house

when I saw another vehicle parked two houses over at the curb. In the Buick La Sabre was my Uncle Thomas and in the backseat to my surprise there sat Stella-Marie and Aunt Louise.

I went to the driver's side window and asked, "How?"

"They saved themselves. I spotted that woman with the gun inside and checked the kid's bedroom to see if I could sneak in when this one comes out followed by Louise," Uncle Thomas explained pointing to Stella-Marie.

"Thank you, Uncle Thomas, for getting them to safety."

"I should have gotten her sooner, but I didn't hear down the pipeline about the hit that was put out on your wife and now you."

"You knew I got married yesterday?"

"I was there, sonny boy. You didn't see me but I saw you safely married. I'm just damn sorry that I couldn't keep her from killing your wife and the baby," he whispered so Stella-Marie didn't hear.

"Take them somewhere safe. I have to go in and get her. She has gone too far she's killed cops and she's killed my wife and child," I insisted.

"Sonny, I didn't know about the baby. I'm so sorry but that is all the more reason I should have a stake in this. You need me or you need back-up let me help you. Please!" Uncle Thomas pleaded.

"Daddy she's really, really crazy! Don't go after her without some other police," Stella-Marie cried.

"I have to baby. She could kill someone else of I don't stop her. "

"You need help she's bad, bad, bad and oh so scary!!"

"I've called for back-up. I'll be safe," I said and it was true but it was also true that I was going into the house before they arrived and nailing that bitch. I wanted her to rot in jail and watch her beauty die away.

"You're going to do this. Aren't you? Okay so take this gun tape this one to your boot to your shin this one to your other shin, and one to your back like John McClain. Here's some duct tape. Don't give me that look Gunner. Doesn't everyone have extra guns and duct tape in their cars? And here's knife for your boot."

"Thank you, Uncle Thomas."

"At least you have lots of guns. Wear your jacket, and put your phone in your front pocket so you can call me, later." Stella-Marie cautioned, "Oh good your badge is already there, put in on your jacket. Don't forget. She needs to know you're a policeman, but be careful daddy. She's mean."

"Tina told me to put my phone there too." I muttered.

"I love you Gunner," Aunt Louise stated.

"I love you all. Thank you for your concern, but I'm going in to get her."

"Just thank me by staying alive and coming home to your daughter Stella-Marie and Louise."

"I will," I said

I then went to my car pulled out my flak jacket and put it on.

~0~

# Chapter 22 – Coming

# Together

As I crept closer to Aunt Louise's

house my adrenaline kicked. My heart began
to beat a little faster. I decided it would be
best to surprise Rita by entering through the
back door. I peeled the back door open
slowly making sure that it didn't creak. I
moved slowly and quickly with my gun
raised.

I heard a peculiar whooshing, sucking sound
in the living room and I advanced slowly
looking for Rita. As I entered the living
room I spotted a trail of blood. I followed
the blood to find Gordon bleeding behind
the sofa.

Gordon seemed unconscious but when I touched his wound he sputtered awake and tried to speak through gasps he said, "The lying bitch is gone. Can't breathe…Sucking chest wound…you need… to put a pen… in so I can…breathe

I'd taken first aid but this was a new one on me though I'd seen it done in many, many, television shows. I remembered that Aunt Louise had an old clear BIC pen from the late seventies or eighties. The clear plastic container would work perfectly to create a suction to make him able to breathe. Grabbing a towel I pressed it into the wound and then ran to the bathroom to grab peroxide. I then seized a knife from the kitchen and the BIC pen and ran back to Gordon. I then googled the technique on my phone and followed it step by step. Then placing a medical tape from the first aid kit across the cut and then taped pads across the initial bullet wound to contain the blood.

"You did it buddy, I can breathe. I think she hit between my second and third rib, missing my heart, or I'd be dead," Gordon said when I finished, but he really wasn't breathing all that well. The chest wound he had was serious, so my next call was for an ambulance and some help.

"I sure hope you're right that's a lot of blood, but not enough for a heart wound. I think you would have bled out by now,"

"Good thing! I'm sorry Gee, she fooled me. I believed every word out of her mouth,"

"I've been there Gordo," I replied, "Remember how Gina fooled me."

"You're calling me Gordo and you know how much I hate that. Tell me I'm not dying."

"You're not dying on my watch."

"So we are still friends?"

"We were never not friends; so stop talking the ambulance will be here soon."

311
S. G. Lee

I came in when she was threatening Stella-Marie I couldn't believe my ears…Gordon inhaled here and then continued his breath coming a little faster, "She killed your girlfriend, Tina."

"She killed my wife and baby," I clarified.

"You got married and didn't invite me?" Gordon stated hurt.

"I did, I'm sorry."

"No, I'm so sorry if I hadn't introduced you to Perita. She wouldn't have been able to blackmail Tina and kill her and your baby…God I'm sorry Gunner," Gordon cried.

"It's not your fault, enough with the sorrys. She has another name in this town and it's the ex- Mrs. Rita Calladen…"

"What the woman who hurt Louise…"

"Yes, her!! Like it should come as a surprise anything that woman would do. Can you think where she could have gone?"

"When she thought me dead, she mentioned a name …Ethan."

"Of course her sons. She's going to get her sons."

"That's right Rita has sons. Perita was divorced, but childless," Gordon commented, his voice dropping off in pain.

"Where is that damn ambulance?" I asked noticing blood pooling more under the towel.

"Don't worry about me; go get her Gunnar," Gordon muttered softly his breath difficult.

"I'm not leaving you until you come out of surgery."

"If you don't go after her now she'll get away. Go get her. I'll be fine," Gordon protested.

"Not until the ambulance gets here."

The ambulance arrived and I almost followed it to the hospital; but the technicians assured me he'd get the best care and Gordon threatened me with breaking our friendship again, so I went after her, *Perita "Rita" Castillo Calladen.*

~0~

## Chapter 23 - Life is a

## masquerade

B y the time I got to the Calladen's, I

saw two cars pull up. One of these was Errol's car, the other Uncle Tommy's. The house was surrounding by a gate with a code that had to be pushed in to admit us. I knew we had to figure out a way to get in but I was more concerned about my aunt and my daughter. What could Uncle Tommy be thinking?

I went over to Uncle Tommy's car, "Where are my daughter and my aunt?"

"They're safe. I had to make sure you were too. I heard over the wire that your pal the FBI guy was shot."

"Yes, he was"

"Rita shot him!" He declared, and then he continued, "Stella-Marie and Louise are safe they're with my best friend, Arnie."

"Who is Arnie?'

"Arnold Ivan."

"The software king? You know him too?"

"Yes, we crossed paths a few years ago. He lives nearby, so Louise and Stella-Marie are close. Don't you worry, nephew. His estate is about 30 miles from here and he has armed guards on his estate. No one gets by them; no one. They're safe."

"How did you get back so fast?"

"I can fly a helicopter and I my friend Ivan loaned me his. I landed the helicopter in the schoolyard two streets over."

"Why are you here then?"

"Come on son. I have the same genes as you. I go where angels fear to tread; charging head on and alone. I can't afford to lose any more family, son."

"Errol's here," I replied.

"I know, I called him."

"And he came? But he doesn't know you!"

"I told him I was your uncle and a fellow cop."

"Does he know who you truly are?"

"No, and he won't know unless you tell him. I've already accessed the scene. Rita's in there with Reginald her son. Her other son, Ethan must be out, but the mayor her ex is on the floor. I think she shot him, maybe once."

"How did you get in?"

"I have this gizmo in my car it finds all sorts of numbers," Uncle Tommy answered.

"You probably shouldn't be telling me that. As long as we can get in I don't want to know. What's with this palatial estate in a suburb anyway?"

"The mayor's family used to own a lot of this land. It's been in their family for generations unfortunately when the mayor's brother, John was murdered he had to sell a lot of it for death duties and to give your Aunt Louise her share."

"How far is to the house?"

"Roughly about two football fields past those low lying trees up that long driveway," Uncle Tommy answered.

"Does he think he lives in England in manor?"

"I think the architect must have used the drawing plans for that monstrosity."

"Damn, what if she sees us coming?"

"She won't I disabled the cameras by putting them on a loop she'll think all is normal."

"Good thinking, thank- you Uncle Tommy."

Errol walked up to us at that moment and said, "Hey boss, so he is your uncle. I thought he was telling the truth. Now how do you want to play this?"


"You and Uncle Tommy take the back after we get near the house. I'll take the front."

"But boss, he's not a Driftwood cop."

"I know, but he can handle a gun and this woman is dangerous. We don't have time to wait. We need to access the scene and then charge in. Rita is holding the mayor hostage and we don't have time to wait for back-up so deputize him."

"The Mayor's in there?"

"It is his house," Uncle Tommy commented.

"Okay," Errol said quickly deputizing Uncle Tommy.

"We're wasting time! Call this in, Errol and then we follow my plan," I insisted.

"Be careful. She hates you," Uncle Tommy stated, "Here you need some back-up."


Uncle Tommy handed me some weapons.

"Gee, whatever gave you that idea?" I asked sarcastically.

Uncle Tommy responded by rolling his eyes.

"Let's take her down." I stated moving towards the house.

~0~

# Chapter 24 – Rita

U ncle Tommy and Errol and I

scampered across the lawn hiding behind trees until we reached the house. Uncle Tommy and Errol went around the back I went in the unlocked front door, gun raised. I took down a man near the front door in a sleeper hold. I hoped that was the only one of Rita's men, otherwise Uncle Tommy and Errol would also be facing her men. As I advanced towards the kitchen, I heard the sound of a shot and I feared what I would find.

In the Calladen's kitchen I found Rita her gun sitting against on the back of Reggie's skull. She didn't see me; as I watched her for a few minutes trying to figure out the best way to disarm her without harming Reggie.

Rita was dressed all in a black and white scalloped tulle shirt paired with a white of the shoulder blouse with three quarter inch sleeves and ruffles. She finished her look with minimal make-up, red lipstick and red spiked four inch high heels. She looked as she had the first time I saw her just like she walked off the fashion pages. I wondered why I even noticed her clothes. She was an evil bitch who deserved a takedown. I felt slightly disoriented as my anger took over. She bested me in a number of ways. I couldn't let that continue I had to play this smart.

I noticed the mayor lay prone on the floor holding his knee cap which was bleeding profusely as long with his thigh. So Uncle Tommy was correct she'd shot, the mayor. I thought. Hopefully the other shot I heard went into the wall.

"Mom, please I haven't gone against you!! You're my mother, why would I?" Reggie pleaded.

"Where's your brother Ethan then?"

"He's probably hanging out with Dillon," Reggie argued.

"Dillon? I told your brother that boy was dirt. Did you call Ethan and leave the message like I told you?"

"I did. I promise, mom."

In slow motion I saw Errol charge in his gun raised and then Rita spun around a gun in her left hand. In seconds Rita had subdued him. Rita then pressed a gun to his temple with her left hand as she used her right hand to continue to push a gun into the base of Reggie's skull. I wanted to fire but that would have given off my position and have put Errol and Reggie in more danger.

"Kick your gun over there," Rita commanded to Errol.

Errol obeyed kicking his gun towards the
back door and then sat next to the mayor
who was sitting in blood holding his right
knee cap.

Suddenly Rita became aware like a six sense
that I was there. Her head swivelled not
pausing from holding the gun to Reggie
skull rotating his body to face me.

"Come to join the party late? I wondered
when you get here Gee. Did Geoff stop you
just a little? Sporting a bullet wound are
you? Or is he dead?"

"No, your man is alive and no bullet wounds
here."

"You're a lucky man then. Drop your gun
first before you come any further or I'll

shoot Errol and then Reggie," Rita
exclaimed.

I didn't want to obey her but Reggie and
Errol's lives were at risk. I put down my gun
at her feet and she kicked it over towards the
front door. I hoped Uncle Tommy could get
us out of this one.

"Sit next to the big baby on the floor's head,
Errol and keep your hands where I can see
them," Rita commanded indicating the
mayor, Ethan Calladen. Her ex –husband,
Ethan held a bloody towel to his thigh and
other his hand to his right knee.

"Why do you have a gun on your own son?"
I asked.

"If I didn't, would you do what I want?"

"Of course I would," I answered.

"Liar, besides Reggie is too hard to control
without a gun. He's too much like his father,

too volatile …the rat!! The big baby mayor is crying on the floor there because I shot him in the leg. Go sit on the other side of him, sheriff."

I complied but I was still thinking ahead I had other choices other weapons my moment would come when she least expected it.

"Not just my leg you hurt my knee too. It God damn well hurts!!!" the mayor cried.

"You blasphemer! Not a good way to be talking to God when you could die," Rita coldly commented.

"Please mom, let me go to dad,. He'll bleed to death. You don't want that really, do you?" Reggie begged.

"I already told you to be quiet, Reggie, while I think," Rita cried.

"Sorry, but if he dies they'll harm you," Reggie stated as if it was perfectly normal for his mother to be holding a gun to his head.

"I'm dying. Let the boy go he friggin' loves you," Ethan Senior begged.

"Put a sock in it Ethan. He's your son through and through. There's no hint of me. He does everything you say; any time you say it. If he hadn't protected Ethan so much, I would have wrote him off years ago. But that will change when I get him out of your sphere of influence. Now quit your bellyaching and tie your thigh off with your belt that might keep you alive for a few minutes," Rita laughed.

"You bitch!"

"Tut, tut is that how you talk to me when I am so generous Ethan?"

"Generous? You fucking shot me; and it hurts."

"It's going to hurt a lot worse when I shoot you in the head," Rita threatened.

"Rita we can end this entire thing, all you have to do is give up," I said pulling a gun from my right shin and then bounding to my feet with the gun in my advancing on Rita.

"You can stop right there. Do you think I'm stupid? I knew you were up to something. Drop your other gun, or I'll shoot my son and then all the other hostages. You know I can do it, I didn't hesitate to order those stupid complicit cops killed," Rita said as if she had eyes in the back of her head.

I did what I was told and threw the gun away towards the front door. Rita lowered the gun and put it in Reggie's back. Good thing she didn't know about Uncle Tommy! Where was he hiding?

"Step over there and sit beside Ethan near his feet… can't have you two too close together. No funny stuff now! I'm a crack shot, ask Ethan."

"Why did you shoot and kill member of my police force and their families?"

"Your police force? Huh!! I did you a favor they were all working for me until they weren't then they all had to go. They liked the perks of a steady salary for looking the other way with my drug shipments. Then Greg had to turn on me even my threat to inform the FBI of his dalliance with that teen didn't deter him. Greg was sleeping with the girl you loved! What kind of a mother would I be if I let that continue?"

"You did that for me?" Reggie asked.

"You are an idiot, Reginald, with shit for brains; just like your dad. Admittedly I would do things for you; but Greg was a valuable entrusted employee that I could control with his vices, until he wasn't. He was going to reveal my whole organization to the FBI and he had back-up with all those other cops. Too bad for him there was a mole."

"A mole? Do tell me more," I begged.

"Maybe I will. Maybe I won't, maybe it will be my parting gift to you. If you cooperate of course, Gee."

"I don't understand how you could do this mother! You shot those kids? That was you?" Reggie asked.

"I didn't do it personally. What do you take me for? I'm not cut out for that!"

"But they were innocent..."

"It's simple. I tried to explain this to you but you just don't listen!! Read my lips!! I had no choice. Greg was ready to turn himself and the other cops into the FBI and Gee. So when Gee arrived as sheriff they would have testify against me and then I'd be in jail. Pinstripes simply don't suit this girl. I hated to order the kids shot but the ends justified the means. Their parents were idiots and the kids knew what their parents were doing and they could testify so..."

Reggie looked really upset and scared; then a mask came over his face and he just became quiet.

"It will be okay Reggie. We'll get you out of this," I reassured him.

"Really Gee, how will you do that?" she laughed, "You don't even have a gun, or two now. I expected better from you; tsk tsk…just barging in with no back-up but Errol. Where's the FBI cavalry, now?" Then she looked at my face, "Damn! You found Gordon. Sorry about that. You know I loved the man! Don't give me that look. I loved him. If you only knew all the things I let slide because I loved him. I mean I'm still here; aren't I?"

"You loved him so much you killed him!" I shouted, I wasn't about to give her the satisfaction to know that he was alive.

"Fuck…I had hoped that you'd save him; but you were slow…too slow. I should blame you, Gee but I somehow I don't. You on the other hand ,you bastard, Ethan; this is entirely your fault."

"What did I do?"

"You divorced me and wouldn't give me my kids, so I had to make money any way I could."

"How does that have anything to do with this?"

"I loved my kids and you ripped them from my arms and poisoned them against me."

"Let's be honest Rita. You didn't love me or your children you just wanted my money, not your kids."

"Liar!! Shut up or I'll shoot you again and I'll make it hurt worse," Rita said her face contorting in anger; as she gestured the gun towards the mayor for a moment.

"You took the settlement quick enough. Don't lie to the boy. If you loved him you wouldn't be holding him hostage."

"I love my little Ethan," Rita stated.

"Not me…not even a little?" Reggie asked tearing up.

"Oh for Pete's sake; you are my son; of course I love you. You're coming with me if you can behave yourself and chose your mother over that moron on the floor. Your father as usual is trying to turn you against me."

"Sorry…mom," Reggie muttered, sounding scared.

"Oh for the love of…"

"How do you think you'll get away with this Rita?" Ethan the mayor asked.

"Shut-up!! My boys and I are leaving this dirty town once and for all. I have money and I can make a new life for us. Sheriff Bullet is going to see that we get away safely. Aren't you Gee?"

"What do you want Rita? A helicopter? A car? A plane?"

"I'm not stupid Gee. I know you have a hostage playbook."

"So what do you really want?"

"My sons, a car or vehicle that will take us to a fully fueled plane; that will take us all to Buenos Aires. There's no extradition there, and you as my hostage till we are ready to take off. So no tricks," Rita insisted.


"But Ethan's not even here, mom."

"Oh for the love of…find him!! Use your cell phone and start calling until you find your brother, you probably know riffraff like Dillon. After all Dillon's a football player too," Rita said holding out Reggie's cell phone.

"Yes, mom," Reggie said obediently taking his phone from her hands and dialing.

Rita then turned her gun on the mayor and placed it between his legs. Errol thought this was the time to make his move and he pulled a gun from his jacket pocket; but Rita was quicker she pulled her gun up and shot Errol in his right shoulder.

"You're lucky I'm in a forgiving mood, Errol. Besides I don't want you dead…yet," Rita stated.

"But you want me dead?" I asked to distract her as I felt Rita was becoming a little unhinged.

Rita twisted her gun around and pointed it at me.

"There's still time for that." Rita laughed, "But if you're really good I'll let you live."

"Why would you just shoot me?"

"There's something about you…an air of tragedy that you carry like a mantel… it makes you so attractive to women. Why do you think Tina fell so hard? Damn that Tina!! She was supposed to stay loyal to me!! Not take your side and turn on me."

I tried not to show my anger at this comment I was conflicted when it came to Tina. I loved her; but in some ways I was beginning to grow to hate her. Yes, she had planned to tell me all that she had done, but she had betrayed me and that betrayal had cost me Tina Marie and now might cost me my life.

"Good, you're angry with her despite her death. If I was another woman I would have made a play for you myself," Rita continued.

"Mom, that's disgusting."

"Oh sorry, Reggie, I forgot you were here."

"You forgot I was here? You have a gun to me."

"He's got a point there, Rita."

"Don't get between my son and me, Gee. Your air of tragedy can't get you out of everything. I still have the upper hand and a gun."

"Of course you do Rita."

"Don't you dare humor me!" Rita screamed
and then reining in her anger she continued,
"Maybe I am blaming the wrong person. If
you hadn't come to Driftwood it wouldn't
have all fell apart. But then again it was
Ethan's idea to bring you here after my rival
killed the sheriff."

Rita then turned her gun from me back to
the mayor.

"Your rival killed the last sheriff?" I asked.

"Doesn't anyone listen to me when I talk?
The son of bitch knew I had the sheriff in
my pocket and he thought if he took him out
he'd harm me. Fool…it might have
inconvenience me a little maybe, but I fixed
him."

"How did you fix him?"

"Must I tell you all my secrets? Suffice to say he's in a pickle with law enforcement and he has no evidence on me; but you Gee you were getting too close and now... "

"You're jetting off to Buenos Aries; can't you enlighten me more about your activities?"

"Since you put it that way...I'll think about it. We have time. Now pick up that phone and call for my plane, Gee. Make it a speaker phone. Tell them no funny stuff or Ethan, Reggie, Errol and you will be dead."

I rang the sheriff's office putting it on speaker phone and said, "Penny it's Gee. We have a bit of a situation here."

"What can I do for you sheriff?"

"You need to call the FBI and get them to send a vehicle that can take Rita and her sons a full fueled plane that can then take them to Buenos Aires."

"Rita? Not Rita Calladen?"

"That's right Pen. It's good old Rita that was behind all of this. Fooled you good, didn't I?"

"You're Perita Castillo? But you were dating that FBI guy…," Penny stated.

"Now it dawns on you. Ha, ha how I enjoyed that."

"I hate you."

"I get that a lot," Rita laughed, and then continued sounding irritated; but perfectly in control, "But that's not very professional now; is it Penny? I have the sheriff, Errol, my stupid ex-husband and my son Reggie as my prisoners so you best get on to finding that plane I want."

"I'll work on it," Penny said.

"You do that Penny dear. You always were the dogsbody so I know you can handle this correctly. So no storming the house, because I've already shot the mayor and his lying in a pool of blood on the floor. I also shot Errol in the right shoulder. The two of them are bleeding out slowly and they need some help; but if you don't hurry and get my plane they won't be the only ones!"

339
S. G. Lee

"You'll get your car and your plane."

"I know that Ethan senior, my jerk of an ex-husband has a plane in the hangar at the Driftwood Airports. Now without informing the FAA it's a hostage situation, Penny get me that plane ready to go and refueled. Oops, while thinking that through I've decided sheriff that you have to come with me to Brazil. We can't have them shooting down my plane because I don't have a valuable hostage."

"The sheriff? I don't think that will work if you keep him hostage."

"Penny dear this isn't negotiable. I'll let him go once I'm safe and not before."

"Fine! I will call back when all the arrangements have been made," Penny stated.

"See that you do but no tricks, Penny. I'll kill them all and take out whoever tries to rescue them. Understand?"

"I do understand and I'll get what you want. I'll call back soon," Penny promised then hung up.

"I don't want to go to Brazil, Rita. I have a life here. A child that needs her father!" I argued, "But if I must I'll stay here and be your hostage. Just let the others go."

Where was Uncle Tommy why hadn't he made his move?

"Don't look at me like that Gee. This isn't a crisis as long as you do as I want. We could negotiate about my all my information once I'm safe. Frankly, despite the fact that your little brat bit me, she's the reason I didn't kill you. That kid has gumption and I kind of admire her in some ways. Maybe if I had a loving father I would have gone looking for love in all the wrong places and have ended up in a life of crime."

"What happened to you, mom?"

Good grief, Reginald do you really think I'd
whine and bellyache about my childhood the
way all those losers do? So I had a rough
childhood. Who didn't? I pulled myself up
and used the men, who sought to use me.
Just like that idiot father of yours over
there!!"

"Didn't you ever love me?" Ethan asked.

"I loved you when we were first married but
then you cheated on me and that was that.
Our marriage saved me from prostitution."

"You were a hooker?" Ethan said horrified.

"Might as well have been. I was living off a
sugar daddy when I met you."

"But you were only twenty when we met."

"I was eighteen, you boob! I had been living on the streets since I was fifteen. I ran away from home after my stepdaddy climbed in my bed. I hooked some but then I found out a sugar daddy would meet my needs and I found one. He was sweet and kind to me but when I met you when he visited Driftwood to look at the old pulp and paper factory. I fell for you, like a ton of bricks. I put some strychnine in my sugar daddy's coffee emptied out his bank accounts and erased any trace of me. Since they had all known me as Candy and since I'd worn a red wig (since he preferred redheads) they didn't know who to look for and I was rich enough to start my new life with you."

"Oh Rita if only I'd known," the mayor responded.

"Men!! You're so friggin' gullible. I spin a story and you believe every word."

"So it's a lie again?" the mayor muttered.

"Maybe there's some truth in it. I know I did love you but then you ruined it all. First you plowed through my money and then you allowed your brother to become mayor instead of you. I hated you after that and vowed you'd never get the best of me again."

"John was a good mayor."

"Ah, but was he a good brother? He lured me to his house drugged me and then raped me."

"You're saying you weren't having an affair with him? That he... "

"Had you going again didn't I? I'm very convincing. Actually I drugged John and climbed in naked beside him."

"Why?"

"John found out about my part in the new criminal organization. He wanted a cut of the business. I wasn't ready to cut him in. I was a small peg on the ladder then. John tried to blackmail me. When that didn't work he threatened to tell you we were having an affair. I pretended I was going to do what he wanted. I let him make love to me and then when he was drugged I silenced him once and for all. I then took the bedside lamp and bashed my head with it and waited for Louise to come home."

"You killed John?" The mayor demanded.

"Who did you think killed him the Easter bunny?"

The mayor looked stunned and Reggie was no better.

"Now look what you've done, you worm. You've upset our son. You understand. Don't you Reginald? I had to protect our life. I thought I could still have my boys, but your father took that away from me."

"It's okay mom. I still love you."

"And I love you Reggie, even though you sometimes disappoint me. We'll have a good life in Brazil. You'll have your choice of the women there to make me a grandma."

"Grandma? The boy is only nineteen years old and you don't look like any grandmother I've ever seen," the mayor quipped.

"I know I don't. That is the point; but I want to raise my grandchildren in luxury."

"You didn't even change a diaper the nanny or I did," the mayor laughed.

"Shut-up!!"

Rita looked like she was going to shoot the mayor; but then she reined it in and said, "I know your game you want me to shoot you again so they'll charge in. I'm not going to put you out of your misery just yet Ethan. But don't be mistaken if someone tries anything else I'll shoot you without even blinking. I'm a much more powerful woman then you ever knew. I run a huge organization I'm not just a cog. Man bow to my feet or I take them out."

"I've never bowed to you and I'm not about to start now."

"That would have impressed me years ago but now Ethan I hold all the cards so you better start cooperating," Rita threatened.

The mayor seemed to shrink down and look like he actually would back down which made me feel more comfortable but I knew it wouldn't last something was going to give. When would my John McClain moment come? I had to get us out of this one and I really didn't trust this crazy bitch not to kill us all in a moment of anger. I shifted my body and Rita turned the gun back to me again.

"Really Gee, are you trying to start something, now?"

"Not at all, just trying to get comfortable," I insisted.

"Likely story, but I'll let it go… for now," Rita then turning to Reggie she said, "You must have found your brother by now."

"I did. He texted he'd be home in ten," Reggie stated.

"How long ago was that? When did he say that?"

"About twenty minutes ago."

"What would scare him Ethan and make him come home? And don't lie, or I'll make you pay."

"I don't know!"

"You do, now tell me!"

"Give me my cell phone off the dresser, Reggie," the mayor demanded, sighing."

"Do it Reggie. Get the phone, but bring it to me. If Ethan gets a text from Daddy saying he's angry, Ethan will come home. He's afraid of the beating he'll get."

"Unlike you I've never raise a hand to our children."

"Really Ethan? You're such a liar I'm surprised your nose hasn't grown ten feet long."

Obediently Reggie ran to retrieve the cell phone. While Rita was distracted watching Reggie go down the hall the mayor spotted my right shin gun. It was only visible because my pant leg had slipped up. The mayor gaped openly then acted easily slipping the gun out of its holster and under his leg. One less weapon for me to grab, but if I tried to take it back Rita would notice. Reggie seemed to take a long time and Rita looked angsty. Personally I hoped the kid had escaped out a window, but Reggie appeared with the cell phone in question.

"Why did it take you so long were you signalling to those cops out there?" Rita asked.

"Hell no, mom. The stupid phone fell on the floor and was kicked under the bed. Dad must have just thrown it down like he always does."

"You're an idiot Ethan. Reggie's right you are careless. You're lucky Reggie found that phone or I'd put a bullet through your head now."

"Now Rita, remember that Ethan is your leverage. I'm a cop so I'm leverage too; but if you put a hole in Ethan's head the tactical squad from the FBI is going to come rushing in here."

"The FBI? Why would they be involved? It's your town."

"You killed an FBI agent. They'd like your blood, luckily for you it is my town."

"So you are a useful hostage, just like I thought," Rita laughed.

Rita then scrolled through the mayor's phone and seemed satisfied as she texted Ethan junior.

"There. I told him you wanted him home now or you'd beat him," Rita smirked.

"See, he'll be back here soon, mom," Reggie soothed.

Rita looked mollified; but then a look came over her face.

"Give me your phone Reginald you didn't give it back to me."

"I left it in the bedroom."

"I don't believe you hand it over Reginald."

Reggie pulled out his cell phone from a back pocket and passed the phone to his mother. Reggie looked scared again and I wondered why. I soon found out as Rita started scrolling the messages on the phone.

"You ungrateful, little monster! How dare you tell your brother that I'm a murderer and that I'll kill him, I'd never harm a hair on his beautiful head. He's the best part of me."

"The best part of you? Is that why you had him running drugs for you, mom? Is that why you got your guy to roofie him? Yes, I know about that mom. You killed all those other kids with the fentanyl; just to keep the sheriff busy and away from you. You harmed Ethan. That's not a loving mom. He spent the last six months in rehab because of you. He was clean before that."

"You fucking, lying, little piece of shit. You're just like your father, a fucking waste of space. I'm not taking you with me; but I'm not letting him have you either," Rita said raising her gun and taking aim at Reggie.

I advanced on Rita trying to grab the other gun off of my shin while I continued moving but Rita spun around getting the drop on me with a high karate like kick. I countered it with a karate chop trying to knock the weapon out of her hands; but it didn't work she had a firm grip on the gun and she wouldn't let go even as her fingers bent at an unnatural angle.

"Time's up for you too, I guess, Gee. Such a shame! I really liked you."

We struggled for the gun; her hand reaching for mine as I made another grab for the gun. Our arms entwined as we danced a merry dance, grappling for the weapon. As our hands both reached for the trigger at the same time, I heard a loud bang that reverberated in my ears. I felt myself spiralling down falling with a bone crunching thunk and a sharp pain like something had kicked my chest. I felt sure something had gone through my flak jacket or under it. Sure that I had been hit I checked for blood and found none. I reached for my cell phone and found my metal case now smashed two bullets embedded in it.

My cell phone case had saved me… that and
my badge. There was a dint in my badge
where the bullet had bounced off and a
bullet embedded in the metal cell phone
case. Tina had saved my life. I couldn't
believe it. Could this be why Tina had
bought a metal case and told me to keep it in
my front pocket? I was stunned and felt a
sense of loss for Tina again.

I pulled myself together I was alive...
stunned but alive. I had a huge metal cased
sized bruise on my chest that would have to
be checked out as per police procedure. But
if I was okay; what about Rita? I had to stop
Rita.

Rita wasn't moving. I reached for her
feeling her body for wounds and found
three. Her eyes were rolled back in her head
and blood poured from her chest. It was
obvious nothing could be done. One or
maybe two of the three bullets had struck
her heart. The third had struck her in the
head right between her eyes. The third was
the kill shot. No one could have survived
that.

I looked over and saw Ethan Junior with Errol's gun in his hands; mostly likely used for the third shot... the kill shot from the trajectory.. The mayor held the other gun. My gun (which the mayor had hidden below his leg) had been used to shoot Rita.

This wasn't good. Ethan junior was trying to save his brother; but he'd already gone through hell because of his mother Rita. The mayor could be excused he had no criminal record and he was trying to save his; but I would be censured because he used my other gun and so would Errol for Ethan using his gun. It was shit-storm of mega-proportions; if the investigators heard this we were all going have legal troubles.

If the detectives found out Ethan junior killed her, he would have to answer to the investigators who would tear him apart before they'd accept the truth. After all he had just left a drug rehabilitation centre two days ago. They'd allude to his drug use and then they'd skewer the mayor too saying he wanted his ex-wife dead and was protecting himself. They'd bring up Tina and how she had ties to Rita.

This was a cluster fuck no there was no two ways around this I was going to lose my job and be disgraced. How would Aunt Louise and Stella-Marie face this? But how could we present this any differently? Investigators would come in and my job would be on the line as well as Ethan Junior's freedom. My aunt's nephew's freedom; he was family how could I deny his need?

Seconds passed as I pondered this but it seemed like minutes. I thought I would have seen the FBI crashing in and controlling the situation but for some reason they held back maybe because all of this occurred so quickly in the span of a few minutes.

"Oh my God! This is so bad!! We can't tell them Ethan shot her," the mayor said as Reggie held his sobbing brother in his arms.

"He only did it to protect me sheriff. He can't go to jail for this he can't!!"Reggie cried wiping away his brother's tears and holding him close.

"We have to protect the boy, sheriff. He feels guilty enough as it is and with his record they might not believe that he shot his mother to save his brother," Errol insisted.

I must have hesitated for a moment because
the mayor chimed in, "Bullet I can be your
best friend or your greatest enemy. Fix this!
Don't think you'll get off Scott-free if you
implicate my boy!"

"I'm still thinking," I insisted.

"You're the sheriff you can fix this," the
mayor insisted again.

I was torn between a rock and hard space.
I'd always followed my personal code there
was right and there was wrong and this was
no different. I turned and nodded at Errol.
He nodded back understanding.

I thought I would have seen the FBI
crashing in, by then controlling the situation
and maybe even finding out the truth; but for
some reason they held back; maybe because
all of the shooting occurred so quickly in the
span of a few minutes; or maybe because
they didn't want to risk anymore shootings.
The odds were ten to one however that
they'd be bursting in soon. We had to fix this
before then.

I told Reggie to take his brother into the
bathroom and wash his hands of any gun
residue. What could I do? I had to protect
my deputy and the mayor's kid did need a
new start.

Errol then picked up the gun with his left
hand and fired using his uninjured shoulder
for leverage as the bullet hit the ceiling.

"This is the story we'll tell to protect everyone," I commanded, "The narration is Reggie was going to be shot by his mom and I struggled with her trying to disarm her. Ethan junior was never here. Errol picked up my gun and fired at the same time the mayor fired the gun. The mayor acquired the gun from me, while Rita was holding us hostage. Ethan Senior saw his chance and sought to save me from Rita. The bullets entered Rita's body after ricocheting off my cell phone case. We were all doing what was necessary in the situation to save Reggie. I didn't see any of this because I was focused on fighting Rita. I'll sneak out the back with Ethan and get him away. You can tell them I've gone for treatment of my wound."

"That will work boss. It's certainly close enough to the real story and Ethan Junior never being here will save his bacon," Errol replied.

"Ethan is out of it dad. It's like he totally checked out," Reggie said coming back into the room dragging his brother Ethan.

"Did you hear what the sheriff said Reggie?"

"Yes, and I'll stick with the story. Anything to protect Ethan! But dad Ethan needs help."

"What do you mean he needs help? I'm the one who is shot."

"Ethan needs to go to a place where they won't be able to talk to him and where he can deal with the trauma of what mom did to him."

"He's right mayor. The kid seems a little traumatized to me and he's going to need help dealing with this. Plus it will be easier for us all to cover for him if he can't talk to the investigators and he has an alibi of being in a facility when this all occurred," I stated.

"Investigators? But you're the sheriff."

"You know the rules we can't investigate our own involved cop shootings. Someone from Larmier County will arrive here and investigate my actions and our shooting of Rita. If we tell them it was Errol who shot her instead of Ethan they'll believe us. His got residue on him but if we take him to a hospital facility you choose and can control. We can fix the situation. Our shooting of Rita will be pegged a good shoot. It's all but rubber stamped. Just take my advice and stick closest to the truth following my storyline."

"Okay, I'll do it. I'll call my friend Doctor Bob Haskell at Meadowbrook. He owes me a favor. He'll check Ethan in and they'll say he's been there for the last week." "First of all we need to get you to the hospital mayor," Errol insisted.

"I'll drive Ethan to Meadowbrook and check him in then I'll report to the Driftwood hospital emergency. You stay here with Reggie and stick to the story, both of you. Tell them I'm headed to the hospital and will give them a statement later." I exclaimed as Errol agreed.

I checked Ethan junior into the facility telling the good doctor that the mayor seemed to think he owned that Ethan was traumatized and believed he had shot his mom but only in self-defence. I only hoped that sticking to that story wouldn't harm the boy more. The doctor agreed to keep the boy under wraps since he apparently knew and respected Ethan's father. The doctor offered to look at my injury; but I refused sticking to the plan. I then headed to the emergency department at Driftwood General.

As I drove I thought about what Rita had said. I should have been happy that she was no longer a problem; but I wasn't she had alluded to a mole in the sheriff department and I had hoped to garner that information. Now there was still a mole and I didn't know who he or she was. When I arrived I made a call to Aunt Louise.

"Oh thank goodness, you're okay. Is Rita in custody?" Aunt Louise asked.

"She's dead," I blurted.

"You're sounding pained. Are you sure you're not harmed Gunner?"

"A little bruised. I'll be fine."

"I'm coming home to see for myself, Gunner," Aunt Louise insisted.

"Stay where you are a little longer. Uncle Tommy's missing and I want you two safe."

"He's missing? Oh no. Did his friends get him?"

"I don't know. That's why I said stay there where you and Stella-Marie are safe."

"I don't like it, but I'll do it. Meanwhile you get seen by a doctor. I don't trust that you're not hurt. You used to try to hide it from when you were a little boy. but I always know when you're not leveling with me."

"Fine, I'll get my bruises checked out. Are you happy now?"

"I'll be happier when I see you for myself, but that will do," Aunt Louise agreed.

"Talk to you later, love you, Aunt Louise."

"I love you too. Bye."

With that I hung up the cell phone and entered the hospital. Hoping no one would question how long it took me to arrive here from the Calladen's.

~0~

## Chapter 25 - Life's Little

## Surprises

I arrived at the emergency and since it was very busy the nurse said, "We were expecting you Sheriff. We thought you'd be here sooner. The doctor will see you now."

The nurse ushered me into a cubical and then handed me a gown saying put this on. . I hated these gowns there was such a gap in the back that your tushy always hung out. I must a face for she said, "Don't worry it's all organic to us we're used to bodies around here."

The doctor came in shortly after I finished putting on the gown and at any other time I might have found her beautiful. She was a very pretty trim, brunette with green eyes, about thirty years with a name tag that read Doctor A. Sutherland. Doctor Sutherland examined my wound and the bruising told me I was lucky even that only two stray bullets had hit me. I told her I wasn't lucky that I was named Stray Bullet. She laughed as I expected. She tenderly probed the bruise then seemed most concerned.

"It's only a bruise," I insisted.

"I'm the doctor; let me be the judge of that," she claimed.

Then as if on cue, I suddenly started to feel what my adrenaline had kept from me, extreme pressure above my ribs and light-headedness with shortness of breath. The doctor rushed me instantly to the CAT scanner and before I knew what was happening I was under the knife to repair a bleed in my heart vein. Apparently the vein had been damaged by the force of the cell phone case and my damaged phone both of which had kept the bullet from piercing my heart. The doctor told me when I woke up that they had got in just in time.

I was very unhappy about this. I have never been a patient person and being a patient I felt made me look weak. However I was soon to find out that didn't make me appear weak at all in fact the people of Driftwood and the investigators now labelled me a hero. Something else I wasn't comfortable with but since it helped with the story we told I reluctantly went along with the adulation.

As I lay in the hospital Penny made arrangements for Tina and little Tina-Marie to be cremated together and buried in with a marker in the Driftwood cemetery. The memorial service for them would be conducted a week after I was out of the hospital.

Penny surprised me with a formatted photo album of the pictures that Aunt Louise and Stella-Marie had taken of our wedding and then she followed it up with pictures of me with Tina-Marie. I touched the pictures and was eternally grateful to Penny for her kind thought. I had a physical remembrance of them.

I was reunited with my beloved daughter who wisely told me not to be so trusting with women they can be bad too! Stella-Marie told me she missed Tina. Aunt Louise said Stella-Marie had nightmares about Rita, but they seemed to be subsiding and that Stella-Marie was otherwise okay.

The investigators took two days to close the case rubber stamping it as a good shoot. I took that as a sign that I could work from the hospital. I ordered Errol to bring my laptop and coordinated and investigation to wrap up Rita aka Perita's Castillo's role in the crimes. I was working hard from my hospital bed when Aunt Louise burst in and kicked everyone out. She then lay down the law to me. She had been talking to the doctor and she was really angry with me.

"How dare you endanger your health this way!! You should be resting. Your heart was bruised."

"I'm sorry?"

"I understand you want to wrap up this case. You need to rest so I'll compromise. Errol can come two hours a day to work with you as long as long as the doctor agrees."

I agreed. I'd learned a long time ago you can't fight Aunt Louise. I'd never win. So I ended up working two hours a day while in hospital. Okay, so I'm lying, I snuck in more time every chance I got and we received a lot of information on Perita aka Rita Castillo from various sources including the FBI.

Gordon had been censured by his bosses at first. Understandably they were not happy he had been with the very person they were searching for but when the news stories started calling Gordon a hero they changed their tune. His closest bosses came up with the story that he had been under cover investigating Perita as a prime suspect. This endeared him to the upper echelons of the FBI and he received a promotion; unfortunately he's working at a desk for the next six months (because of his injuries and because he's being punished.) As for me I recovered quickly (in less than a month) still wondering what had happened to Uncle Tommy and trying to figure out whether Rita was yanking my chain, or if there was really a mole in my sheriff's department. From all the records I had gone through it all seemed that the people that had worked with Rita were gone. These were the cops that she had murdered. No testimony came from the arrested associates throughout Colorado or anyone else of anyone who seemed to have ties to Driftwood's police department. The FBI concluded that Rita had lied, but I vowed to keep an eye on my officers. Driftwood's police department would be safe from the criminal elements takeovers I vowed.

One morning as I returned to work for the first time after the shooting, I found out. Uncle Tommy sat in the front seat of my car.

"Where have you been?"

"Nowhere of my choice." He answered, "You are looking better."

"I'm looking better? When did you last see me?"

"A couple of days ago; you were sleeping."

"Where have you been?"

"One of my handlers nabbed me. He's no longer my handler. His boss censured him for his failure to protect two police officers from a dangerous felon Rita and then luring me away with a knockout drug. You can thank me now that made your buddy Gordon look better and I got them to give him a promotion. "

"Your handler actually gave you a knockout drug? How?"

"The bastard injected me. He wanted me to give them more information that I simply don't have. He thought he could just kidnap me then tie me up and inject me with sodium pentothal and get any answers he wanted. He was in for a surprise let me tell you. He kept me for three days before I escaped, that's why he's in hot water now," Uncle Tommy stated cryptically.

"So you have a new handler?" I asked changing the subject.

"Sort of."

"You either do or you don't Uncle Tommy."

"I have a former FBI agent, a former S. A. I.C. (special agent in charge, like your buddy Gordon) looking after me and my interests and reporting back to them to keep them off my back."

"So this agent will keep you safe?"

"I'm finished all the testifying, I'm going to enjoy life now."


There was something Uncle Tommy wasn't telling me and I waited for the other shoe to drop.


"I'm going to stick around in the area. That is if you don't mind after I let you down."

"Nonsense, you were kidnapped. You didn't let me down."

"At least my wife came in handy."

"What wife?"

"Annie. She helped you didn't she?"

"I don't know any Annie," I proclaimed.

"Sure you do. She saved your life, my Doctor Annie Sutherland. I've taken her last name in my new life."

"What does your new handler think of this development?"

"Well considering my new handler is all handsy it's not a problem."

"Doctor Sutherland is your wife and your handler?"

"Yep. She's going to continue to work at the hospital and I've bought a ranch just outside of town. Your daughter will be able to ride my horses there if you allow it."

"I think she'd like that," I answered.

"So you have all the information on Perita Castillo now."

"Did you know who she was?"

"I knew she was operating in Colorado. I didn't know that she was in your sphere."

"How did you know?"

"I still have my contacts but I've let you down nephew; but I'm going to make it up to you. I promise you."

"Do you know anything we don't know about Rita?"

"Let's see she was running a drug organization for Demonio."

"Yes, we have that information. It's an Argentinian and Mexican collaboration to run drugs through Canada and the United States. Rita's great uncle had ties to the leader in Argentina but he's now saying that he doesn't even know any of them."

"I heard the FBI is now doing that end of the investigation."

"The FBI is best at taking over. Gordon is doing some of the work at his desk position but the legwork is being done by someone else," I answered.

"And it's almost wrapped up? I heard they arrested some of the key Mexican players but the Argentina end is going to walk. They think they've got all the dealers and suppliers throughout Colorado that were working with Rita but you know there's always one who slips the leash. "

"That's more than I've heard. All I know is that we've choked off the supply here."

"Do you really believe that?"

"No, they'll always be another dealer or supplier to step in. I'll have to be vigilant and keep eyes and ears out to tramp down the drug trade in Driftwood."

"Good thinking nephew; at least it will keep you busy and working."

"Are you being sarcastic?"

"What do you think? See you in an hour at the memorial," Uncle Tommy stated and then in matter of seconds had exited the car and disappeared.


Just before I entered the memorial a familiar figure took my arm and pulled me aside.

"You think you have something on me now don't you Bullet?" The mayor exclaimed in an angry tone, "I want you to know that two can play that game. I can go to the authorities at any time and tell them you coerced me into giving that statement and omitting my son's involvement to protect yourself. Just remember that I can be an ally or an enemy."

"What brought this on Mayor?" I asked sounding surprised but really I wasn't the man was really a slippery eel.

"I started thinking about the sweetheart deal you have now hero of Driftwood. You were involved with one of the players too!"

"My wife was coerced by Rita. None of us knew that Rita was manipulating us. But even if that weren't true, I'd do this for my Aunt Louise."

"Your Aunt Louise? What has she to do with this?"

"Aunt Louise still considers your sons, her nephews. So that means that Reggie and Ethan are m family too."

"You really mean that," the mayor said surprised.

"I do and I won't tell any of this if you don't mayor, so let's call a truce. You have nothing to worry about unless you turn on me, then we have a problem."

"I have the upper hand," the mayor insisted.

"You'd like to think that but anything that happened after I was hit by Ethan's bullet could be argued that I didn't see or register. After all I had a traumatic injury. I was I shock."

"If you think that will fly..."

"Oh it will, but only if you push me into a corner, mayor."

The mayor looked like he wanted to argue more but Aunt Louise was waving at me from the door so I added, "You do realize you are interrupting the memorial for my wife and daughter don't you?"

"Sorry. I just wanted to be clear. Now that we are I'll let you go and follow you in to say my goodbyes." The mayor exclaimed.

"We're clear."

I hoped the mayor meant what he said I didn't need his kind of trouble that could end my career even if it would also end his at the same time. I would keep him close as I had read the Art of War in my sickbed. The Chinese general Sun Tzu was right, keep your friends close and your enemies closer at least that's what I figured he was saying in his philosophy. So I'd keep the mayor as close as friend and keep an eye on him protecting myself and my own. I had discovered much to my surprise the back up of my I –Phone recording in my cloud account and it had recorded everything; if I went down he'd go down too.

I went into to the church to find a full house.
The memorial for Tina and Tina-Marie was
well attended it seemed most of the town
turned out. Press from all around the country
confronted me when I came out of the
church. Though the townspeople tried to
protect me I decided to address the press.

I briefly told them of the bravery of the
mayor and of my deputy Errol Ward saving
Reginald and Ethan from their mother.

"What about the fentanyl crisis is it now
over in Driftwood?" asked a reporter.

*"We have made numerous arrests and have
broken up the supply of fentanyl and its
other forms for now but there is always a
new supplier and a new drug. The fentanyl
crisis will never be over this is an epidemic
make no mistake about this!! Take the case
of an estimated 4,149 people in Ohio who
died from unintentional drug overdoses last
year that's a 36 per cent increase over
2015. Ohio has been the hardest hit in the
United States. We don't want that
happening here in our small town of*

*Driftwood, but it could. We've had deaths from this scourge and will continue to have deaths unless we take steps to control the fallout."*

"But we're not a huge town," argued a reporter.

*"Size does not matter; this drug is deadly. This crisis started with the mistaken impression that opioids were non- addictive which were prescribed frequently in the past by doctors and even in the present,easily. These patients can become addicts and do. Your brothers your sisters your neighbours are fighting their way out of these addictions but they need help. These opioids are too easily accessible and are ever changing making them harder to track. For instance the DEA is now concerned with a new form an analog called acrylfentanyl. Acrylfentanyl seemed to have associated with more deaths because it takes more naloxone to reverse an overdose than just fentanyl. Driftwood and many other communities have lost a number of young people to this plague. We*

*can't arrest out way out of this. This is a man-made opioid 100 times more powerful than morphine."*

"But didn't the World Health Organization listed fentanyl as an essential drug?" asked one reporter.

*"Yes and when more citizens are dying every month from overdoses of illicit fentanyl it's easy to lose sight of the fact that prescription fentanyl is an important drug for patients. It has been listed on the essential medicine list. There are people who need access to these medicines but they have to be prescribed with caution and used with caution. Fentanyl patches and methadone are needed for the treatment of cancer pain. So we need to find alternatives that are not as addictive.""*

"I don't understand! The DEA wants to restrict it," another reporter muttered.

*"That's the problem with this crisis there are many opinions, some conflicting and this is not just Driftwood's problem. It is not only a national crisis but a world crisis that we need to address it head on. Even the U.N. has now declared it the most dangerous substance in the world. There were roughly 20,000 U.S. overdose deaths in 2015 from fentanyl and its derivatives according to the CDC and there has been an increase since that data was collected. China's ban of carfentanil, furanyl fentanyl, acrylfentanyl and valeryl fentanyl from being legally manufactured and sold will help, but we must be vigilant. Suppliers pop up and new drug operations will persevere but make no mistake we will put a stop to this."*

*"We want to start up a conference with mayors across Colorado to address this problem as they've done in Canada; and also liaison with police forces and health officials throughout Colorado to share overdose data and hopefully be alerted and be able to have a better response to the crisis and stem the tide of this opioid drug crisis. The FBI has helped us in this*

*endeavor by reaching out to China to stop
the influx of the chemicals used to make
fentanyl. However we need to educate the
public and provide a place to help the
addicts get off the drugs. I am also starting
construction on a rehab facility in
Driftwood that will help them with the
proceeds of my wife's estate. The
foundation in my wife's name will also
provide naloxone to front line workers to
prevent overdoses and deaths. This
foundation will operate in an older
building temporarily downtown until the
new Doctor Tina Bullet Foundation for
Drug Rehabilitation opens next year.
Parents talk to your children and other
family members about these drugs. Tell
them that they don't know what the drug is
they are getting and that they really are
taking a chance with their life every time
they use one of these drugs recreationally.
Talk to them about opioids and how easy it
is to become addicted in a short period of
time. Talk to them about the signs of an
overdose and how to get help immediately
at those signs. The life they could save
could be family or friends. I carry a
Naxolone kit that is because I want to be
able to save someone's life. It will now be
mandatory for officers to wear protective*

*equipment including a respiratory mask, safety glasses or goggles, nitrile gloves, and long sleeve shirt or jacket while conducting drug searches and seizures. After all we want to keep our officers safe too. This drug fighting equipment will be provided by the Doctor Tina Bullet Foundation for Drug Rehabilitation free of charge for the first five years."*

*"If you should please carry a Naxolone kit, too it could save their life. Most of all have an open dialogue with your kids. Hopefully with these steps we can help some people recover and stem this tide."*

"Are you suggesting we should supply the drugs to these addicts?" Someone shouted at me.

*"No, I'm not suggesting that we supply addicts with their drug of choice but I am suggesting we direct these addicts to help so they can get clean and sober. If they can..."*

"So the center, the Tina Bullet Foundation will do this?"

*"Hopefully we will help a lot of people. Thank you for your time that is all."* I concluded.

I was rewarded with applause but I knew that we had a long way to go. Driftwood would never the quiet town I thought it would be no town could. Crime was human nature in some and I could only hope to stem the tide.

"How are you really dear," Aunt Louise asked.

"I'm fine," I stated.

"I'd like you to meet someone, she's just your type," the mayor said.

"Really Ethan! My nephew just lost his wife and babe and you're trying to set him up at their memorial?"

Why was he putting this show on in front of Aunt Louise? Oh no, I think the mayor had feelings for her. He wanted to look good in her eyes. A complication I didn't need.

"I've swore off women. I'm all about the job now," I declared.

"I'm sorry Gee. You saved my life I'd like to make it up to you since I feel responsible," the mayor admitted.

"None of us could have known about Rita," Aunt Louise insisted.

"Aunt Louise is correct. We leave the past in the past and we move forward," I declared.

"At least I haven't lost my job. And my constituents have sympathy for what happened. "

"Good then my job is secure too."

"Of course it is Sheriff you're the hero of Driftwood. You stopped a mighty felon," the mayor said aloud so others could hear.

The mayor was protecting his own ass for now and I was still the sheriff. I wasn't complacent I knew he still had his own agenda but I would protect myself. Stella-Marie was coping with the loss of Tina as were we all. I was still coming to terms with my loss. Some days I was angry some days just sad but I had my work and that kept my mind busy. And so ends my first year in Driftwood, Colorado I tip my cup of coffee to many, many more.

~0~

## Excerpt from Untraceable

## Preface:

Penny Ambercrombie loved her

family's ranch and she loved riding her horse; but she loved Driftwood even more. Frankly working for Sheriff Bullet the next year had been exciting; but she was happy that there had been a lull for the last few months. The tragedy of the sheriff losing his baby girl Tina-Marie had brought back too much to her of her own tragedy and losing her own daughter, Lorna to leukemia. She had even considered going back to her therapist but then she had discarded the idea. All she needed was to ride her horse, Bucky (real name Buchanan Stirlingshire the third). He had been a race horse at one time but he had never lived up to his reputation. Penny had bought him before they could send him to the slaughterhouse. With love and

attention Bucky had blossomed and was a
fine horse for someone who was a rancher in
their spare time like Penny was.  There had
been a changeover in the properties near the
ranch as families had lost interest or the
money to run big ranches anymore. She
barely knew the neighbors anymore.

She looked towards the east and saw forest
and thanked the fact that developers hadn't
come forth and developed that land. The
truth was the Ambercrombie's owned part of
the forest and were not about to part with it.
Sometimes it felt like the only place Penny
could be alone and one with nature. She'd
ride Bucky to the edge and then tie him to a
tree and just wander just a little into the
forest to think. She wouldn't be long and
then Bucky wouldn't mind.

Penny let Bucky have his rein and they
galloped towards the forest area in the edge
of the Ambercrombie property; before they
got their Penny pulled Bucky up short as she
stopped to examine the sky. Penny had
heard a sputter then watched as a small
plane seemed to drop from the sky and then

a load bang was heard as it crashed in deep in the forest near the Ambercrombie ranch.

Penny took out her cellphone from her pocket and dialed the sheriff's office. So much for her day off and thinking quietly in the forest soaking up nature; she thought and then felt selfish. It was possible whoever was on board that plane was already dead but maybe not so she had to do all to save them if she could.

"Sheriff Bullet? A plane has gone down in the forest near my property. You need to alert the FAA and get some officers out here to assist any recovery efforts. I'm on my way to help. Okay see you soon," Penny said into her cell phone.

Penny then tied up Bucky and entered the forest following the crackling sound. She hoped that the fire would not spread and trap them all.

Penny heard the sound of moans and
quickened her pace. Entering a clearing she
spotted the wreckage. She at first though the
small plane had broken into two pieces but
then she realized it was three. It appeared
that the pilots were dead but as Penny
looked around for passengers she saw a seat
up in a tree. She would have to wait to save
whoever was in that seat. Then she spotted a
woman still buckled into her seat. Her head
was lacerated but she appeared to be
breathing in and out from a distance. As
Penny advanced on the woman she
recognized her; she seen the woman's
pictures in all the tabloids, that golden
blonde hair which normally fell to her
shoulder in distinctive waves was now
matted with blood and her signature fashion
scarf around her neck also seemed coated
with blood. That worried Penny she knew
she had to get closer to the woman to
checkout her injury and hopefully save the
woman's life.

Penny gasped as she got closer for she knew
she was correct and this was Paris Ivan, the
daughter of Arnold Ivan, the software king.
As she advanced towards her Penny heard

the sounds of an All-terrain vehicle and as she followed the sound she saw then proceed into the crash site. Good she could use the help to find any other passengers she thought but before she could even get close enough to Paris the man dressed in black leather from head to foot, his head cover with a helmet snatched Paris' scarf pulling it tight and began to strangle her.

"Stop, police officer," Penny cried grabbing a rock since she didn't have her service weapon.

The man lifted his head and starred at her but didn't stop. Then Penny heard anther ATV behind her and she turned her head slightly to see where I was unfortunately another man in black leather had snuck up on her and he struck a glancing blow across her head. Penny fell to the ground clutching her head and seeing double. She tried to regain her equilibrium but when she tried to stand she felt the blood rush to her head and she slumped in a stupor on the ground.

Before she gave into the state of unconsciousness she heard, "Don't kill her she's a cop."

~0~

*To be continued look for this book in December 2018*

*If you have enjoyed Stray Bullet please think about leaving me a few words in a review where you purchased this e-book.*

*Sincerely S. G. Lee*

# Excerpt from ~ Penny Saved

# A Murder Earned- Chapter 1 –

# Bloody Shoes

*"A penny saved is a penny earned" ~*
*Benjamin Franklin*

T he blood streaked across the floor, but

he had carefully sidestepped it. Stupid bitch!
She got what she deserved. How dare she
defile his Angel's property? He hadn't left a
trace...had he? No, he was too clever by
half.

A voice he didn't recognize interrupted his thoughts, "I didn't spot you entering. Working late, dear? Of course, I forgot; you have an early opening tomorrow."

The man strode closer to the killer and the body lying on the floor, "Wait a minute, you aren't the lady. Who are you? You shouldn't be here," the man continued clearly alarmed.

"You shouldn't be here either," the murderer insisted.

"You, you killed Megan. I'm telling."

"Really? You know this was something you shouldn't be allowed to see."

"I'm leaving. I didn't notice anything," the man lied, witnessing the blood.

"I'm sorry pal. Wrong place, wrong time!" the killer answered.

The homeless man ran dodging racks, finally deciding to hide behind some shelving. The killer ran after him, puzzled for a moment because he could see no trace of the homeless person. The murderer then laughed, as he realized how foolish the vagrant was being, his stench gave him away. He subdued the man with a Taser gun. Waiting seconds he then pulled the man from his hiding place. Taking ties from within his pocket; he fastened the man's arms and feet. Satisfied that the homeless person was now trussed up like a turkey, he smiled.

"P...P....P...Please! I don't want to die!" the man cried, visibly sweating and starting to shake.

The man tried to kick out his legs and arms but failed.

"You've heard about fate? Well sorry but this is your fate, buddy!" the murderer explained.

"P...P...P...Please, I'm begging you! Couldn't you let me go? I won't tell! I'll move to another city. Besides who would listen to a homeless man?"

"Someone would. My Angel would."

The homeless man then smiled as if to gain trust from this killer, "You won't hurt the lady who owns the store, will you?" he asked.

"I would never harm my Angel. How dare you?" the killer responded outraged.

"S...S...S...Sorry! I didn't mean to insult you! Please just let me go. I'm harmless ask anyone...."

"What is your name?"

"Why do you need my name?" He asked looking puzzled then reconsidering he answered, "My name is Al."

The killer put his gloves back on and smoothed them and then turned his back on his victim.

"You're going to kill me now. Aren't you? Just don't harm the sweet lady who owns this store. Will it hurt?" the man asked resigned.

"I would never hurt my Angel. She is sweet isn't she? Unfortunately that also makes unscrupulous people take advantage of her."

"I promise I would never take advantage of her kindness. I wouldn't!!! She's the best part of my day and this city, Happy Valley, Ontario. She picked me up from the gutter and helped me."

"I know you wouldn't and it hurts me to do this. Tell you what though, I'll make your death painless because I like you, Al," the killer offered, feeling suddenly sorry for the man. Then he checked himself. Living on the streets was hell; maybe he was doing the guy a favour? Yes, of course he was. Taking a pill bottle out of his pocket and opening the dispenser, he placed some in a coffee cup he took from the sideboard. He filled the cup with the tepid coffee from the coffee pot, stirring the pills in rapidly.

"C...c...c...couldn't you let me go? I won't tell and I'll watch over her when you're not here."

"Sorry, times up, Al. Here now, drink this coffee," the assassin commanded placing the mug at Al's lips.

Al tried not to drink and spit some of the coffee out, but the assassin plugged his nose and the cup was soon empty.

"Admit it Al, you had a crappy life. Just give in and go to the light. I hear good things wait there for people like you," the killer stated.

Al tried to fight some more, but he soon found it was losing battle. Al's breathing slowed as he slipped into a deep sleep and stopped breathing altogether. His age and living on the streets made the pills work fast.

Now what to do with the body? The killer thought. His Angel must not find this man's remains here, bad enough he left Megan's body here for his Angel to find. He couldn't hide Megan though she needed to be found. Every needed to know she suffered for her crime. Maybe even his Angel would see Megan's evil and protect herself from people like that. This man, Al however knew his Angel and she cared about him. It was so like her to look after the homeless. He could let her cry over Al. Where could he put the man so he wouldn't be found?

The dumpster of course...the perfect place for Al! The day after tomorrow was garbage day. Covered in garbage no one would find Al.

~0~

## *The next day*

## *Lily*

Ominous clouds replaced the

morning's sunlight turning the skies to shades of deep purple and navy blue, streaked with gray. Lily Kelly stared at the sky for moment, and then departed the courthouse doors in Happy Valley, Ontario, Canada, skipping down the steps. The city looked its age of over a hundred as the buildings downtown looked old and decrepit. If only the town could find some money to fix downtown Lily thought.

Then her mind turned to Amelia, her cousin and best friend. Amelia needed Lily to support her in her grief. Lily had a fight with her husband Horace again this morning about how much time he was spending at the office and how much time she spent supporting Amelia. Lily was always working, and so was Horace, so how much time was Rose their fourteen year old daughter really getting?

Lily had won in court, but all she could think about was her family. Everyone needed her and she felt like she was being pulled in three different directions. Something had to give and it looked like it was her job. She would have to cut back on some of her work. Her family had to come first.

Lily stumbled some more over the steps only stopping from hurrying across the courtyard to her office, when her heel broke on her shoe. Today was supposed to be about her victory after her win in court; but it appeared with her expensive shoe's heel breaking, she was mistaken. They ought to get the ruts in the paving stones fixed; that was her reflection as she cursed her bad

break. What did they say about omens?
Maybe she should have taken a hint from the
heavens' darkening? She noted as her bad
luck had seemed to get worse with the
arrival of some reporters.

"Ms. Kelly, give us a statement about the
Rockwood case?" yelled one reporter.

"Ms. Kelly, how does the Sulimani family
feel about your victory?" yelled another.

One bold reporter stepped forward, "Crown
Attorney Kelly, congratulations on your
win. Was it hard to try a case which
involved a council member?" asked Paul
Knight from the local television station,
thrusting a microphone in Lily's face.

"Anyone who commits a crime in Happy
Valley will be tried by the Crown with the
full force of the law, despite their office. So
no, I did not find it difficult to do my job,"
Lily replied testily.

"Thank you, Ms. Kelly. What does the Sulimani family think about the judgement?"

"Amani Sulimani was five years old, when Zebadiah Rockwood's truck went through a red light. His truck struck the back of the Sulimani's SUV killing her. He then left the scene pursued by good Samaritans, who wished to stop Mr. Rockwood from continuing driving drunk: a pursuit caused by Mr. Rockwood's actions, which put a number of lives in danger."

"Will the family be comforted with this conviction?" queried another reporter.

"Amani Sulimani existed as their only child. Mr. Rockwood's conviction will not bring her back, but hopefully will bring some peace of mind to her family knowing he will be behind bars." Lily answered.

"Do you sense, given your own personal tragedies that you'll be able to get a sentence fitting the crime?"

"My family's history does not come into my trial cases, only the person's guilt."

"And when will sentencing take place?" asked another reporter.

"Sentencing will take place next month."

"Thank you Ms. Kelly. This is Paul Knight reporting, with an update on the Zebadiah Rockwood's drunken driving case. Zebadiah Rockwood was a long time council member here in Happy Valley. He took a leave of absence to deal with his legal issues. Mr. Rockwood was charged with impaired driving causing death, two counts of failing to remain at the scene of an accident and dangerous driving last December. When asked about the conviction today Mr. Rockwood and his lawyer issued a no comment. We will have the complete story for you at six pm. Paul Knight reporting for CHPV-TV."

Lily hated speaking on camera, even though it was part of her job as the Crown attorney, so she was glad the scrum had been completed.

She hated sounding tough and unyielding but it was all in the description of her job title. She had fought difficult challenges to get this job and she had to work hard and fight hard to keep it. After all there were aspects of her job her she loved like putting the bad people that would harm others away. The press was gone and she was now free to go to her office to file her reports and leave early. She crossed the street, entered her building and went straight up to her office.

"Victory is mine!" Lily Kelly cried triumphantly as she walked into her office.

"So you won?" asked Colleen Finn, her administrative assistant.

"Yes, I bested that idiot, Michael Taylor. He thought he would beat me in court. He actually believed his client would win."

"Good for you, boss, I knew you would nail his lily white ass to the wall. He's such a scumbag lawyer all his clients seem to be as guilty as hell."

"Colleen! Language! But thank-you," Lily answered, showing pearly white teeth.

Colleen looked expectantly at Lily and she felt stupid did she miss something? Oh the joke! Lily hadn't laughed at Colleen's wit.

"Funny, I got it. Zebadiah Rockwood's sentencing takes place next month, but he will be held until then; no bail, no goodbyes to his favourite watering hole. As the Crown, I'll recommend the longest sentence I can get that he can serve. It's victories like these which make my job worthwhile. I don't know how much satisfaction this will give that little girl's family, but at least they'll know her killer remains in jail. He can't take another life again, because he will be incarcerated."

Lily went over to her desk and sat down.

"Can you imagine Michael Taylor, tried to use the defence that Rockwood was not drunk. Just tired? He claimed Rockwood drank only after the accident, while driving his company's truck; so the company couldn't possibly be responsible,"

"I believe you told me that before," Colleen commented, "However I'm glad you proved he'd drank so much before getting in the truck. That proved he was legally under the influence when the accident occurred. I hope I was some help in that aspect."

"Yes, you were invaluable."

"Thanks, Lily."

"It's still early; only nine forty-five, and my day's clear until what, two-thirty?"

"That's correct." Colleen replied.

Colleen checked a day planner, frowning, "Is everything okay, Lily? You seem a little down."

"Everything is fine. Amelia's grand opening starts at noon, but I promised to be there sooner if possible. If I go right now, I'll surprise her," Lily grabbed her coat to leave.

"I'm glad she's doing so well. Although after what happened, Amelia needs the encouragement. Please tell her, I'll try to get to her store another day. I hope her store has great success."

"Thank-you, I will tell Amelia. Hold all my calls Colleen. Unless it's urgent then call my cell."

"I'll do that. What time should I say you'll be back?" Colleen responded to a departing Lily.

"Tell whoever asks that I'll be back after two p.m..."

"And if they ask where you are?" Colleen questioned.

"Tell them I'm meeting with a witness," Lily replied with a wink.

"If there's cake bring me back a piece. Please, boss?" Colleen begged.

"I ordered a cake, but it's not supposed to arrive until one thirty so we'll see. I'm leaving now. Remember only urgent calls to my cell phone." Lily cautioned, leaving through the front door.

She twisted her shimmering brown hair back up into its traditional bun. Pulling out her cell phone, she dialled Amelia's store. There was no answer. How odd! Amelia must be busy putting out last minute stock.

~0~

## *A few minutes ago*

Alone male walked into the store. His left hand held a gun while his right hand steadied it. He strode in with caution. His dark brown eyes dart from corner to corner, searching for an assailant. His well over six-foot tall frame slouched. Ruggedly handsome, with dark brown hair clipped short to his head; he was dressed in a dark blue jacket and dress pants; a badge is also clipped to his belt buckle. Finding the scene secure he putting his gun away and pulled a pair of gloves out of his suit coat pocket and a pair of booties, which he slipped on his shoes.

He checked the victim. No pulse. Advancing forward, he bent down to check the second woman; her phone still in her hand, her head bloody. He noted the second victim was still breathing, though unconscious. He looked around, as if waiting for someone. Deciding they weren't coming yet, he took out a mini recorder. He started scanning the scene and speaking aloud.

"This is Sergeant Detective Emmett Rogers. I am at the scene of a homicide, at Quirks, one forty five Maple Street. A woman lays sprawled out across the floor. The woman's arms are positioned underneath her, as if to break her fall.

The back of her head and her long blonde hair are streaked in rusty-brown blood, as well as her clothing below the hair. Blood pools across the floor spiralling out in two long streams. Footprints are noticeable, as if someone stepped through the drying blood. The weapon appears to be a pair of scissors, found beneath the victim. I have marked both of these."

The man spoke aloud as he walked around, carefully avoiding contaminating the evidence, by stepping over a paper cup.

"A coffee cup... possibly one of those lattes is overturned. I'm sure the forensics team can determine this if necessary. Its contents are also spilled on the floor and countertop. Coffee is spilled at the front door and possibly on the shoes. The second victim's shoes are not on the bruised victim, but on the floor. The shoes can be found near an overturned ladder, at the front door. It appears the woman, who appears unconscious, may have been carrying a ladder and toy stock to place on the shelves, when she slipped in the blood.

The man paused to think.

"This might be a setup by the second victim to cover the actual crime. The woman, however, seems to have the victim's blood all over her clothes and hands like she crawled through the blood. I believe there are two possible scenarios here. One the owner of the shop, one Amelia Kelly (the unconscious person), murdered her employee or unknown victim and set this up to appear a perpetrator broke in and killed her accidentally hurting herself in the process. Or two... it is at it now seems that she stumbled on the crime scene and harmed herself."

He pulled out a notebook again and examined the room taking some more taking notes.

"Is it a robbery gone wrong? It is too soon to tell. The store owner will be en-route to hospital as soon as the EMTs have arrived. Interview to follow. The time is now ten twenty a.m.," he concluded turning off his recorder.

He examined the room scribbling on his notepad.

~0~

## *Now*

## *Lily and Detective Emmett Rogers*

T he man's eyes turn and his vision

focused completely. A woman entered the store. His eyes took in her tall and slender form and her long shimmering brown hair, pulled into a tight roll. He noted she was closely followed by the Emergency technicians and gave a sigh of relief. The woman entering the store had brilliant blue eyes. He had a feeling she often turned heads, even dressed as she was, in her business attire. But he noted something about the way she walked screamed money and upper class.

"Oh no, Amelia!" she screamed and tried to rush to Amelia, but was stopped by the man's arm.

"This is a crime scene ma'am. We don't want you disrupting our evidence. Let the EMTs and detectives do their job. Then you can go to ...you're er...friend?" Sergeant Detective Rogers commanded.

"Crime scene? What has happened?" Lily asked politely, wanting to be cooperative.

"Ma'am, I'll know better after I assess the scene. Until then, please remain near the front door." ordered Detective Rogers briskly.

"I promise I'll stay out of the way; but at least can I get her Adrienne Changs?"

"What or who, are Adrienne Changs?" said Detective Rogers looking totally perplexed.

"Shoes, those shoes right there!" Lily pointed to a pair of heels lying behind the yellow tape.

"You're worried about shoes? Woman! Do you have any idea of what's going on here?" Detective Rogers snapped, shaking his head.

"You sexist pig!" countered Lily under her breath,"Men!" Losing her temper now and louder she continued, "Those shoes are worth five hundred dollars! And she probably wore them for what a half an hour? And you want me to walk away and leave them to be destroyed in some kind of liquid!"

"Liquid that's blood! And five hundred dollars for shoes? Is she crazy?" Detective Rogers asked dumfounded.

"No! She's not crazy. How dare you?" Lily asked suddenly outraged.

He was smug wasn't he? Handsome yes, but oh so smug, she questioned herself. That wasn't important. Amelia was injured on the floor and he questioned her? Instead of letting her go to her cousin! What was wrong with Lily? Why was she so worried and focused on the shoes? They were only shoes. Amelia was injured; who cared about footwear?

"Sorry, ma'am, the shoes are evidence now. Name? Occupation? Address?" Detective Rogers barked, ignoring her statement.

"I want to see your identification first, and then you'll get the information," insisted Lily.

"I am Sergeant Detective Emmett Rogers," the man revealed, showing his police badge.

"Oh that's funny," Lily uttered laughing, "If you and Amelia were introduced it would be Aem and Em."

Lily followed this up by hysterically laughing and then alternatively crying. What was wrong with her? She never lost it like this. She always appeared a professional. She had seen crime scenes. She could handle this. Couldn't she? Amelia would be okay. Wouldn't she?!

"Get a hold of yourself Lily. You have embarrassed yourself," Lily heard this voice in her head, she recognized as her father's. Odd how her Dad's voice, came back to her now, she rarely saw him, since he lived in Prague and he only called about twice a year.

"Ma'am, what you are saying is not remotely funny. Are you all right? Put your head between your knees if you feel lightheaded. I think your friend's relatively fine. She might have a head injury and possibly a broken leg, but she'll be okay." Sergeant Detective Rogers then turned to the Emergency technicians (EMTs) to seek confirmation demanded, "Right?"

"Should be. But head injuries can be serious," the one EMT replied.

Sergeant Detective Rogers shot him a disapproving look.

"Yes, the Sergeant Detective is right. She'll be fine. She'll be taken to the hospital for treatment," the Emergency Technician agreed, finally.

"See...what did I tell you? Now that we have that out of the way; I need to see some identification and then get some answers to my questions. Name? Address? Occupation? The reason you are here?" Detective Rogers barked at Lily.

"Amelia's my best friend and more. This should have been the greatest day of her life, her opening of her new store; a one of kind toy and collectibles retailer. A grand opening and now it's ruined. Who did this to her?" Lily asked, uncharacteristically wringing her hands and still trying to regain her calm, as thoughts of Amelia's demise threatened to enter her mind.

"Ma'am, she slipped in blood. She hit her head on the floor and on the ladder. No one harmed her. She did this to herself," explained Sergeant Detective Rogers.

"I realize she's clumsy, but she didn't put blood there to trip in," defended Lily angrily.

"No, the blood was spilled by whoever killed the woman behind the counter."

"Someone is dead behind the counter?" Lily responded shocked and surprised.

"No comment; as I explained Ma'am this is an active crime scene. Now as I asked before what is your name?" Detective Rogers insisted forcefully again.

"Lily Kelly-Brooksfield. My husband is Horace Brooksfield, the mayor. We live down the street on Beaconfield. Do you want the number? It's nine hundred and sixty-two." she replied condescendingly.

"If you're Mayor Brooksfield's wife… then you're the Crown Attorney." Coming to this realization, Sergeant Detective Rogers hid a sigh.

"Please update me on this active crime scene, now," commanded Lily pulling back her shoulders.

Emmett Rogers put on his professional face and smiled. The smile was just so warm and inviting that Lily felt warm all over. Lily frowned back at him; she was just felt so angry. This cop who grinned back at her was the biggest reason. She was a married woman. She shouldn't be attracted to a cop who apparently existed to give her grief and solve a murder. She threw back her shoulders again. It was okay to look at someone attractive, she excused herself. Everyone looks, and most of the time it meant nothing. It's only if you acted on any attraction it became wrong. She would never act on the temptation. Besides he appeared to be the most annoying man she'd ever met.

"Ma'am, you know I can't fill you in on any of this case. You'll have to recuse yourself from this case, as you're familiar with the crime scene." Detective Rogers emphasized, once again interrupting Lily's thoughts.

"Why don't you just come out and say what you think. You consider me a suspect," Lily uttered.

"A lot of people are suspects in my book. I have to make a case for them committing the crime or I have to eliminate them as suspects. And don't attempt to solve this yourself; amateurs just get in the way." Detective Rogers explained, his eyes wandering.

Lily was slightly amused. Detective Rogers thought she wanted to insinuate herself into this murder investigation? She might not have before that comment, but she did now. He seemed to be focusing on Amelia or Lily as his prime suspect. Lily knew neither of them had committed this murder, so that meant she had no choice but to find out for herself who had committed this crime. She would pretend she wanted nothing to do with this situation, even as far as passing it off to her underling Barbara. After all she could always investigate behind the scenes.

Spotting the emergency technicians Detective Rogers exclaimed "Oh good, the ambulance has arrived to take the victim to the hospital. Now can we can get down to brass tacks; you can fill me in on these people and anything else you know or have held back from me."

"I want to go with her," Lily protested.

Lily pulled herself back taking several steps back putting distance between herself and this cop. It was odd, how alive she felt when she jousted with him. He was a cop investigating a murder and she was married.

"Stop this now Lily!" She told herself.

"Ma'am, I realize you want to go see your friend. Before I could release you from the scene, I need something from you. We need you to identify the other victim. Maybe you'll recognize her when I turn over the body." Detective Rogers explained, softening a little, as he slipped on another pair of gloves.

"Only if you'll stop calling me Ma'am. Call me Lily or Crown Attorney Kelly, but not Ma'am. It makes me feel eighty years old."

"If it will get you to identify the victim...thank-you Crown Attorney Kelly."

"Let's look, shall we?" Lily agreed.

Lily took a breath as she gathered herself to observe who lay there dead. She gasped as she stared over the counter to see the back of the woman's head. She covered her mouth in horror.

"Good grief! I never realized they appear so alike from the back," replied Lily shocked.

"Who do you think she looks like ma'am?" demanded Detective Rogers.

"What did I say about ma'am? Don't they give you sensitivity training at Police College? You want to know who this is? This is Megan, Megan Fowler. She's an employee of Amelia's. But she works evenings she's...is....was a college student. I can't believe this is Megan. Megan is such a sweet girl and worked part-time to be able to go to school and support her mother. Why would someone kill her? Do you think it's possible someone mistook her for Amelia?" Lily rambled, tears slipping from her eyes.

"That's a possibility, ma'am. We will explore all aspects."

"I know the drill, Sergeant Detective Rogers." Lily gave the detective a mock salute, "Why can't you admit that they mistook Megan for Amelia?"

"We don't have any of the facts yet, Ms. Kelly," replied Detective Rogers.

"What about Amelia? Is she in any danger?" asked Lily. "If I were to speculate, I suppose that could be a possibility," Detective Rogers answered non-committally.

They both watched as the technicians gathered the evidence and blood samples and took pictures before the body was taken away.

"Will someone be assigned to guard her and keep her safe?" Lily asked getting exasperated.

"That's in motion, Crown Attorney Kelly," Detective Rogers explained, trying not to sound annoyed that she's telling him how to do his job.

427
S. G. Lee

Detective Rogers and Lily turned as another cop swaggered into the store. Burly and well over six feet tall, his hair was dark like Detective Rogers. Unlike Detective Rogers, this man preened like a peacock; Lily was aware of the type. Guys like him smiled with their mouths and not their eyes. They thought all women should admire them and only them. She noted his smile went as far as his lips.

"What have you got here, Emmett?"

"Nothing you need to be concerned about, Brad," Detective Rogers replied, obvious tension showing between the two.

"You should be able to get some great publicity out of this one," Brad said loudly to Detective Rogers.

Brad then strutted over to the murder scene.

"It's my case, Brad," Detective Rogers insisted.

"I'm not trying to interfere," Brad persisted walking around, "I just thought if you needed some help I would lend a hand. It doesn't look like something you could handle on your own."

"I don't need help, thanks, Brad. I don't need you messing up my crime scene." Detective Rogers declared "I've got it all under control.

"It doesn't look that way to me. I would solve this case quickly. You could use me in your corner," Brad continued.

"We don't need you. Now the Crown attorney is here, so I have it all in hand. Goodbye, Brad." Detective Rogers practically spat.

"Ah, the lovely Crown attorney Kelly is here. Can't go now," Brad exclaimed trying to sound charming but failing miserably.

"And you are?" asked Lily putting her full aristocratic chill in to her voice.

"I'm Brad Owens, at your service, Attorney Kelly. Sergeant Detective Brad Owens. I use to be Emmett's partner," Brad explained smiling and pointing to Detective Rogers.

Detective Rogers rolled his eyes. "Thank God you're not anymore," He stated under his breath loud enough for only he and Lily to hear.

"So what do you think, Crown Attorney? Was it a robbery gone wrong?" asked Brad.

"I'm not sure. Why do I bother to tell you this? This isn't your case," Lily commented suddenly not willing to share with Brad.

She didn't know why. Something about his smile, and the way Emmett Rogers had reacted to him made her dislike him. Brad's smile was phony, like a used car salesman. It was slick and slimy. That wasn't fair to used car sales people. Lily was sure they were more honest than this phoney, Brad Owens. Lily had come across a lot of people in her job. She certainly felt she was a good judge of character. In fact, she could spot a phoney a mile away. Detective Emmett Rogers, unlike Brad Owens, appeared like he knew his job. She'd heard of him many times, but had never run into him on the job until today. Thank goodness for the Internet on her phone. He was a dedicated cop. He had done his time and had come up through the ranks, strictly on merit. Detective Rogers didn't seem to like Brad Owens and that was reason enough for Lily not to trust him.

Emmett Rogers had an exemplary record as a police officer; she trusted his instincts and knowledge over this smarmy, Detective Brad Owens. He'd get to the bottom of this. Lily wished he would let her leave soon and check on Amelia. They had spent their teen years together and were as close as sisters. She'd always felt responsible for Amelia, being two years older. She wanted to make sure Amelia was okay.

"Okay. Well if you don't need my help, I'm leaving because I have work to do. There are other crimes to investigate." Brad answered leaving, "See you around Emmett."

"Not if I see you first," muttered Emmett under his breath.

"So am I free to go?" Lily demanded.

Emmett then offered her his pen.

"I have your address, so as long as you sign here in my notebook. "You are free to go," he said gesturing.

Lily glanced over at Detective Owens and watched him leave before reaching for the book. She then signed her signature with a flourish. Detective Rogers scanned the signature, thinking momentarily it was just as elegant as Lily. He shook his head, reminding himself to stay connected to reality.

"So I am free to go, Detective?" Lily repeated.

"I'll be checking in on your friend, of course, and I may need to follow-up with

you later, but as of now, you are free to go."
he smiled, already exhausted.

"I would expect nothing else from you,
Detective Rogers."

As she got into her car, Lily breathed a sigh
of relief she had finally been able to leave
the store. She buckled up her seatbelt and
put her car in gear.

Backing the car up, Lily pulled out into the
street and narrowly missed getting hit by a
car, she didn't view. Luckily the other driver
slammed on his brakes. She noticed the male
driver shouting, "Stupid woman driver" as
she read his lips in her rear view mirror. He
was justified in his anger. It had been her
fault, but she didn't have time to dwell.

She headed down the road toward the
hospital; despite her resolve her mind
wandered. She thought about poor Megan's
mother getting the news of her daughter's
death. It would kill Lily to get news like that
about her adopted daughter, Rose.

What kind of monster kills a young woman? Why did, whomever it was, have to kill Megan? It wasn't a robbery, she'd read in Detective Rogers' notes, when he gave his notebook to her to sign her statement. As Lily drove, more questions flooded into her head. Was Amelia the real target? Megan certainly appeared like Amelia from the back.

Amelia didn't appear too hurt. Maybe she suffered a concussion? Concussions could be serious; she knew from her readings. The EMT hadn't said Amelia was in serious condition though. Not that the EMT could explain before Emmett Rogers got on his case. Revving the engine, she waited impatiently for the light to go green. Once Lily reached the hospital, she could reassure herself, Amelia was all right.

~0~

# Excerpt from Love's Labour's

# Won

Coming to book form soon available in e-book
now

Preface:

### <u>Love's Labour's Won</u>

# S*arah sought a job,*

*Biting back a sob,*

*Her love and life,*

*All constant strife,*

*And filled with unbroken sorrow,*

*Like there was no tomorrow.*

*She thought her future,*

*Safely to be assured,*

*Instead of that Sarah found,*

*Many wonders to astound,*

*The world changed forever,*

*Yet the pull of a tether,*

*For the prize she sought,*

*And the joy and pain it wrought,*

*And all that she had done,*

*Was "Love's Labour's Won"*

*By S.G. Lee*

# Chapter 1 - Want Ads

Life was getting Sarah down. She was twenty one years old and what did she have to show for it? Did she have a career? No, she didn't. Did life produce a boyfriend, husband or children? Another no! Or even a significant other? She had no one, no one to care if she lived or died. She had worked so many dead end jobs; too many to count.

She had once been a Wal-Mart Greeter and even spent a winter as a telemarketer selling lawn services for the upcoming spring. She failed miserably not making that job a success either. Numerous hang-ups ensued and no sales.

They kept her for a month and then said…"I'm sorry you're not working out."

Like, duh. She didn't complete any sales.
She had to make a living somehow.

She scanned the want ads. There remained
lots of jobs for coffee servers, but she was so
tired of smiling andserving food to people.
Then she spotted the ad, the ad which made
her sit up and take notice.

*Companion wanted.*

*Must be young presentable and personable.*

*Apply by phone at 555-5555 only serious
inquires need apply.*

*Must have two references*

What was this some kind of weird scam
luring young woman to their peril? Really,
how dramatic was she being?

Sarah normally ignored such an ad, but she
was getting short on cash and the rent was
due next week.

She didn't have the eight hundred and fifty
dollars the landlord wanted for this

dump…err…wonderful furnished apartment. She'd be out on the street if she didn't earn some money. It wasn't like she had a lot of friends, which she could ask to crash on their sofas. Melanie would have let her, but she was off on a modeling job in France. Melanie had sublet her apartment to a yuppie couple that obviously didn't know Sarah.

Should I or shouldn't I call? Sarah thought. I mean was it safe? What if the employers subsisted as white slavers?The people Gran were always warning her about growing up? Gran's notions bordered on the ridiculous, of course. So I should just seize the opportunity. Sarah thought. Gran was gone and so were her worrisome and outdated ideas. Sarah looked at the ads again.

*Barista wanted must have previous experience and two references.*

*Must be prepared to clean and carry up to 40 pounds of product.*

The ad's specifications were a new take on the job. They were warning people that they would be heavy lifting. Hmm, generally they told you this when you started the job. But forty pounds, what the heck?

Were they having the baristas carry coffee beans? There had to be another job offer somewhere in these online sites. She scanned the ads once again.

No nothing in the ads but a companion job. A companion job didn't sound so bad. Did it? She needed a job and jobs were scarce that she qualified for right now. She had to at least try to get the job didn't she? She took a huge breath and dialled the number.

"Hello," the voice said on the other end of the line.

A real live person answered instead of the answering machine Sarah expected. Sarah took another deep breath.

"Uh I'd like to apply for the job; you placed in the Free Press." She replied with all the enthusiasm she could muster.

"I see… and what makes you believe you're the person we are looking for?" Asked the voice on the other end of the line

"I like people and people like me. I am often stopped by strangers and they always seem compelled to tell me their complete life histories," Sarah replied.

"Uh huh, and how do you respond to these indignities to your peace and quiet?" asked the voice.

"Well I am aware not everyone would listen, I find it fascinating to hear the stories people tell and to just listen if that's what they need. In some way I feel I can help them. It's not an intrusion," Sarah answered without even thinking.

"I comprehend one such as you, may have led a very difficult life. People do not always return the kindness to that you seem to offer so freely. You are an old soul," replied the voice sounding distinctively male, and little too familiar.

"Well…I don't know if this is odd or what but a long time ago I decided I liked me. If others find me a Pollyanna; a person who is too kind, too naive for the world, that's their problem. I like being different even if others think me odd, I can only be me. Oh, I can't believe I'm telling you this, in a job interview no less. Now you'll never hire me and I'm sorry I've wasted your time, sir." Sarah responded embarrassed and about to hang up.

"Miss, please don't hang up. I think you are an excellent potential candidate for this rather unique job."

"You think I might be the person you want?" asked Sarah incredulously.

"Well clearly my employer would have the final say, but you sound as if you might make my short list of candidates."

"Not to make you mad or anything and lose my chance at this job; but don't you think you should know more about me?"

"I am a very good judge of character. That's why my employer trusts me in this manner," stated the man with an almost mesmerizing voice. Sarah felt herself believing every word he said.

"Wow, you must be in a prestigious job," replied Sarah without thinking again.

"The only possible drawback to your employment might be your tendency to forthcoming with your thoughts. Do you do this often Miss?"

"Miss Sarah Dexler, and no I don't usually blurt out everything. There is simply something about you."

Sarah realized her blunder. "Sorry I'm doing it again I don't know what has come over me. I promise I'm not typically like this and would guard myself with your employer."

"Never fear Miss Dexler. I'm a good judge of character and you seem to be nice and kind. My employer needs kindness, and someone who will listen most of all. You said you do that with strangers. You listen and help others, so that makes you a candidate we simply must see."

The man suddenly sounded very interested and in the next second he surprised Sarah with, "So would you be available for an interview tomorrow at 3 PM?"

"Yes, of course," Sarah became tentative. "I guess I could."

"Obviously given the generalities of our ad some applicants have been taken back and would like assurances of our trust worthiness. My employer, though he wishes to remain anonymous until the candidates are found, will be quite happy to provide references for himself.

Confidentiality agreements are signed as well. These, of course, will be provided at the interview stage. Interviews will be conducted at our temporary office at 1000 Park Street. We look forward to seeing you there Miss Dexler. Goodbye," the man ended the call abruptly.

Sarah closed her cell phone and thought… how strange this man appeared so mesmerizing on the phone He even seemed to snatch thoughts from her head. It was all a bit odd. Then as she thought some more she realized even stranger he had forgotten to share his name. Had she distracted the poor man? Why had he forgotten to share his name? His English upper crust accent sounded so prim, proper and professional it seemed even peculiar to her now that he did not reveal his name. Still, she hoped this job would pan out or in a few days she'd be begging on the street corner.

~0~

## *Chapter 2 - Venimus, Vidimus, Vicimus*

S arah was in a hurry. She tried on every

outfit she owned for this interview. Most of her wardrobe now lay strewn across her bed or floor. She finally settled on this black pantsuit. The tailored jacket was flattering and her pants that went with the jacket sculpted her rear end. Not that was necessary in an interview but it gave her a lift. She felt like a model in this outfit. A tall shapely model, because of these four inch heels on her black sandals. They had cost her quite a fortune when she was pulling in a paycheque, but they were worth every penny. Sarah felt beautiful and hope her confidence would translate into a job. She really needed this job.

She entered the door at one thousand Park Street. The building was one of those non-

descript glass buildings without about forty
floors. She entered the building and realized
the man on the phone had not given her the
office number only the building number
address. Without the office number she was
lost. She could take the elevator but to
where?

Sarah was in near tears thinking maybe the
whole conversation with that man was a
joke, a terrible joke on her. She spent her
last five dollars to take a cab, so she
wouldn't be late. She was lost.... the job was
lost. Oh no even worse she'd be out on the
street in a few days.

No, she couldn't let that happen. She had
told the man on the phone she was good
with people. That she could charm total
strangers into telling their stories, so here
was the time to prove it. She'd find the
office. It might take a little talking; asking
people questions that would lead to the
office number. But surely being late would
be excused when he realized he forgot to tell
her the office number. Sarah began by
talking to the receptionist at the desk in the
hallway. She approached the young woman
and she was almost taken aback. The
receptionist appeared gorgeous her hair a

beautiful honey blonde and cascading down in corkscrew ringlets. The receptionist's bright blue eyes were like diamonds and red lipstick finished the face that could launch a thousand ships. She was dressed in a very tight red dress. It didn't seem quite appropriate for the office, but who was Sarah to judge? Sarah couldn't help but wonder if this was the type of beauty that they hired here if so she was in trouble. She couldn't compete with someone so incredibly lovely, or wear those oh so revealing clothes.

"Hi, my name is Sarah. I have a little problem I'm hoping that someone as knowledgeable and as intelligent as you are, could help me with," Sarah began.

" That's so flattering you think I can help you. People tend to treat me like a bit of an airhead because I'm a receptionist it's my job to assist people. I guess my parents didn't do me any favours by naming me Brandy," babbled Brandy breathlessly while snapping her gum.

"Oh, your name is Brandy? You know, some say Brandy is better than fine wine," Sarah piled on the charm.

"I'm not... you know.... so if ...you know if that's what this is all about you can stop right there. Nothing against your preferences, but I'm seeing a guy," replied Brandy awkwardly misunderstanding.

"Oh no....no .... Really, there's nothing to worry about. I am straight too. I'm here trying to get a job. You see, I applied for this job, but the man on the phone forgot to tell me the office number where the interview is," explained Sarah.

"That's difficult because there's tons of offices in this building. Do you know what the guy looks like?" asked Brandy looking at her red painted fingernails and sliding a nail file over them.

"Sadly no, you see I talked to the man on the phone. He had an upper crust British accent though. Does that help you identify him for me?" begged Sarah.

"Oh you are so in luck today." Brandy replied, "We have only one guy who talks like that here. Mr. Poundstone. He's conducting interviews today too so he is probably your man."

"Oh thank you so much Brandy, you don't know how much this means to me. Oh wait a minute I have a coupon for a free coffee, here this for you," answered Sarah digging the coupon out of her purse.

"But if you're looking for a job you must need the coupon."

"I wanted to let you know how much I truly appreciated your help," Sarah insisted sincerely.

"You are a really nice person Sarah; I hope you get the job. Maybe we can share a coffee break when you do. You know... if you end up working in this building. Now the office number for Mr. Poundstone is 304. And just because I want you to get the job, if anyone asks for the number because he forgot to tell them I won't tell them," Brandy insisted winking.

"Oh no, that wouldn't be right," asserted Sarah, although delighted. "If they ask please tell them. If this job is meant to be I'll get the position."

"Did anyone ever tell you Sarah, you're too nice for your own good?" asked Brandy, as Sarah walked towards the elevator.

"Yes, people do say I'm too nice. But I can't be any different than I am," Sarah answered turning back to Brandy. Sarah then entered the elevator waving goodbye to Brandy.

The elevator reached the third floor and Sarah glanced at her watch, she realized she wasn't late at all; it was only 2:55 p.m. She was early, how amazing. She stepped off the elevator to find a room full of women of varying ages, shapes, sizes and colours. Sarah couldn't help but noticing the other women appeared all extremely attractive.

Oh, so I'm not the only one up for the job, Sarah thought as she entered into room. If she had it her way when she left today she'd have the job despite all these beauties. No second interviews, or third interview. This wasnt a beauty contest after all. She would win this job. She was as sure of it as she was that her name was Sarah Dexler; Sarah thought proudly as she remembered the family Dexler motto."*Venimus, Vidimus, Vicimus*". It meant "We came. We saw. We conquered!

Sure, her ancestors had blatantly borrowed the saying from Caesar, but it was a good motto to live by and inspired confidence. Of course, if you could use your God-given charm and win the day why shouldn't you? She didn't think you had to use your attitude violently or cruelly, like a sword. A charming disposition worked as well or better than the sword and without drawing blood.

Sarah steeled herself marched up to the receptionist and confidently said…"Sarah Dexler, I have appointment at 3 pm."

"Yes, Miss Dexler, your name is here. Please take a seat. Mr. Poundstone will be with you momentarily," the receptionist said hardly looking up from her desk.

The office door opened and a congenial looking man came out. If Sarah were to describe him she would describe a dignified Santa, maybe an Edmund Gwenn style from Miracle on 34th Street. His appearance was stylish and dignified, like an upper crust Englishman, suiting his voice on the phone. His suit was a gray Burbury throughout. His hair trimmed short and he had a tiny white moustache. He seemed to be in his sixties.

"Miss Dexler I presume?" Mr. Poundstone looked straight into her eyes.

"Yes, I am Sarah Dexler," Sarah stood tall and threw her shoulders back, holding out her right hand which he clasped firmly with both his hands.

"I am Harry Poundstone. What a great pleasure to meet you in person. I worried I had steered you wrong as I remembered not giving you my office number. But I can see you are as good as your word and you obviously found me. Please do come into my office so we can discuss the particulars of this job and your qualifications for the position," said Mr. Poundstone, while still smiling.

"Certainly, I would be happy to Mr. Poundstone," replied Sarah while stepping into his office.

Mr. Poundstone continued to smile even more broadly, almost unnerving Sarah.

"Miss Dexler I didn't want to tell you in front of all those job applicants, but we decided to give the job to you," Mr. Poundstone declared with great flourish.

"Me? But you didn't even interview me? Are you sure?" Sarah was shocked but rambled on, "Well, of course if you are sure or you wouldn't have said so. Oh I'm doing it again. There's just something about you that makes me do that. Oh did I just say that aloud. Sorry," Sarah, blurted, and then blanching, asked…"Do you still want me for this job?"

Mr. Poundstone couldn't help but be amused.

"Miss Dexler. Or may I call you Sarah?" asked Mr. Poundstone.

"Please do, Mr. Poundstone," Sarah replied

"Please, would you care for some of this freshly steeped tea? Or, would you prefer coffee?"

"Yes, I would love some tea, two sugars and a little cream please," answered Sarah

"Huh, exactly how I made your tea. Most people prefer milk rather than cream. It's Harry actually. Please call me Harry. Mr. Poundstone is so formal," expressed Mr. Poundstone, and then followed quickly with, "Where do you see yourself in five years Sarah?"

"Well I could lie and say I see myself in an executive position but the truth is I want it all. I want a career that fulfills me and I want children and a husband."

What a weird start to the interview, Sarah thought. Why, oh why, had she mentioned she desired a husband and children? Was she sharing things that were too personal? Were there bounds that were being overstepped ?There had to be something in the tea, a truth scrum perhaps? What was it about this man? What caused her to blurt out exactly what she was thinking? What possessed her?" He would think she didn't want this job and would leave at the first opportunity.

Sarah continued thinking knowing she needed to reassure Mr. Poundstone her priority was this job. "Oh, but I can tell you I see this position as a real opportunity to gain experience…"

Sarah wanted to continue but could not. She could not hide her suspicion and was suddenly compelled to ask "Did you put something in my tea to make me tell you only the truth and in fact say everything I am thinking?"

"No, but I'm finding this conversation absolutely amazing," Mr. Poundstone replied smiling and Sarah suddenly found his constant smile slightly creepy.

"What's amazing?" asked Sarah bravely, "That for some unknown reason, I believe that you have the power to mesmerize and draw words from people?"

Mr. Poundstone just grinned even wider like he knew a secret, a secret that Sarah didn't know but needed to uncover.

"Holy cow, I can't believe it. That's it isn't it? You have some unusual power and I can feel it. You can get people to tell you what they are really thinking," Sarah exclaimed while truly surprised by her own words.

Mr. Poundstone reached into his jacket and pulled out a pocket watch which he proceeded to open. The watch was gold and attached to a long chain.

"This is truly amazing. I have never encountered anyone with such acuity. Two minutes, that's all it took for you to perceive the unusualness of our conversation. Most people who have any ability require days to detect my power, but you became aware it within less than two minutes."

Mr. Poundstone's next words shook Sarah to her core.

"He said you would be the one. I heard glimmers of your abilities in our phone conversation, but he was absolutely right. This is so truly, truly astonishing." His voice became high pitched with excitement, almost maniacal, and belied the dignified image he had shown earlier.

"Uh…Ok… I'm going to leave now." Sarah had become slightly frightened of the nature of Mr. Poundstone's behaviour, "But no harm, no foul."

"Oh please my dear lady, do not be frightened of me or my employer. I know I am not explaining this well but we've looked so long for one like you…"

Sarah found this last statement even more disturbing.

"That's okay but I think I'm going," Sarah replied reaching for the door handle.

"Please Sarah, I beg of you, give myself and my employer another chance. Wouldn't you like to find out the real reason why we chose you? Don't you want to be aware of the untapped power that you alone hold?" Mr. Poundstone begged again with his voice once again deep and compelling.

"No! If you have some deep dark plan for me you can just forget it," Sarah turned the doorknob and continued to try to make her escape. "Quit trying to compel me. I know you're doing it. I don't understand how you're doing it but I can grasp you are doing it."

"I apologize but it is sometimes hard to turn off one's gift," Mr. Poundstone stated calmly. "Did you ever wonder where you came from? Who your parents were? Who were your other relatives? Sarah, we know you started life in Foster Care."

Sarah retorted, her fear changing to anger. "How dare you? That…has nothing to do with a job interview. How did you access those records? You didn't even have my social security number?"

"I know a lot about you Sarah Marie Dexler. For instance I know your real last name is Maidenstone. The Dexler's adopted you when you were four years old, and isn't the truth, before they adopted you, you did not speak."

Tears formed in Sarah's eyes and her anger grew. "I'm going to report you and your agency to the Better Business Bureau, the police, and a lawyer; in that order. You have absolutely no right to snoop into my life."

"I've hurt you and that was not my intention. I know your grandfather and if he could have found you, believe me, he would have. He would have taken you from that foster home. It really wasn't his fault. Your parents disappeared without a trace in America. They were British citizens, born in Coventry, England. Your grandfather was not even aware of your existence. He found out six years after they had perished, that his beloved daughter and her husband had died. He went crazy with grief, and we despaired that we would never get him back again. But he did recover over time, albeit never to the same contented state. But, he discovered by searching through numerous records that she had a given birth to daughter; that daughter was you. And he asked me to find you."

"So this was all a ruse? There is no job? Of course there is no job! Why…why am I still here? Did you hypnotize me? All this because you say my so called grandfather wants to meet me?"

Sarah was going to tell Mr. Poundstone, he was a very bad man, but he cut her off.

"Needless to say, your grandfather waits anxiously to meet you in person. Moreover, he is well aware of your current predicament and has an exciting job…mmm…opportunity, he wants to discuss with you. But I'm afraid, I have been forbidden to share the particulars with you at this time."

"I don't know about this. None of this seems right. A strange man tells me I possess a grandfather, a grandfather who didn't come forward to me when I was young? And now he wants to meet me? And then he expects me to just take a job from him?" Sarah composed herself. "I just don't know. This is a lot to take in."

"Think about meeting him. Please," begged
Mr. Poundstone. "You won't be sorry if you
agree to this meeting. Your grandfather is a
wonderful and wise man."

Mr. Poundstone couldn't help but smile
slightly at the corners of his mouth but he
kept his eyes penetratingly fixed on Sarah's
own deep gaze.

Mr. Poundstone mused out loud, "What if I
go tell the other applicants to come back
another day for an interview for the actual
job I brought them here for?"

"Please don't keep them waiting. If there's
an honest job for them at least interview
them. I can wait in the lobby," Sarah replied,
relieved the other women were not being
duped. And, she realized, she was not
surprised Mr. Poundstone sensed her
concern for those who unwittingly helped
him in his duplicity.

"No, please, I have another office here, I'll
interview them there. Just please… take
your time. Have a cup from the freshly
steeped pot of tea and I hope you'll make the
decision you will see your grandfather,"
begged Mr. Poundstone while leaving the
room.

"Fine... I'll wait...but I'm still not sure," Sarah exclaimed with exasperation to Mr. Poundstone's departing back.

In a room next to the one where Sarah waited, a man watched through a two way mirror. From his side he could see her seated in the chair in front of Mr. Poundstone's desk. The man was mature, his hair greyed at the temples and sides but with a shock of black hair that ran through the middle of his thick mane. He was tall and stood over six feet, possibly as tall as six feet six inches. He was broad shouldered and lean looking while surprisingly well muscled.

He looked to be about sixty, or maybe sixty five years of age, but he moved with the ease of a much younger man; as he paced back and forth with his focus on the mirror. Dressed in a suit tailored perfectly for him, he exuded confidence. He seemed mesmerized as he intently surveyed Sarah though the glass. He appeared somewhat amused, that he knew Sarah was unaware that she was being watched.

The door opened to the chamber, where the tall man stood watching. Mr. Poundstone walked into this room with a much different demeanour, than the one he displayed when he had earlier greeted Sarah. Mr. Poundstone lowered his head and seemed hesitant to approach. He moved forward cautiously as if any misstep could trigger an explosion like bomb in a minefield.

"This is the one? This is she? No mistakes this time?" the man demanded harshly while taking a seat.

"Yes, my lord, this is the one. I promise there has been no mistake this time. As promised, I supervised this one myself," replied Harry Poundstone, his voice very subservient.

"Good. What did you tell her?" asked the tall man.

"I told her you were her grandfather and you kept looking for her, just as we rehearsed. I told her you grieved for her mother and searched for her as soon as you knew she existed."

"Marvellous Harry, a falsehood that is so close to the truth is always so much more believable," said the tall man pleased.

"I hope this makes up for the failure of my operatives last year?" asked Mr. Poundstone meekly, obviously seeking approval.

"It does if this is truly her!" replied the tall man, Sarah's grandfather. "Does she show any essence of her mother? Or is she only tainted by him?"

"The taint is there my lord. I am sorry my lord…but if there is any of you in her I see none of it." Mr. Poundstone cowered as he said this, expecting to be castigated. He was all too familiar with the consequences of failing to please his master, through words or deeds.

"I'm sure you are mistaken. She is of my line after all. I think I have seen glimmers of myself. If not, while then it is decided," pronounced the tall man, dismissing the matter.

"Must we, Lord Eccklestone?" Mr. Poundstone dared to ask.

"Are you questioning me? You dare to question me?" demanded Lord Eccklestone.

The tall man's face turned purple and his rage consumed the entire room. To Mr. Poundstone it seemed as if darkness surrounded him, only broken by the fierce glower of his lord's penetrating eyes.

"No sir, of course I am not questioning you. I would never dare," replied Mr. Poundstone submissively, mollifying him.

The pair continued to observe Sarah unbeknownst as she waited anxiously in the adjoining office. Sarah found herself consumed by many thoughts that raged incessantly through her mind. A grandfather searched for her? She had family, but a family that took this long to come forward? Could the story really be true, that he just couldn't find her until now? What an incredible story, much like a fairy tale. Those usually didn't end well.

What of Mr. Poundstone? He was to say, a very unusual man. True. Still there was something not quite right about him. At times she felt he seemed a jovial Santa Claus, but could it just be a false persona? If Mr. Poundstone wasn't who he pretended to be, then how could she trust that this man would put her in touch with her real grandfather?

Maybe she should just leave. But, if he did know her grandfather and he could put them in touch maybe she should give him a chance? Mr. Poundstone was distinctly odd, almost chilling with this strange power he had. He actually eluded she might have one as well, a power. That, of course, was ludicrous stuff and definitely nonsense. Then there was the fact that he had snooped in her personal business.

He had found out facts that she had never told anyone. It was like stripping her bare. She wasn't happy about that. What did she really know about these people? Only what he, Mr. Poundstone, had told her? She had already found out he had a power that made people believe and do what he wanted them to do; so why was she sitting here waiting for Mr. Poundstone? Or waiting for this man that claimed to be her grandfather?

How trustworthy was a man who manipulated people with some spellbinding ability and made them do what he wanted? She suddenly became afraid again. There was something definitely not quite right about this and she felt it down to her very bones. If her grandfather had truly wanted to meet her there was no need for this deception. And why were so many people interested in a companion job? And why were they all attractive young women? These thoughts had just entered her mind. What had prevented these thoughts before?

There were just too many things that didn't
add up here.

So what was wrong with her that she hadn't
bolted all ready? Mr. Poundstone had used
some of his power on her; that was the only
explanation. The power that she was starting
to believe he really possessed. Was it some
kind of hypnotism? She was leaving now,
this very minute, before something bad
happened.

Just then the door opened to Mr.
Poundstone's office and Sarah watched a
man enter. He was tall, dark haired and
mysterious looking. His hair was raven
coloured, his eyes blue and piercing and his
gaze centered on her. He was muscular and
dynamic looking and he just seemed to be
one of those people that drew upon all eyes
upon them. Simply put, this man radiated
power and one could not help but put all
focus on his presence.

It was odd though when he came in the
room it was like time stopped. She looked at
the clock on Mr. Poundstone's desk and
realized that it wasn't as if time had stopped,
it actually had. The circumstances were
getting more bizarre for Sarah the more she

went along today. Had she really gotten up this morning, or was this all a dream?

As she gazed upon the man he spoke…"Come on then, we have to leave now." he requested of her.

"We…we have to leave now? I don't think so. I have had enough with you weird people. I don't understand what is going on but I'm not going anywhere with you," Sarah reacted, annoyed.

"I don't have time to explain this to you. You deserve explanations, but we definitely don't have time. This only lasts so long. It takes so much power and energy, that it's very draining. We have to go now. We have to be away from here before I lose my power, which could be at any moment," said the man urgently.

"Again with the power? I'm getting out of here but not with you. I don't want to see any of you weirdoes ever again," replied a disgusted Sarah.

"Fine, just come with me now. Let us leave and get away now!" pleaded the man.

"I don't even know your name. I'm not going anywhere with you. I'm going home,"

Sarah's anger grew and she was very determined to get away.

"They know where you live. They want something from that you don't even know you have," The man then said cryptically "They are not nice people. You don't understand the lengths they will go to or the things they have done."

"Enlighten me then," Sarah demanded.

"I told you there isn't time. Please I beg of you, come with me now."

"And you are? And I should come with you because? I'm tired of this. You and all these other people just come into my life making impossible demands."

"You can do things that aren't possible or real. Oh…just go away and leave me be"

"My name is Demetrious Blackstone and we are sort of related. I promise I'll tell you more once we are away from here." Then seeing her face he added, "I know all of this is difficult for you to understand and I will explain when we get away from here but we must get away now."

He then took Sarah's hands and pulled her to her feet. Moments later they are out the door. Sarah wasn't sure how they got to the waiting room so fast. Or even why she didn't fight back and resist but here they were. In this room Sarah saw all the people she had before, but there was still not a ripple of movement. Time was stood still and it seemed as if only they moved through it. It was all so unreal and peculiar. Demetrious opened the front door of the building and they passed out into the street. Cars were stilled, not moving at all as time and space stood still. Not even a breeze blowing. Sarah was amazed and frightened all at once. What was going on?

"How long will this last?" asked Sarah.

"Not much longer. We must be long away when it stops. He will know it was I and come after us," warned Demetrious ominously.

"I'm going home," insisted Sarah, afraid but determined.

"Do you not understand their fierce abilities? Don't you understand the danger you are in?" Demetrious asked, staring at Sarah. Then slowly searching her face he sighed and said…"No, of course you don't. How could you know that there is a great peril to you here? This man, who is your grandfather, is a kin to a vampire. He finds power from innocents, from those who are not aware of their power. He then takes their power from them and not in a pleasant way, I assure you. What he leaves of these people is a nothing but a zombie like creature; a creature that only exists to obey their lord and master; your grandfather. Or, if he chooses, they are left a broken soul whose mind is completely stripped, so they function only on a basic  primitive level."

Sarah did not believe her ears and denied everything the man was saying.

"This is all so utterly ridiculous. I'm starting to think that Mr. Poundstone drugged me, so I'm very glad you got me out of there Mr. Blackstone. I thank you for everything you have done so far but I'm going home. Now!"

"I am sorry I have to do this to you. I wouldn't if it wasn't necessary to protect you. But you don't even realize the great power you hold and how and what could happen if someone as unscrupulous as your Grandfather got a hold of that power."

Demetrious gripped the back of her neck gently with the fullness of his hand and Sarah began to feel light headed. Slowly the world seemed to fade away and she fell into a deep unconsciousness.

~0~

## Excerpt from Dreams Can Kill

## Chapter 1- Survival

T he rain pelted down on me, as I

struggled to come to my senses. My head felt like it had split in two, as if little lumberjacks had taken up residence. I opened one eye. The world spun sideways like a ride at the fair. I tried shutting one eye, then the other. I nearly fell back to sleep. I opened my eyes again, fighting the sleep which wanted to overtake me. I shuttered my eyes again, as my stomach protested. My whole body manipulated, bruised, bent and broken like some old rag doll discarded.

Sleep...sleep would solve my problems, my brain protested. No! I had a reason I needed to stay awake and alert...A little sleep, a part of me protested again. No, I must stay conscious. But I remained so tired. I dragged myself across the pebbled ground. My right leg stuck out at an impossible angle, obviously broken. I saw by lifting my head slightly and turning it that there appeared to be a road up ahead. I had to get to the road. If I dragged myself that far, surely I would be rescued?

But it was oh so hard, to drag yourself backwards, when you couldn't perceive where you were going. Oh no, what if he came back. He would finish me off...finish what he had started.

He who? Who was this person, who left me to die? Why couldn't I remember? Don't panic… the thing to do is right now is to reach help; then and only then would I be safe. I caressed large pieces of gravel which cut into the back of my head. I sensed I was close to the road. I reached out with my good hand and touched a paved surface.

I knew I didn't have much strength left. I
experienced the energy drain quickly
leaving my body. I tried to fight the drain,
but the world faded to black.

~0~

## *Chapter 2- Time Flies When You're Having Fun*

I opened my eyes slowly. A tube

appeared to have been inserted in my arm, feeding me intravenously, another tube down my throat as well. The lumberjacks in my head had been replaced by a dull achy sensation, as if I wasn't quite there. I suffered from weakness all over, but my body didn't have the same sensation, as when I had blacked out on the road. My leg felt whole again and yet my leg didn't appear to be in a cast, or slung up on a tripod. How much time had passed? This definitely looked like a hospital room. The walls were pale white and I lay in a single bed. I rested in a private room how about that?

A nurse in a white cap entered the room. She grabbed my wrist and she proceeded to take my pulse. Alarmed, she stared straight into my face, "Well! Look who is awake. Welcome back to the real world," she proclaimed.

I tried to speak and realized the tube in my throat prevented that. Why was a tube in my throat I wondered? How long I been here? I assumed I looked scared because the nurse explained in a soft voice, "There, there honey, you take deep breaths, easy now."

"Why don't I go get the doctor? He can come and have a look at you and remove the tube from your throat."

I tried to nod my head in agreement but my head moved like lead. It seemed like eons before a man in a white doctor's coat appeared at my bedside. He appeared tall and lanky; with dark curly brown hair and warm deep blue eyes. Without any preamble he announced, "We will now remove this tube. Take a big breath now."

The tube came out as I gagged. Now I could ask the questions which plagued me.

"How did I get here? And where am I?" I tried to ask, croaking out the words, as if my voice hadn't been used in a while.

"Speak slowly. Here, have sips of water," answered the doctor.

"How did I get here?" I repeated, sure that I had been speaking clearer because I had taken a sip of water.

"I don't know who found you, but an ambulance brought you here in critical condition. You had a broken leg, some broken ribs, and a fractured skull."

"I came here in critical condition? So I've been here awhile?" I asked shocked.

"Yes, you've been here awhile. You were at a different hospital first. You are in Andrews' clinic now."

"Your condition appeared to be perilous there for some time. They lost you twice. We had placed you in a coma to let your brain swelling go away. Then we didn't know if you would ever come out of the coma."

He continued to explain like he couldn't quite find the words. But why would a doctor have trouble explaining a medical condition?

"I guess time flies when you have fun," I stated flippantly, hiding fear I didn't quite understand and becoming puzzled.

Why did he say first they then we? Hadn't he been there?

"I would like to examine you to see how you're doing now and get an update on your condition."

"I'm good. As you can see," I answered in response.

"I don't know if you even realize, but your speech isn't as clear as you think. You're slurring your words," he stated. "I'm sure the words will come easier in time, but I'd like to check your reaction time and some other physical reactions."

What could he be talking about? I wasn't slurring my words. Was I?

The doctor began his examination. A flashlight flashed deep into my eyes. I blinked in response, as the light, so bright, made my eyes hurt. His response seemed to be to write down something on the chart, and pick up my wrist to take my pulse and blood pressure. He then listened to my chest with his stethoscope.

I moved my head and tried to sit up, but the effort zapped all my remaining strength. I surprised myself at how I felt like a newborn baby. He continued his examination. I grew tired but fought the sensation. If I closed my eyes for a moment, would the feeling would go away? I closed my eyelids and fell fast asleep.

I ran over hills. The night appeared so dark, and ink black; I could barely view two feet in front of me. My feet stumbled, as I tried to see the uneven ground in front of me. My palms clenched with sweat, as my heart pounded like the organ would jump out of my chest. I turned around, my eyes darting from side to side searching for my pursuer. No sign, but I knew he wasn't far behind.

My hair in a high ponytail, whipped at my
face, as I picked up the pace in my flight. He
seemed close enough, that I had the
sensation of his breath on my neck… so
close he might reach out and touch me. I
turned again to see if I could glimpse him
near, and I saw a man. But what puzzled me
was what materialized in the man's face.
Where his face should be, a gaping black
hole yawned.

How could this be? The thought plagued me
only for moment, as fear gripped me and
survival instinct kicked in. Realizing if he
caught me I would be killed, I ran stumbling
over rock and uneven ground. When the
inevitable happened, I tripped falling to my
knees. He had me. There was no escape
from my fate. I would die now. I struggled
as he grabbed my left wrist twisting my arm.

This appeared no dream, I might awake
from; he had me now and he would kill me.
I twisted slightly trying to free my wrist but
he grabbed my other wrist and shook me
slightly saying…, "Quite a dream you were
having, but a dream none the less. Nothing
can harm you now."

I stared into his face and slowly his look changed, from the faceless man, to another face entirely. This wasn't the man in my visions; the demon in my nightmare. I knew in my heart this remained an altogether different kind of man.

This face with smiling blue eyes radiated warmth, and kindness. His face stayed gentle, not violent. I had been dreaming and had mistaken his touch for the man in my dreams. I flushed with embarrassment.

"You are quite awake now? I won't harm you. Now, do remember me?"

I stared at him, slowly waking up, and realizing where I was.

"I'm your Doctor, Doctor Andrews, at your service, my lady. We met before when you awoke from your coma," he continued speaking softly, and gently, bowing at the waist and smiling.

Shouldn't I have recognized him immediately? Heat rushed to my cheeks, as I turned red in embarrassment.

I was a fish out of water. I didn't like the way I reacted; like something had happened and all was a secret to me. I liked to be in charge of my life every aspect, and right now it seemed like I appeared in charge of nothing.

"How long have I been here?" I whispered, trying to speak louder.

"I would have said it's a lot longer, than you think," he replied cryptically.

"Do you always answer a question with a question? I want an answer for my query," I demanded angrily.

"What do you remember?"

"I believe I asked you to stop making this an interrogation. If you must know, I remember waking up a little while ago the nurse came in and then you came a little later," I answered exasperated, wondering what could be wrong with me. I didn't get angry so easily. Did I? Why did I behave this way? Everything he said seemed to make me angry.

"Your little while ago was two days ago...," he explained, breaking off as if afraid to say more.

"But that's impossible..."

"You fell into a restorative sleep. It is not uncommon for patients who have been in a coma to do so."

"Two days? I slept for two days?" I commented incredulously.

"Yes," Doctor. Andrews stated.

"How long was I in a coma?" I asked worried to hear what he might say.

"What month do you remember?"

"You have to be in charge, don't you? Questions! Questions!" I replied, delaying the answer. I was suddenly afraid that I'd been in this coma far longer than I realized, and grew angrier.

"I know you're scared. Are you sure you want to know? The information can wait," he insisted.

"I'm not scared," I lied with false bravado, "I remember quite clearly the month is March."

"It is the eleventh of September nineteen hundred and seventy-one. Do you remember what happened the day of the accident?" he asked.

"That's not possible. I can't have been in a coma for six months. Why do you lie to me?" I spat at him.

"I know it's hard to assimilate but time has passed and it is September," he insisted softly, but firmly.

"Why do you persist in a lie? What do you have to gain with this preposterous story?" I demanded; still not ready to believe this.

"Exactly what do I have to gain? Sharron, I'm not lying to you," he stated sadly.

Until that moment I hadn't given any thought to my name, but as Doctor Andrews called me Sharron, I realized I wasn't even sure if that was my name. I didn't have a clue what my name was. My name might be Sharron, but I didn't recall the name. My name could be Mary, or Angela, or any other name in the world. If I had a surname,

I couldn't remember it either. A huge blank spot stood where any recollection should be.

How could my last memory be of March, but I still had no recollection of my name, er names? This was normal after a long coma. I decided.

Perhaps my memory had been so underused, and only had temporary gaps? Or I was hungry? Yes, it had to be one of those things. A temporary aberration of the mind... No need for me to worry. No, need to share any such information.

My memory was only hiatus. That had to be the answer. Give it a few days and my memory would all come back. There was no need to tell the doctor, especially since my recollections would all come back. Absolutely not, I reasoned.

After all what good would it do to tell him? He'd look at me either with sympathy, or call in a shrink. I wanted none of the sympathy, and whispered glances which would follow. So I had a few memory gaps, nothing to worry about. It was perfectly normal after a coma, I reassured myself.

"What will you do with all this information Sharron?" asked Doctor Andrews suddenly concerned.

"I must admit the information was a bit of a shock to find the month was September and not March, but I'm over the surprise. "I'm hungry what does it take to get food around here?'' I demanded, quickly changing the subject. Besides I was ravenous.

"I think you can start some light foods, some soft foods, Jell-O soup etc.," Doctor Andrews spouted. Turning to the nurse he commanded, "Nurse get a light meal for my patient."

"Certainly Doctor," the nurse replied, coming into the room rather quickly, at his summons.

Just when I thought I had successfully gotten rid of the doctor, he turned around and said... "I know you are rather tired and hungry right now, but I'm sure you to want to discuss these revelations later today."

How could I get him to change his track? I didn't want to discuss my memory loss with anyone. I wasn't ready for anyone to find out I didn't know who I was. If I told him, would he treat me like a mental patient?

No, I wasn't going to tell him, or anyone. I needed to fake what I remembered. They'd never know, I couldn't remember. I would then have the time to accept this myself, and hopefully everything would come back. No one would ever have to know.

Wait a minute, did he know, I didn't remember? He talked about the fact I'd been in a coma, but had he given me any knowing glances? I gave him a sideways glance. Deciding he didn't have a clue about my memory problem. I plotted to keep it that way.

"There is not a lot to talk about; but if you want to we can discuss my medical condition we can get to that later," I replied, hoping he would take my response as an agreement and leave.

Luckily for me he took the hint. Maybe he would even forget to come back and discuss this later? No, I hoped for too much, but he did look convinced that I'd talk to him later. Good then he'd go away.

"I will return later, Sharron."

He then left taking his questions with him. I breathed a sigh of relief. Now alone with my thoughts, surely I'd conjure up a memory or two. First I would cat and refuel. That would help the memories, as well as my stomach.

I stared at the food the nurse had brought in. I'm starving to death and the nurse gave me not enough food to feed a rabbit? I tried to pick up the spoon and found my hand wouldn't cooperate.

"Would you like some help?" the nurse asked kindly.

"I can do it myself," I responded stubbornly.

Although I had found it difficult to raise my hand to my mouth, that soon became easier. I found by clamping my hand around the spoon I could manage to feed myself. It was then I realized how much work I had ahead of me. The nurse watched, so I smiled at her like everything was fine. She smiled back and left.

I soon made short work of the food and wanted to move on to the therapy I recognized I needed. I would set the memories, or lack of them aside, and working on building up the muscle tone and abilities I'd lost. When the body restored itself, I would begin to remember. I understood without being told, that I had to begin like a baby to exercise my limbs and I wanted to start immediately. Let's be honest. I realized I could remember something. I grasped now that I was an impatient person, at least when it came to doing things I had to be doing. I called the nurse on the call bell to ask about therapy and exercises.

"Yes?" I heard a disembodied voice somewhere over my head say. Momentarily puzzled, I then realized the voice came from an intercom.

"Sorry to bother you but when can I start therapy? I need to get my limbs moving," I explained.

"Dear, you are barely out of coma. I'm sure your doctor would want you to build up your energy first. Or wait at least until you started solid foods."

She sounded surprised and had a hint of censor in her voice. No support there. I wanted those six months back, but clearly that wasn't going to happen. Move on, I told myself. I'd wasted six months sleeping, time to fight back and get back into fighting form as they said. But who had said that?

I somehow knew I was a fighter. I'd have to do everything myself; something I knew I always did. But how did I know that?

I thought about what would work, and what limbs need to work. My hands needed to a work out. Okay, they need to grip. How do you make hands stronger?

You give them something to grip. Squeezing something soft, medium soft, would work. Where to get something to work my grasp? I couldn't even get out of bed. My limbs were useless, absolutely useless.

My hand shook in weakness, from forcing the stupid thing, to do its job and feed me.

All of this began to feel hopeless. ..No, I wasn't some stupid helpless female. I had to figure out a plan. You're on your own, I told myself, nothing new. You can overcome any odds. Think, Sharron, think!

How about some finger exercises? Slowly working each finger, and then in tandem, I would get back movement. I began the exercise I devised. It sounded so simple when I had thought of how to exercise the hand, but painful and tiring. Work through the pain, I told myself. Isn't that what you've always heard?

I forced myself to do the exercises for what seemed like hours, until I couldn't take the pain any more. Then I decided to exercise my arms. Gripping well enough to pull myself up to the bar over my bed, I reached I'm with my right hand to grab the pole. My fingers won't cooperate. My fingers are weakened and my grip slipped. Damn it! Even simple exercise was impossible.

"Nothing is impossible," a voice spoke loudly in my head. But whose voice did I hear? My memory had fled, if it was ever there. I only comprehended the voice had been someone I loved, and respected. Was this a father, or a father figure? I knew I was bone weary, and a great sea of lethargy stole over me. It would be counterproductive not to take a nap, I reasoned. Surely a short nap would restore my energy and I would begin again.

I closed my eyes soon I began dreaming. At first the dream appeared happy. I viewed myself in a beautiful home and grinning at someone I couldn't see.

I smiled and felt great joy, but the sky grew dark and I found myself outside on a field. The moon overhead slowly covered by clouds, and I grew terrified. Something was wrong. The faceless man chased me once more. I ran over rocks and streams and more rocks. He kept coming and coming. I knew he'd soon be on me. He nearly had me when I willed myself to wake up saying… This is a dream and I want to wake up now.

I awoke gasping for air like I had been running a marathon. A strange man sat by my bed. His hair appeared dark, practically black, greasy, and slicked back. He had black thick glasses that he peered over like they were a prop.

An oversized suit coat in plaid and matching pants completed the picture. Despite his harmless appearance, he struck terror to my heart. What gave me the idea he put on this persona, like a piece of new clothing? I think it was his face which seemed to give it all away, like he tried too hard to portray someone he wasn't.

As I gazed at him, he jumped from the chair he sat and exclaimed…"About damn time you woke up out of the coma Sharron. I thought you laze there forever."

He then continued, as if choosing his words carefully, "Oh Sharron, this is the most wonderful day of my life." Then he pulled me to him, fiercely.

"Let go of me, this instance. Who do you think you are? I said don't touch me! And quit acting and looking around there's no audience for your play," I blurted out, before I stop myself.

"Sharron that's not funny. Quit joking. You always had a wicked sense of humour, but I'm not laughing." the man stated, sounding annoyed and grabbing my wrist.

"I said let me go, and I meant every word. Now kindly take your hands off me," I demanded at the top of my lungs, struggling unsuccessfully to free myself of the grip, he now had on my wrist.

Taken back by my yelling, he let me go, but he still continued to treat me, like a bug under a microscope. Suddenly switching gears, his face changed. It was if a curtain went down over his face. He took on a concerned look and then a hurt look. I admit he nearly had me fooled.

I started thinking I had forgotten a boyfriend, but surely I wouldn't suffer from such bad taste.

He wasn't my type. He seemed quite violent too. I wouldn't have been so foolish to get mixed up with a weirdo like him! Would I?

"Sharron quit staring at me that way you're making me uncomfortable. I'm not amused here...Wait a minute you're not kidding

.You don't recognize me at all. You don't recognize your fiancé?"

I recognized somehow that he was put on an act. No, I wasn't engaged to him. If I had been it would boggle my mind. He had to be lying, I decided. Why I didn't know, but I knew he lied.

I had no sparks with him. In fact something about him gave me the creeps. He repulsed me and made my stomach hurt. He certainly didn't sound sincere. He put on an act ... but why? He grabbed my wrists again, once again in a vice grip. I struggled valiantly, but his grip tightened and I couldn't handle his fierce clutch in my weakened stated.

"Let me go you, caveman. I don't know you and what is more, I don't ever want to know you," screamed at him fighting frantically.

"Sharron you cut me to the quick. Why do you say such things to me?" he whined, letting go of my wrist, but gripping my arms even tighter.

Maybe it was because of my dream, but suddenly I was terrified. Why did they leave me all alone with this crazy man? Where was everyone else? Couldn't they hear me shouting?

"Let me go. Let me go....Don't touch me," I yelled at the top of my lungs, and then screamed, hysterically "Help me someone help me."

As I started to pull harder frantically to be free he stilled held fast. What kind of evil demon had me in his grasp? I tried to bite him, but that was impossible; finally in the answer to my screams were footsteps running. Seconds later a nurse and Doctor Andrews entered.

"Let my patient go immediately. I said let her go," Doctor Andrews growled, pulling the man's arms behind his back.

I breathed a sigh of relief. I was safe. Doctor Andrews had saved me.

"I wasn't hurting her! What kind of a man do you think I am? Gee, I have more bruises than her. She acted crazy, so I grabbed both her arms to calm her," the man explained, sounding plausible.

Surely Doctor Andrews and the nurse who followed him in, didn't believe his act?

"Your technique doesn't seem to have calmed her, but it certainly frightened her," Doctor Andrews said, checking my blood pressure and heart rate.

"You can't tell me what to do. She's my fiancée I can speak to her anyway I want," complained the man, loudly.

"You've upset my patient. Her blood pressure and heart rate is elevated as well. This is not good for my patient, so I can tell you what to do. What is your name?" demanded Doctor Andrews.

"Titus Brown is my name and Sharron is my fiancée," the man replied a little too quickly.

Doctor Andrews consulted his clipboard. He pointed to it and then announced, "This is the approved register and you're not on the list. Leave now, Mr. Brown, or I'll have security escort you out of the facility."

"I'm not going anywhere. Who do you think you are?"

Mr. Brown showed his true colours, I thought. They would trounce him faster than you could say Jack Robinson.

"Mr. Brown, so far I've been pleasant. The nurse has already called for a security guard. I suggest you leave now and don't come back, or you will find yourself with a trespassing charge and jail time," Doctor Andrews said through his teeth.

"I'll be back with my lawyer and you'll be sorry," Mr. Brown menaced.

Two security guards entered and forcefully removed Mr. Brown from my room. I began to shake like a leaf. I tried to stop, but I grew frightened. Someone had tried to kill me and that is why I was in the hospital. What if it was Him, Mr. Brown?

They wouldn't let him take me when he talked to his lawyer? Would they? Words I hadn't want to share, spilled out of my mouth, first in torments, and then at a screeching level.

"I don't know who the heck he is, but I do know I don't know him. I'm not his fiancée. Don't let him come back lawyer, or no lawyer. I don't want to see him. Someone did this to me! I wouldn't be surprised if the person was him!" I guess I appeared a little too hysterically and forcefully, because the next thing that occurred was Doctor Andrews plunged a needle into me.

"Please, please don't. It's not necessary, really. I'll be good," I pleaded too late.

"It's a little sedative. I don't like your colour, your blood pressure, or your heart rate. You've had a nasty scare and your body isn't able to cope with this right now. Calm down now," he said comforting "Go to sleep."

"I think I hate you," I replied vehemently.

"That's okay, you can hate me if you need to," he answered, smiling.

Damn him and his handsome smile! Something about the grin, made me want to smile back and tell him all my secrets.

"Don't leave me alone. He might come back," I pleaded as I drifted into a deep drugged sleep.

If you enjoyed Stray Bullet please consider leaving me a few words at your favourite retailer and if you liked the excerpts and would like to read more of my books please check out one of my other books listed on the next page at Amazon

Sincerely S. G. Lee.

~0~

## List of Books by S. G. Lee

### *Murder Mysteries*

Love's Labour's Won

A Tiger's Heart Wrapped in a Player's Hide

Reborn – a novella~ prequel

A Penny Saved A Murder Earned

A Diller A Dollar A Really Dead Scholar

Betty Blue Lost Her Holiday Shoe

What Will Poor Robin Do?

The Kelly Murder Mysteries-Book 1-3

A Stitch in Time

Stray Bullet

Dreams Can Kill

Stray Bullet

## Short Story Books

Murder Most Fowl

Jack be Nimble

Day of the Dead

Legends, Folktales and other Stories

The Stuff of Nightmares

ObsessionX2

## Christmas

Christmas is Calling

The Christmas Card

The Christmas Angel

Visions of Sugarplums

## Poetry

A Poetic Touch - The Human Condition

## Children's Books

Mare the Hare due out December 2017

~0~

Stray Bullet

**506**
**Stray Bullet**

www.ingramcontent.com/pod-product-compliance
Lightning Source LLC
Chambersburg PA
CBHW051934020726
47501CB00001B/115